EXT

DATE	ISSUED TO	
B 6 21 7 ½		
HS 324 8/9		
T219 9/4		
B1107 12/24		
V203 3/2		
RZ 3/4		
FR67 8/2		
CM02 7/6		
AS 8/10		

Murder in Passy

Murder in Passy

Cara Black

THORNDIKE PRESS
A part of Gale, Cengage Learning

GALE
CENGAGE Learning™

Detroit • New York • San Francisco • New Haven, Conn • Waterville, Maine • London

GALE
CENGAGE Learning

LIBRARY OF CONGRESS CATALOGING-IN-PUBLICATION DATA

Black, Cara, 1951–
   Murder in passy / by Cara Black.
     p. cm. — (Thorndike Press large print mystery)
     ISBN-13: 978-1-4104-3793-8 (hardcover)
     ISBN-10: 1-4104-3793-0 (hardcover)
     1. Leduc, Aimee (Fictitious character)—Fiction. 2. Women
private investigators—France—Paris—Fiction. 3. 16e
Arrondissement (Paris, France)—Fiction. 4. Paris
(France)—Fiction. 5. Large type books. I. Title.
PS3552.L297M7985 2011b
813'.54—dc22   2011006620

Published in 2011 by arrangement with Writer's House LLC.

In memory of Madame Aufrère,
Anne-Françoise's great aunt
who loved Passy,
and for the ghosts.

ACKNOWLEDGMENTS

My deep thanks to: forensic pathologist Terri Haddix, M.D., Vincent O'Neill, Jean Satzer, Dot Edwards, Barbara, Jan Gurley, M.D., Max, Susanna von Leuwen, Elaine, Libby Fisher Hellman, Jo and Don Metz, and the amazing Ailen, Katie, Mark, Bronwen, and Justin at Soho.

In Paris: Colonel Michael McGurk, American Embassy, Paris, André Rakoto, Service Historique Ministère de la Défense, Chateau de Vincennes, Sarah Schwartz, translator extraordinaire, Gilles Fouquet, Carla Bach, toujours Anne-Françoise Delbègue, Gilles Thomas, underground specialist, Julian Pepinster, of the Paris Métro, the GIGN unit at Satory, Versailles for the visit and expertise, Vassili, gracious Silvie Briet of Eau de Paris, Nathalie and Benoît Pastisson, generous beyond words.

Un grand merci in Passy and Auteuil to Anne Bordier, Lynn Green-Rutannen for our walks over the years, Arianne Rosenau Levery for sharing her "village," and Claude Pasquét.

On the Basque front, La Maison Basque de Paris, Jean Damien Lesay, and in Bilbao, Elizabete Bizkarralegorra, huge thanks, and Ondo Izan.

Always in my corner, James N. Frey, Linda Allen, my son Tate, and Jun.

Words feel inadequate for the debt I owe my late, dear editor Laura Hruska. Her guidance and knowledge over the years were a gift. *Merci,* Laura.

"What is irritating about love is that it is a crime that requires an accomplice."
— CHARLES BAUDELAIRE

■ ■ ■ ■

PARIS
NOVEMBER 1997

■ ■ ■ ■

Monday Early Evening

The doorbells tinkled as Aimée Leduc stepped inside the cheese shop from the cold and inhaled the warm, pungent odors. A radio blared the evening news: ". . . evading seven roadblocks erected after the shootout in the *Imprimerie Nationale* documents heist. In other breaking news, a radical faction. . . ." She shivered, nodding to pink-faced, rotund Victor, standing in his white apron behind the counter. Bombings, shootouts, she hated to think what else — and to make it worse, just before the holidays.

"World's gone crazy." Victor shook his head. "The usual?" He gestured to a runny rind on grape leaves standing on the marble-topped counter: "Or this?"

Aimée tasted the Brie dripping on the white waxed paper. *"C'est parfait."*

She emerged from the shop into the evening mist and rounded the corner toward her office on rue du Louvre. The reflections of the furred yellow orbs of streetlights glowed on the wet pavement.

"About time, Leduc." Morbier, her godfather and a police commissaire, his black wool coat beaded with moisture, paced before her building door. An unmarked Peugeot with a driver, engine thrumming, waited at the curb.

"More like five minutes early, Morbier." The chill autumn wind cut a swathe through the street of nineteenth-century buildings. Passersby hurried along, bundled in overcoats.

A look she couldn't read crossed his face. "We've got a situation in Lyon. I'm late. You've got the file, Leduc?"

Forget the apéritif she'd expected in the corner café! She brushed away her disappointment. So they would do the exchange in the cold, wet street. She handed Morbier a manila envelope containing the supposed ten-year-old letters and photo of her "brother" Julian. It was time to let the professionals handle the only copies she had, so she could find out once and for all if they were genuine. "A week for lab authentication, Morbier?"

In return, he showed her an engraved business card reading POLICE PAPER FORENSICS DIVISION HEAD PAUL BERT.

18

"Bert's the leading forgery expert. That's all I know."

She nodded; she couldn't push it. He was doing her a favor.

"Time for a quick espresso?" She pointed to the lit windows under the café's awning, which was now whipping in the wind.

Morbier shook his head. Under the thick salt-and-pepper hair, his face appeared more lined in the streetlight; dark circles showed under his eyes. "You think life finally makes sense, then . . . *alors,*" he shrugged. "*Pouff,* it turns upside down."

"What's wrong, Morbier?" She wished they were inside the warm café with its fogged-up window instead of standing in the wind. A siren whined in the distance. "A case?"

"Can't talk about it, Leduc."

As usual. The streetlight revealed his cuffed corduroys, his mismatched socks, one brown, one black. Morbier was no fashion plate. He hadn't made a move toward his car. Unlike him. She sensed something else bothering him. His health? "Did you have that checkup like you promised?"

"Something's going on with Xavierre," he said. "I'm worried."

Taken aback, Aimée fumbled for something to say. She remembered him with his

19

arm around Xavierre, an attractive older woman with dark hair. Xavierre's laughter, warm smile, and scent of gardenias came back to her.

"Worried over what?"

"She doesn't answer her phone," he said.

"*Zut!* I don't either, half the time," she said. "You're reading too much into it."

"I need to know what's going on."

She'd never seen him like this, like a lovelorn shaggy dog. It was not often that he shared his personal feelings.

"Her daughter's getting married soon, *non?*" Aimée rubbed her hands, wishing she'd worn gloves. "You told me yourself last week. She's busy." A cloud of diesel exhaust erupted from the Number 74 bus as it paused to board passengers.

"Xavierre's holding back," he said. "Something feels wrong, Leduc. When my gut talks, I listen."

"Like what? You're thinking she's in danger?"

"She's fond of you," Morbier said. "Help me out, eh?"

He hadn't answered her question. "But what can I do?"

He pulled a police notepad from his coat pocket and wrote down an address. "Do me a favor. Her daughter's wedding rehearsal party's tonight. Go there and talk to Xavierre. She'll open up to you. If I hadn't gotten called away to this investigation —"

"Me?" Aimée interrupted.

"How many times have I helped you, Leduc?" he said. "Better get going, the party's started."

Why did she always forget that Morbier's favors had a price?

He pointed to the leather catsuit under her raincoat. "I'd suggest you change into a little black dress, too."

"*You* dispensing fashion advice, Morbier?"

But he merely said, "Can I count on you?"

She nodded. And then he climbed in the waiting Peugeot. A moment later it turned and its red taillights disappeared up rue du Louvre. Some kettle of fish, she figured, if they had to summon Morbier to Lyon.

She hit the numbers on the digicode keypad; the door buzzed open. She was tired out: it had been her first day back at work after a month's recovery from the explosion that had laid her low on her last case. Her shoulders ached; she had a report to file. And now this. But she couldn't ignore the urgency in Morbier's voice.

On the third floor, she unlocked Leduc Detective's frosted glass door. Instead of the dark office she expected, she caught the sweet smell of juniper logs and welcome warmth emanating from glowing embers in the small marble fireplace. "What are you doing still here, René?"

René Friant, her partner, a dwarf, swiveled his orthopedic chair, his short fingers pausing on the laptop keyboard. "Catching up," he said. "How did today's surveillance go?"

He was worried about their computer security contracts, as usual.

"I think you'll like this." She slotted the VCR tape into the player. Hit PLAY.

René's large green eyes scanned the screen. With an absent gesture, he brushed at the crease in his charcoal suit pants, which were tailored to his four-foot height.

"Good work." René grinned.

She'd had a tête-à-tête with the VP of operations and had planted the video camera in his office, along with a data sniffer on his office computer's input cable. Now they could monitor his less-than-transparent budget transactions remotely. Their client, the CEO, needed proof of embezzlement.

"So the VP took the bait?"

"Like a big hungry fish, René." She crinkled her nose in distaste. "The things I do for computer security!"

René shrugged. "And for a fat check, too.

We should be able to document the VP's sticky fingers in the corporate cookie jar and wrap up our surveillance by Friday, write our report, *et voilà.*"

He was excited, as always, on a new project. She hadn't realized how much she'd missed work while spending a month on her back. She had been wounded and René hospitalized after being shot. But René had recuperated at a seaweed Thallaso-therapy, a cure courtesy of national health insurance. Noticing his glowing complexion, she wished she'd done that too, instead of attempting to master the new encryption manual while she recovered.

"I need to run an errand for Morbier." She glanced at the time. "Back in an hour. Then I'll lock up."

"Leaving now? You just got here."

"*L'amour,* René."

"Eh? Another bad boy? Don't you learn —"

Was that anger in his voice? She ignored it.

"Not me. Morbier's worried about Xavierre, wants me to talk to her," she said. "It's complicated."

"You're serious?" he said. "We've got an account to update. And there's this case."

"Do you think I don't know that?" she

said. The last thing she wanted was to go back out into the cold. "But Morbier called in a favor."

She took the half-empty Orangina off her desk, tore off a piece of baguette from inside her bag, unwrapped the white waxed paper, and scooped up a runny wedge of Brie. Dinner.

"Help yourself, René." She went behind the screen and unzipped the black leather catsuit, peeling the buttery leather from her thighs. She found her little black dress with the scooped neck, vintage Chanel, in the armoire and hooked the last snap under her arm. She clicked open her LeClerc compact and applied a few upstrokes of mascara.

"Armed in Chanel." René shook his head. "You look tired."

So obvious? She noticed the circles under her eyes and dabbed on concealer, ran her *rouge noir* nails — for once newly lacquered — through her shag-cut hair. She had blond highlights this week, at her coiffeuse's suggestion. She checked the address on the map in her Paris plan. "40 rue Raynouard, that's in the 16th *arrondissement.*"

"Très chic," René said. "Look, it's your first day back; let me give you a ride."

"But it's out of your way," she said. "I'll grab a taxi."

"Morbier's my friend too, Aimée," he said, sounding hurt.

"That's not the issue, René."

His health was. He was still using a cane. The case she'd dragged him into last month had resulted in his injuries; she didn't want that to happen again. "No reason for you to get involved."

"But I already am." He shut down his laptop. "My car's out front."

To their left, the arms of the Seine wrapped the Île de la Cité in a turgid gel-like embrace. Arcs of light from the gold-crowned Pont Alexandre III glittered on René's Citroën DS windshield as he shifted into third gear. The dark masses of trees lining the quai whizzed by, blurring into a row of shadows.

Concern dogged her as she recalled the tense edge in Morbier's voice, the tremble in his hand. She doubted he'd had that checkup. She pulled her anthracite-gray faux fur tighter. The heated leather seats toasted her thighs.

It was late, she was tired, and part of her wanted to get this over with. The other part wondered what Morbier's gut had told him.

"Morbier thinks she's seeing another man, *n'est-ce pas?*" René turned onto a wide avenue with tall limestone Haussmann buildings like silent sentinels to the *quartier,* which was bordered by the Seine and the Bois de Boulogne.

"I don't know," she said.

"But that's a special thing, eh," René said. "Older men offer the devotion of a lifetime, as Oscar Wilde said."

More to it than that, she thought as they drove past closed upscale boutiques. Past Franck et Fils, the darkened department store where her father had bought her Catholic school uniform, and the shuttered café opposite where they'd had hot chocolate, something she longed for on a night like this.

René turned onto a street canopied by trees. The next narrowed into a high-walled lane; no doubt it had been a cow path in the last century. It still amazed her how these enclaves existed, tucked away, the remnants of another world: the old villages of Auteuil and Passy, where once Roman vineyards had dotted the hills, thermal springs — celebrated for curative properties — had beckoned seventeenth-century Parisians, and where Balzac, penniless and in debt, had written while hiding from his creditors.

René turned the corner and pulled over,

and the Citroën shuddered to a halt. She stepped out of the car into a biting wind under a sky pocked with stars. It was a cold clear night.

"Quiet, *non?*" René said.

"Deafening." Only the chirp of a nightingale could be heard as the fallen chestnut husks crackled under their feet.

Now the *quartier* housed embassies in old *hôtels particuliers* amid exclusive countryside-like hamlets of the moneyed who could afford tranquility.

Aimée pressed the intercom at the side of the high wall fronting No. 40, which was bathed in pale streetlight.

"*Oui?*"

"Madame Xavierre?"

"You have an invitation?"

She felt uneasy and cleared her throat. "Commissaire Morbier asked me. . . ."

"*Un moment.*" Aimée shivered as dead leaves swirled around her ankles. Voices and strains of classical music drifted through the intercom. René's breaths showed like puffs of smoke in the night air.

A moment later, the grilled gate buzzed open.

They stepped into a small garden, a *jardinet,* fronting a Louis Seize–era townhouse. Trellised ivy climbed the stone façade. Twin horseshoe stone staircases ascended to the entrance of this small jewel of a mansion. Even wearing vintage Chanel, she didn't feel comfortable in this kind of place.

René whistled. "Not bad, Aimée. We win the Lotto, we can live here too."

Morbier, a dyed-in-the-wool Socialist, with a *haute bourgeoise* girlfriend? Opposites did attract. Several Mercedes were parked in the gravel driveway, which ended in a dark clump of buildings.

After buzzing the door, they entered a black and white tiled foyer. Beyond open double doors, a high-ceilinged room revealed a chandelier. The clink of glasses drifted toward them.

René unwound his Burberry scarf, putting his gloves in his coat pocket. Then he stopped. "You're paler than usual, Aimée. Sure you want to go through with this?"

She applied Chanel Red to her lips. Blotted it with a torn deposit slip from her checkbook. "Better?"

Determined, she strode inside, where she saw a blue banner hung across the gilt-paneled wall. It read BON MARIAGE, IRATI ET ROBBÉ in silver letters. Inside, the closeness of body warmth lingered. Coming from the cold into the stuffy room made her feel light-headed.

Where were the other guests?

It was only 7:30, but the cake had been cut. Smudged Champagne flutes stood on the sideboard. Only an old couple remained: a man wearing a formal black dinner jacket, a woman in a black dress more suited to a funeral. They'd seen sixty a long time ago.

René tiptoed to reach for the last of the Champagne. His fingers couldn't quite reach it. Aimée, with a deft swipe, took a flute of fizzing rose Champagne and handed it to him.

"Vintage Taittinger. Not bad." He shot Aimée a look. "But not what I'd call Morbier's crowd."

She agreed.

The old man, cadaver-thin and shrunken in his black jacket, winked at her. Already well into the Champagne, he had a happy glassy look in his eyes. "Don't tell me," he said. "You're another cousin, eh?"

"We come in four-packs, like yogurt," Aimée said as she scanned the room. "You don't just marry the daughter, you get the family."

A petite young woman, dark hair knotted in a clip, wearing a slim red skirt and a silk blouse, stepped into the room. Her large dark eyes were hesitant. The man took a look at her, grabbed his wife's hand, and left.

Odd.

"*Excusez-moi*, are you Irati?" Aimée asked. "I'm Aimée Leduc."

A blank stare greeted her. Had she made a mistake? Aimée noticed clenched white knuckles clasping the silk blouse. Then the girl gave a little nod.

"Sorry to bother you," Aimée said. "I know you're busy. But Morbier asked me to speak with Madame Xavierre."

Irati smiled. "Not at all. This gives me a good excuse to extricate *Maman* from the temperamental caterers. Now I can escape upstairs and sleep. My fiancé, Robbé, escaped already." Her voice quavered; she paused. "But I know you, don't I?"

"I'm Commissaire Morbier's goddaughter."

"Of course." A look Aimée couldn't decipher crossed her face. The tinkle and crash of plates sounded from the kitchen. Irati clenched her fists together.

"*Pardonnez-moi,* Aimée," Irati said and left the room.

René downed his Champagne. "A real love feast, eh? Temperamental caterers, a wedding party of geriatrics, a sweet girl. And we rushed out into the cold for this?"

She wondered herself. A cigarillo moldered in a crystal ashtray. Beside it was a half-eaten slice of *gâteau* Basque oozing with cherries and almond filling.

Aimée caught a whiff of gardenia, felt her shoulders grasped, and then Xavierre's warm cheek pressed on hers in a flying kiss. "Aimée, delightful to see you."

Xavierre's peach silk scarf framed her shoulders. Matching lipstick, a hint of blush, and arched brows in an unlined face. Not one dark hair out of place. If she was surprised, she didn't show it except perhaps by a little jump in the pulse at her neck, barely discernible in the dim light.

Aimée introduced René. Xavierre shook René's hand, holding his in her own peach nail-lacquered fingers, her gaze level, not averting her eyes as do most people confronted by a dwarf. "Morbier late as usual? As you see, the guests have left."

"*Désolé,* Xavierre, I'm his messenger." She hesitated, sensing a tautness in Xavierre, an undercurrent. "Can we talk in private?"

She took Xavierre aside near the tall salon door and lowered her voice. "A last-minute investigation came up. He asked me to tell you in person."

"But why? He went to too much trouble.

I'm fine."

"You didn't answer your phone." Aimée hesitated. "He worried. . . ."

"My phone?" Xavierre blinked. Then laughed. "*Zut!* I guess I forgot to charge it."

Aimée nodded. "I forget all the time too. But is anything wrong? I mean. . . ."

A line tightened at the corner of Xavierre's perfectly applied peach lipstick. "Have you ever planned a wedding on two weeks' notice?"

Aimée shook her head, feeling awkward. Did that explain it? She couldn't ask Xavierre if she was having an affair. Not her business. But she could put in a good word for Morbier. "I've never seen Morbier so happy, Xavierre."

Xavierre smiled, squeezing Aimée's hand. Her look was wistful. "But we met more than twenty years ago. He hasn't told you? A *coup de foudre,* love at first sight." She gave a little sigh. "My marriage, his, children, divorce got in the way. But when I ran into him last month, we reignited. It was as if we'd never said good-bye."

A phone trilled from the hallway. Xavierre's eyes clouded. There was a flutter of fear in them. Her shoulders tensed, and then she seemed to relax. Aimée heard the click of heels in the hallway and then Irati answering the phone.

Xavierre sighed. "I've got so much to do for the wedding on Sunday. I'll reach Morbier later. I think it's better if you go now." Xavierre took a deep breath. "You understand, *non?*"

Aimée could understand. But not the flicker behind Xavierre's eyes and the tight smile. Family problems? Or something else?

"Maman?"

"You'll need to excuse me." And without another word, Xavierre left.

Aimée heard footsteps coming from the kitchen. A moment later, Irati stood at their side.

"*Maman*'s upset; let me apologize for her," Irati said. "The wedding plans, stress of relatives, endless. Me, I'm calm. Supposed to be the other way round, *non?*" She gave a short laugh.

Short and forced, Aimée thought. What undercurrents are flowing here? she wondered.

"Maybe it would have been easier if Morbier had been here," Aimée said.

"Nothing would help." Irati blinked, then looked away, distracted.

What did that mean? Time to disregard tact and force the issue. "Morbier was worried she was having an affair," Aimée said.

René shot her a look.

"You're saying my mother would —" Irati said.

"Me and my mouth," Aimée interrupted. "Please forget you ever heard that, Irati." Aimée paused. "Your mother's upset. Can I help?"

"Right now I wish this were all over," Irati said.

Not exactly the excited bride-to-be, Aimée thought. "What's wrong?"

Pause. "Robbé and I wanted to keep it simple. But you didn't hear that either." Irati took Aimée's arm. "In Basque, when things go badly, we say it's like cobwebs: just brush them away and get on with it. I'll see you both out."

Outside, the crisp biting wind met them. The air cleared Aimée's head, but did not dispel her unease. Xavierre was hiding something.

"What do you make of that, René?"

"A tempest in a teapot," he said with disgust. "Morbier's over-reacting."

She wished she thought so too.

"But, considering the Taittinger," René said, smiling, "not a totally wasted trip."

Fir branches scraped the wall, their scent released into the crisp air. Beyond, at the side of the house, was the service entrance.

A dim glow shone from windows, pooling yellow on the gravel.

"Give me a moment," she said, unable to get rid of her sense of unease. "I'll be right back."

She walked over the gravel toward the kitchen's back windows. For a moment she sensed a presence. A feeling that someone was watching them. As she was about to look up from the crunching gravel under her feet, she heard a squishing sound. Her shoe's pointed toe was mired in softness. Leaves, and something else, clung to her red-soled Louboutin heels. Then the smell hit her. Dog poo!

Great.

She heard the gate click open.

"*Un moment,* René."

She leaned against the stone wall, took the penlight from her bag to see to clean off her shoe, and shook her head. "My brand-new heels, too!"

In the penlight's beam, she saw by the tan smeared dog poo several reddish-brown congealing clumps on her shoe sole. She grabbed a twig to scrape it all off. There was a coppery metallic smell. She looked closer.

Blood.

Her hand froze. "René," she whispered.

"What now? I'm cold." He let the gate shut. His gaze traveled the penlight's beam, which traced a reddish-brown trail of droplets over the gravel path along the ivy-covered wall.

"I don't get it." René shook his head. "It's late. Let's go, Aimée."

From behind the house, Aimée heard a car start. The rumble of a diesel engine, the spit of gravel as it took off. She tiptoed ahead, rounded the corner, crouched under the windows. Shadows flickered. She saw movement inside the house.

"It's not our business." René stood behind her next to green garbage bins by the short flight of back steps.

"Shhh." She leaned toward him, tugged his elbow. "He thinks we left."

"Who?"

"The figure watching from the window," Aimée said, pointing at the house. "He heard the gate close."

Hunched down, she poked with the twig, noticing that the blood had darkened. It had semi-clotted in the cold night air. The blood was not fresh, but not old enough to have dried. She followed the blood spatter trail on the gravel around the corner to the garden.

Her penlight beam illuminated the

evening-misted hedgerow, a tangled fragment of peach scarf, and, farther on, a figure slumped among the gooseberry bushes against the stone wall. Fear jolted along her spine.

"Xavierre?" Her throat caught. "You all right?"

But the cocked angle of Xavierre's head, the scarf twisted tight around her neck, and her unblinking gaze told Aimée that Xavierre wouldn't answer now. Couldn't.

"My god, René! Call the SAMU!"

He flipped his phone open.

Horror-stricken, Aimée untied the scarf digging into Xavierre's flesh. She felt for a pulse. None. Frantically, she made quick thrusts to Xavierre's chest.

"Maman?" Irati's voice came from the open French doors. "Telephone for you."

Too late.

Wind rustled the damp leaves tattooing shadows across Xavierre's pale face. "What's going on?" Irati said. "What have you done to my mother?"

"Her heart's not beating, Irati."

"I don't understand." Then a piercing scream. Irati knelt down by Xavierre's lifeless body, stroking her mother's cheek. "You killed *Maman!*"

"No, we found her like this." Aimée

turned to René, who'd knelt beside her. "Tell the *flics* to hurry."

Choking sounds came from Irati. "What do you mean?"

"I heard a car pull away, then saw blood," Aimée said. "Who was in your house, Irati?"

And then she felt Irati's fists punching her. "*Non, non* . . . this can't happen!"

Aimée caught her arms and pulled her away. "Let's go inside."

Irati shook Aimée's hands off. "And leave her in the cold?"

Aimée noticed the snapped twigs, bent bushes, the flattened grass feathering the gravel. She saw damp footprints and something that glinted.

"Please. I'm sorry, but it's better if we don't touch anything."

Before she could check the bushes, a thump came from behind her and Irati sprawled, collapsed, sobbing on the dirt.

Aimée paced in the closet-sized upstairs sitting room. Twenty minutes, stuck in here, after giving her statement. Her heart ached for Morbier. His phone didn't answer.

Below, flashing blue and red lights bathed the townhouse in an eerie glow. In the rear, bright white lights set up at the crime scene painted the back in stark detail. Xavierre's

body had been removed; *le Proc,* the pros-
ecutor, had come and gone; technicians in
jumpsuits had finished combing the gravel,
the bushes, the stone wall. One by one the
lights shut off, and the crew packed their
crime-scene kits.

Already? She opened the latticed window,
breathed in the frigid damp air. Snatches of
conversation rose from the terrace: ". . .
classify a crime scene by what it tells me.
This shows low planning, high passion, as
opposed to high planning, low emotion."

Footsteps. The door opened and Lieutenant Hénard, the middle-aged, angular-jawed
duty *flic,* entered. One look at the window
and he shut it and pulled the velvet drapes.
He sat down at the escritoire on a gilded
chair too small for his large frame. Aimée
expected it to snap.

"Sit down, Mademoiselle," he said.

"Did you find the wounded person?"

"Mademoiselle, I need a clarification of
your statement." Hénard didn't look up
from his notes.

"But he or she can't have gotten far," she
said. "The blood on the gravel —"

"We're handling this investigation, Mademoiselle," Hénard interrupted, consulting
another page in his notebook.

She'd almost welcome a cocky Brigade

Criminelle high-ranking detective to question her instead of this by-the-book plodder. His pen scratched over the paper.

"Mademoiselle Leduc, please explain those bruises on your arm."

"But I told you," she said. "You have my credentials."

Hénard pushed Aimée's PI license, with its less-than-flattering photo of her, across the polished desk.

"*Merci,* but of course you realize it's in your interest to cooperate."

"Lieutenant Hénard, I already explained," she said, tapping her heels. "Poor Irati went into shock. Denial, anger I think, but she lashed out as I tried to calm her. I wanted to remove her from her mother and not disturb the scene. Ask her."

Hénard consulted his notes. "In shock, yes. She had trouble calming down enough to answer all our questions. The police psychologist sedated her."

"Of course my colleague, René Friant, confirmed my account." She stretched out her arms. "Look, do you see any scratches, marks other than a bruise? Xavierre fought her assailant, her fingernails were broken. But there was no blood on her. What about the half-dried blood spatters on the gravel?

40

The figure I mentioned standing at the window?"

He snapped his notebook shut with a sour look. "We're quite aware, Mademoiselle. That's all for now."

Shutting her out, standard police procedure. "Have you notified Commissaire Morbier yet?"

"Command handles notification."

"He's my godfather." She leaned forward. "If there's any possible way I could speak with him. You know, coming from me —"

"Noted, Mademoiselle," he interrupted. "Now join the officer in the other room."

In other words, go home. Typical. Stonewall a witness after taking his statement.

"But you're questioning the guests who'd attended the party, the caterers?"

"Let the professionals do their work, Mademoiselle," Hénard said, an edge to his voice.

She wanted to tear the notebook from his hand, read his notes. Instead, she smiled. "My father was a *flic;* I'm acquainted with —"

"This way, Mademoiselle." He cut her off, opened the door, and gestured downstairs.

In the dining room, Irati's wedding banner still hung from the ceiling. Aimée's heart caught. Now, instead of a marriage, it would be a funeral. The cherries had congealed on the plate of *gâteau* Basque.

She excused herself to use the bathroom in the hall. Inside, she paused until she heard retreating footsteps, then climbed on the marble bidet's rim. She opened the tall bathroom window to the terrace. Still in conversation, the inspector was huddled with a crime-scene technician. The technician was smoking; a plume of gray smoke rose, lazed, then dissipated in the night.

"Called to a case like this last night," the tech said. "Classic signs."

"Coming to conclusions already?" the inspector said.

"A beautiful woman strangled with her own scarf?" He paused. "It's a common scenario. Her man's jealous, reason clouded by anger. They fight, it gets out of hand. An hour later, drunk, full of remorse, he confesses." He paused. "Crime of passion. In theory, of course."

"Says who?" said the inspector.

"The *mec* left evidence," he said. "They always do."

"Circumstantial," the inspector said. "Unless you convince *le Proc* otherwise."

"You call the item we found embedded in fresh footprints circumstantial?" A pause. "I hate to say it, but this one's not good news."

42

His voice drifted away.

She tiptoed forward on the bidet, teetering on the edge. The gloved crime-scene technician moistened his thumb and forefinger, then tamped his cigarette out between his fingers, stuck the butt in his pocket, and shot a look at his team. "We found this. It must have been dislodged in the struggle."

"Got his name on it, then?" a voice said. "Handy, eh? We can go home."

That quick? Was it what she'd seen glinting in the dirt?

Loud knocking erupted on the bathroom door. "Mademoiselle Leduc?"

She stepped down, flushed the toilet, and looked in the mirror to tame a stray eyebrow. She tried to calm the trembling in her hands.

In the hallway, a blue-uniformed *flic* guided her to the kitchen, a remodeled state-of-the-art wall-to-wall marble affair. "We'll contact you for further questioning if needed."

She bit her lip, wondering about the item discovered by the crime-scene tech. "Do you know if there's a suspect?"

No expression showed on his face.

"But the footprints outside, that would explain —"

"And I explained to you," he interrupted,

"exit through the kitchen."

The *flics* were barking up the wrong tree. She felt it in her bones.

Family photos were pinned on the corkboard by the kitchen pantry. She paused, saddened at the snapshots of Xavierre and Irati in happy times at the beach in what looked like the Basque countryside, with sheep and snow-tipped mountains. She glanced behind her. The *flic*'s back was turned. She unpinned the best photo, one of Irati smiling and Xavierre taking a picnic basket from the trunk of a car, and slipped it into her pocket.

A bruised night sky hovered above the walled driveway. Cloud wisps obscured the moon. The cold air seared her lungs. Still shaken, she pulled her coat tighter.

"Such a tragedy," René said outside on the gravel, shaking his head. "Let's go. My body's numb. You look cold."

She surveyed the driveway, the back gate. "Did you notice a catering truck when we arrived?"

René shook his head.

"Neither did I." She paused. "Something's different."

An empty space lay ahead of a dark maroon two-seater Mercedes coupe. "Another Mercedes was parked here, remember?"

René stomped his feet in the cold, nodding, interest in his eyes. "That's right. Sedan. Nice model, too."

She glanced at the window, pulled the photo from her pocket. She stared at it, then showed René. "Like the one in this photo?"

René nodded.

She ran over to the *flic,* who was now striding ahead to a waiting police car. He was speaking into the microphone clipped to his collar.

"Officer, may I speak with Hénard?"

"Hénard's gone. We've been called to an incident, Mademoiselle."

"Another Mercedes was parked here." She pointed to the tire tracks.

"A priority call. But we have your statement, Mademoiselle," he said, static erupting from his collar microphone.

"But you don't understand. I think this car —"

"The crime-scene technicians examined the area, Mademoiselle." Blue lights flashing, siren whining, his car shot over the gravel and out the driveway.

"What a rats' nest, Aimée," René said, gunning the Citroën into the narrow lane. "Poor Morbier."

Sadness weighted her down, thinking of

her godfather hearing the news via official-
dom.

René hit the brakes as a cat, a charcoal
shadow, streaked across the street. He
downshifted into second and hit the horn,
turned the corner, and sped up.

"Don't you think it's better if the news
comes from you?"

She took a deep breath and tried Morbier's number again.

"No answer, René."

"Give it a few minutes. You need to explain
what we saw. He'll know what to do."

She was prepared to do just that, but for a
couple of small problems: his phone didn't
answer; he was in Lyon. And he'd enlisted
her help; he'd suspected something.

She cleared her throat. "Of course, but
that missing Mercedes. . . ." She sucked in
her lip. "I heard it pull away."

"Me, too." René nodded. "A diesel with a
knock, right before you found Xavierre. I
know what you're thinking. But would the
murderer be stupid enough to steal the car
and think it wouldn't be traced? That Irati
wouldn't notice?"

She needed to think about that.

"That is, if the murderer took it," René
said. "Doubtful."

"No harm in finding out, René."

"What can you do, Aimée?" René stopped at a red light. "Trace the car?"

"Not officially. The *flics* made it clear they don't appreciate interference." But with a little charm and luck, she could. "Take a right." She switched on the interior light, reapplying her lipstick in the visor mirror, and dabbed Chanel No. 5 on her nearest pulse points.

René shook his head.

"Any other ideas, René?" She snapped the compact shut. "I'm playing it by the —"

"Hem of your skirt. Like usual, Aimée."

He shifted into first. She saw the set of René's jaw. His white-knuckled hands on the steering wheel. "What's wrong?"

"Xavierre's Basque, *non?*" He checked the rearview mirror. "Last week in Biarritz a Basque was murdered after church, right in front of his family. Some ten-year-old vendetta."

Another angle to consider? "Nothing points to politics here, unless I'm missing something."

"*Everything's* political with the Basques. Murdering tourists on the Costa Brava is their specialty." René pounded his fist on the steering wheel. "Like my cousin. He was fifteen, on a school holiday on the Costa Brava, when a bomb ripped his bus apart."

She'd had no idea. "I'm so sorry."

" 'Sorry' doesn't bring him back," René said.

"You never told me. But that's ETA, the Basque terrorists," she said. "Pull over there."

She pointed to the small, storefront-like Commissariat de Police across from the darkened Marché de Passy, the indoor market. The Commissariat, a vestige of the old neighborhood, had a blue, white, and red flag whipping in the wind in front of it and a plaque on the light blue door. This remnant of the former village faced the market, not the designer shops and haunts of the wealthy.

René exhaled. "I don't get it. Didn't you already give a statement to the *flics?*"

She nodded, combing her fingers through the blond streaks wisping behind her ear.

"Yet we're parked in front of the Commissariat and nothing else looks open." René pulled on the parking brake.

Outside the car window, a figure walked by on the pavement. Alert, she watched. Only an older man, his cap low on his head, wearing a long wool coat, walking his dog, pausing every so often by the gutter. Otherwise, the street lay deserted.

"Time's crucial," she said. "Investigational

red tape bogs everything down. Filing crime-scene reports can take up to twelve hours. I need to know whether the missing car's important or not."

She hoped she sounded more confident than she felt, that he didn't notice the trembling in her knees.

The Mercedes. She had to find the Mercedes. An hour and a half head start, and the *flic* hadn't even listened to her or noted it down. Irati wouldn't notice that the car was missing until too late.

"Irati's under sedation," she said. "When she wakes, she'll be desperate. Frantic."

"Exactement," René said. "Who wouldn't be? A daughter losing her mother. . . ."

She felt the buried pain in her heart. That little pain that never went away. Aimée's American mother had abandoned her when she was eight years old.

René averted his gaze. "My turn for sorry." His mouth tightened.

She smiled and touched his hand. "It's all in the timing."

"Timing? How?"

She shouldered her bag. "I don't know yet." She reached for the door handle. "But I'll find out."

She paused and caught his hangdog look. His pale face.

"Your hip bothering you, again? What's wrong?"

"What's *right,* Aimée?"

The windows fogged, and he hit the defroster.

"This murder. Morbier," he went on. "But I worry about you," he said, "that you'll get involved just as you're recovering your health." René turned on the defroster full-blast. "Not that worrying does any good."

She shuddered. This was the last thing she wanted, with a business to run, ongoing projects, clients, and pending proposals. She'd just spent a month on her back, and she needed to catch up. "Did I go looking for this?"

"Xavierre's murder's not your fault, or your responsibility," René said.

"But I owe Morbier," she said, biting her lip. "I failed."

"Failed? She kicked us out, remember?" René said. "It's more important for you to support Morbier in his grief."

She nodded. But if she didn't track down this car, do something, she'd get no sleep.

" 'In the river of life,' as Saj says, 'all things merge,' " René said.

"And that makes it easy?" she said. "Have you heard from him yet?"

Saj, their part-time hacker, had gone on a

well-earned vacation: a meditation retreat in southern India.

"He's at the ashram in Pondicherry, as far as I know. He won't respond to e-mail during meditation courses." René's clenched fists gripped the steering wheel. A faint sheen of perspiration showed on his face.

Best to keep his mind off what had happened. She remembered him in the hospital, how she'd almost lost him. Never again. "With Saj away, you need to check the data sniffer feed, René."

"For once, you're being practical?"

She twisted the leather strap of her bag. "Don't you need to prepare?" She squeezed his hand. "I know you, René."

"You do?"

The atmosphere became grave. For a moment she couldn't read his expression. But she couldn't think about that now. She had things to do. She opened the car door. "Places to go, René."

And miles before I sleep, she thought, keeping her trembling hands in her pockets as she traversed the zebra-striped crosswalk.

"36 85 RS 75." Aimée read the Mercedes license plate number from the photo in her hand. A smiling Xavierre and Irati posed with a red-and-white picnic basket and rolling hills in the background. "A maroon Mercedes sedan, say two years old. Diesel."

"You don't ask much, do you, Mademoiselle Aimée?" Thesset cleared his throat. "Me, here in the Commissariat with two men, two others out responding to calls. Do you think I've got nothing to do?"

Thesset was approaching his mid-fifties. A career *flic* who'd graduated from the Police Academy with her father and Morbier, now edging toward retirement in the Commissariat, mostly preoccupied with disturbances of the peace or robbery by a disgruntled servant.

"Looks quiet to me, Thesset."

"Heated up tonight," he said. "Murder of some *haute bourgeoise* matron. They're calling it a crime of passion. Shows you never can tell what's going on behind the gilded doors."

Her shoulders tensed. Not good. It sounded like the crime-scene techs wanted to go home early, shelve the investigation to low priority, and discount other motives.

But she'd worry about that later. The timing between the car pulling away and Xavierre's murder wasn't a coincidence. She needed Thesset to trace the car before he or the investigators finally connected the dots tomorrow.

"Crime of passion sounds convenient," she said.

"More like they wanted to warm their *derrières.*" Thesset shrugged.

"Any leads yet?" she asked offhand.

"Not my call. Or my turf."

A twinge of guilt passed through her. Here she held a photo of the dead woman in her hand. But Thesset could search without making an official report. And if she'd jumped to conclusions, say the old couple at the party had borrowed the Mercedes, no one would be the wiser. No harm done. No record.

"I'm not supposed to do this, you know."

"But you're the pro, Thesset."

Thesset's expertise lay in navigating *Système D,* the catchall term for getting things done. He was efficient behind the thick-lensed gray-framed glasses mounted on his beaklike nose, his misleading sallow jowls and permanent squint. "Like a pigeon," she'd once said to her father at the Commissariat, and he'd put a finger over his mouth. "*Shhh.* We call him that, but never to his face."

"*S'il vous plaît,* Thesset. I'm asking on behalf of Morbier."

She heard the fax machine come to life behind the wooden partition, tried to ignore the acrid cigarette smoke spiraling from the ashtray on the counter, the empty pack of Mentos crumpled near the phone.

"Let the old coot request this himself."

"*Très compliqué,* Thesset." She leaned forward as if in confidence. "A delicate situation, if you know what I mean. Morbier's lady friend's daughter fell in with a bad sort — a vindictive type. Now he's her ex and out on parole. He took her Mercedes tonight. The daughter wants nothing to do with him, no accusations, just her car back. No urge to make a report and land him back in prison and deal with recriminations on his release. *Compris?* A small favor, Morbier said. He counted on you keeping it quiet. Unofficial."

"Sounds like a soap opera," Thesset said.

She wished it were, but figured it wouldn't be the first time he'd gotten a request to keep *haut bourgeois* linen clean.

"Me, I've got work to do," Thesset said. "Tell Morbier to get on it himself."

"*Mais,* Morbier's in Lyon." She expelled air from her mouth. Tried to look helpless and without a clue. Not hard. "Some big investigation," she said, playing it to the hilt. "I don't know what, but he asked for my help."

Thesset squinted behind his glasses. Put

down his pen.

"Lyon? That circus?" A cough, then he cleared his throat again. "Better him than me."

What did that mean?

"*Et alors,* in that case," Thesset said, "I'll see what I can do."

The change in Thesset's attitude intrigued her. "What's happening in Lyon?"

"Nothing I want to know about." He shrugged.

She left it for now and flashed a big smile. "Then how about a trace through traffic division? The patrol cars in Bois de Boulogne, little things, the usual."

"Usual?" He snorted. "If you weren't taller than me now, I'd take you on my lap, like I used to, and tickle behind your knees."

She'd loved that. "And give me the hiccups."

"Like I said, you don't want much, do you?" A sigh. "I'll put the alert out to my boys on patrol."

"How long will it take, Thesset?"

"To find the car?" He shrugged. "Two minutes, two hours, two days. Depends."

The murderer could have abandoned the car. But casting a wide net, a maxim on the force, would find it sooner or later. Regular patrols cruised the neighboring Bois de

Boulogne, a stretch of forest double the size of New York's Central Park. The big lung of Paris, locals called it, a park honeycombed with roads, horse trails, the Longchamp racing course, and also Brazilian transvestites offering their services on the fringes, a frequent issue with the consular staff of the numerous embassies dotting the 16th arrondissement. YOU PLAY, YOU PAY, headlined a recent scandal sheet over a transvestite's blackmail demand, complete with compromising photos. Immediately hushed up while the junior consul was packed off to his home country.

She wished her shoulders weren't aching with fatigue. And that she could provoke Thesset into revealing some details about "the Lyon circus."

"Morbier promised he'd return tonight," she said, hating to lie.

"Don't count on it," he said. "Between you and me, Mademoiselle Aimée, who knows. It's three branches all jockeying for credit. A mess."

"Anything to do with the news on the radio?"

"*Salauds* killed a *flic*. And you know what that means."

A priority. All forces would be centered on a policeman's killing.

"Morbier's a Commissaire Divisionnaire now; Lyon's not his turf."

"It's not for me to say." Thesset's eyes suddenly seemed shuttered. He was holding something back. Impatient, she tapped her nails on the police blotter and noticed a chip on her newly lacquered pinkie.

Thesset's jaw tightened. Papers rustled from behind the partition, a filing-cabinet drawer shut. She shivered in the cold unheated reception area at the scuffed wood counter.

"Aaah. But on the radio." She thought for a moment trying to draw him out. "Those roadblocks? *Bon,* what can you tell me?"

"Every branch's salivating to get the *flic*-killer, that's all I know." Thesset pounded his fist on the counter. "The *flic*'s wife's eight months pregnant. Poor thing."

Sad. No doubt the *flics* were seeking vengeance. With all forces concentrating on the murder of one of their own, she realized, Xavierre's murderer could slip under their radar.

Through the open door in the rear office, she saw a blue-uniformed *flic* pull a fax from the printer. "Thesset, look at this."

"I'll ring you later," she said. "*Et merci,* Thesset."

Aimée snapped her bag shut. Thesset disappeared into the office. She paused behind the divider, her ear to the smudged glass, and overheard "damned ETA terrorists . . . acting up again."

Then the door closed.

ETA, the Basque Nationalists. Xavierre was Basque. Was there a connection? Had that worried Morbier?

The street lay quiet, apart from water rushing in the gutter. Typical of the staid *quartier:* not even a café open. But a perfect *quartier* for terrorists to hide in, in a tony residential district where everyone minded their own business. And never a taxi when you needed one, she thought, scanning the empty street. She shouldered her bag, her only companions a streetlight and the low, distant moan of a cat in heat.

Around the corner, a lone taxi paused at the intersection. Thank god. She caught it before the light changed.

"Île Saint-Louis, *s'il vous plaît,*" she said, giving her address, and popped her last two Doliprane aspirin, dry-mouthed, in the back seat. Fifteen minutes later, she punched in the digicode of her building, a seventeenth-century soot-stained townhouse on the quai, and stepped into the cobbled court-yard. Beyond the ancient pear tree, she noticed with relief, the windows in her concierge's loge were lit.

"Late and breathless," frowned Madame Cachou, her concierge. "As usual."

Aimée leaned down to pet Miles Davis, her bichon frisé. His wet nose sniffed her ankles. "*Désolée,* Madame. Work. Traffic." Murder, but she left that out.

"Good thing!" said Madame Cachou. "With my bursitis, I can't walk Miles Davis up and down three times a day."

Madame Cachou, a chronic complainer, was growing worse in her old age. Framed in the doorway of her loge in the courtyard, Madame handed Aimée the leash from the wall hook. Miles Davis emitted a low growl, which reminded Aimée of her shoes, the dog poo.

"Un moment," Madame Cachou said. "There's a package for you."

Warmth emanated from Madame Cachou's loge, a steaming cup by an armchair near the *télé* showing the late-night France2 news. Aimée's tired body ached and she couldn't wait to get under the duvet. An announcer spoke as a scene flashed on the screen: dark sky punctuated by lights, yellow crime-scene tape, a narrow lane bordered by high walls. Her shoulders tightened. She recognized those stone walls. The walls of Xavierre's garden.

"The Police Judiciaire refused to issue a statement regarding the murdered ex-wife of a prominent attorney found tonight in her bedroom in the 16th arrondissement."

Bedroom? She dropped Miles Davis's leash.

"Sources close to the investigation revealed that attention is being focused on the victim's relationship, referring to it as a crime of passion. The source indicated that a suspect was about to be detained."

Crime of passion? The hair rose on the back of her neck. The media and the *flics* had gotten it all wrong.

"Last time," Madame Cachou said. "Building regulations don't permit receiving business correspondence here, Mademoiselle." She pointed to a yellowed paper of building regulations as she handed Aimée a Frexpresse package.

Always a stickler for rules, her concierge. Aimée glanced at the return address. Infologic. Work-related files she could handle tomorrow.

"I bent the rules, but . . . ," said Madame Cachou, "seeing as you're recovered, fit, and back at work, no more."

She wished she felt fit instead of exhausted. More worry lodged in her head

60

over this turn of events with respect to Xavierre. The pain of telling Morbier . . . but he certainly must already know by now.

She trudged up the worn marble stairs to her door. Darkness, a chill, and rising damp from the Seine outside met her in her empty apartment. She kicked the radiator. Then again, until it sputtered to life. She hung up her faux fur, tossed the Frexpresse package on the hall table with her bag, and wedged off her heels. Miles Davis pawed at them. "Not this pair, furball."

She picked them up. A dark brown-maroon blotch stained the candy-red insole. Ruined. She'd never get the blood out.

And then it struck her, piercing the fog of tiredness in her mind: she was holding the proof right in her hand. The killer's blood. Her spine stiffened. She took a plastic baggie from the hall escritoire drawer, slipping her high heels inside. "They go straight to the lab in the morning. Good call, furball."

TUESDAY MORNING

Morbier's tobacco-stained fingers trembled as he lit his second Gauloise. Why couldn't he feel numb? Numb like the victims' families he'd broken the same news to countless times, more times than he liked to remember. And he remembered every one. Their shocked faces: ". . . but it can't be"; then his words sinking in. The collapse into tears.

Why didn't he even feel anger, hurt, grief? Instead he floated, as if out of his body. His mind blurred when he should be analyzing Xavierre's last words, rethinking her every action.

There was so much to do, so many facets to consider in the investigation, so much to concentrate on: the crime-scene results, lab tests, questioning the family, any witnesses, speaking with Aimée. But here he was, spinning his wheels, waiting in the Préfecture's office for Suffren. The last person he wanted to talk to. Now or ever. Suffren's office afforded a view of the green-brown Seine. Not a corner office, but a sign of the favor he'd attained in the six years since Morbier had almost sidetracked his career.

The longer Suffren kept him waiting, the more he wondered at the abrupt summons that had taken him from the Morgue, wishing that his last view of Xavierre hadn't been her wide red-veined eyes, her delicate neck red and bruised as she lay on the stainless-steel morgue table; that the creeping feeling of helplessness would subside; that he could do something to bring the smile back on —

The door creaked open and Suffren, a man in his early forties, whip-thin, brunette with a stripe of white hair showing above his ears, gestured for Morbier to sit down. Suffren kept his cell phone glued to his ear, emitting occasional hmms and grunts. Only once did he look up and give a small apologetic shrug.

Upstart, out to prove himself, has a chip on his shoulder were the comments Morbier recalled from Suffren's file. Morbier's review team, singularly unimpressed by Suffren, had passed on his application based on his low scores on the officer examination.

If Morbier remembered this, no doubt Suffren remembered with venom. Morbier settled in the upright wooden chair, wishing he could go to the crime lab. He tried to push that aside, get the interview over with, a formality. He needed to channel his nervous energy into the anger he knew would come . . . so as to find out who'd done this.

Suffren hung up the phone and studied the view outside his window for a moment. In the pale lemon morning light, a lone seagull squawked on the quai and clouds floated over the jagged Left Bank rooftops.

"Commissaire," Suffren said, leaning forward, tenting his fingers. "You had a known relationship with the victim. Physical evidence found. . . ."

"*Oui,* of course, I do . . . did." Morbier leaned forward. "You're handling the investigation?"

"That thing of yours for the ladies, eh? I remember . . . didn't your Arab mistress, one of them . . . I forget, die in Marseilles?"

Insult, inference, intimidation, Morbier knew well the standard interrogation techniques. He used them himself. Determined, he steeled his nerves to get this questioning over with so the investigation could proceed.

"Mouna left me years ago," he said. "Two

years later, she was caught in crossfire in the Belleville riots."

"It's coming back, yes, Mouna," Suffren said, flexing his tented fingers, his voice layered with innuendo. "Her daughter Samia was murdered not much later in Belleville, in 1994."

"*Our* daughter," Morbier interrupted. His fists clenched in his corduroy jacket pocket.

"A brutal slaying, if I remember. And your grandson. . . ."

"Marc lives in Morocco with his paternal grandparents."

Morbier balled the handkerchief in his pocket.

"Quite a protracted custody battle over little Marc, *non?* Allegations surfaced concerning . . ." he paused. "Abuse, I think."

"Get your information correct, Suffren. There was no abuse. His Muslim grandparents alleged religious and educational discrimination." Morbier kept his breathing steady with effort. "I paid Marc's Catholic school tuition instead of sending him to the mosque school. The court threw the case out. But in another legal round, well, two grandparents beats one." Morbier kept his gaze steady. "But you know all this; it's in the open file on your desk."

"Murder follows the ones you love, *non,*

Morbier?"

Suffren was wasting no time, Morbier thought. So he'd descend to his level and get right to it.

"Maybe you think it's clever to knit these incidents together," Morbier said, "but they won't make a sweater. My grandson's father was convicted of Samia's murder. He's serving the next twenty years in Clairvaux. Didn't one of *your* new team put him there? Quit wasting time."

"But I'm establishing a pattern, the history over a period of years."

Word for word from the Police Academy textbook. Morbier tapped his worn heel. He'd be bored with this, if it weren't for his underlying unease. His frequent refusals to play police politics over the years had won him more enemies than friends. He kept important players happy and his head down, doing investigations his way. Most of the time. But he realized he'd ticked someone off big-time if it had come to this.

"Either get creative, Suffren, or find a new playbook, but get on with it. Then look for the real killer."

Suffren glanced up. "Creative. That's good. I like that. But you beat me to it. Eh? No TGV ticket record to Lyon; matter of fact, you arrived an hour late . . . enough time to strangle her."

"What?" His shoulders tensed. "You're calling me a suspect?"

"Tell me why you dismissed your driver."

Now it had gotten real, Morbier realized.

"How I run my investigation, that's my business."

"Why hasn't this come up in your notes? Meanwhile, a Lyon investigation team member noted your flustered . . . *non,* pardon, disheveled appearance, and that you turned the team over to the second in command."

Morbier could bluff this out. He had to.

"It was so the investigation could proceed," Morbier said. "I delegated according to the surveillance information received."

"But you were late. Can you account for that time? Where were you?"

Morbier averted his eyes. "Talk to Inspector Laguardiere."

"But I can't, you see; he's on medical leave."

Merde! Another hernia operation? His bad back? Laguardiere spent more time in the hospital than out of it.

"*Et alors,* handle it through the usual channels. I understand you've got to rule out people close to Xavierre —"

"But Laguardiere is the proper channel,

as you know," Suffren interrupted. "Why don't you reconsider your answer?"

"I can't discuss the ongoing investigation." Morbier shook his head. The fur-like fabric pellets in his corduroy jacket pocket were ground to lint now.

"But we need to establish your whereabouts. Very simple, and much less painful than the alternative."

"Check with Laguardiere. He'll tell you it's —"

"Disturb the man after his heart attack yesterday? With pulmonary thrombosis and surgery scheduled?"

"I'm sorry to hear that. I didn't know." Morbier shrugged. All the old dinosaurs like him were en route to the cemetery. "After his recovery, he'll clear this up." Morbier made to stand. "If that's all?"

Suffren grimaced as if in pain. "If that could only take care of the discrepancy. But I'm afraid this gets in the way." He held a clear plastic evidence bag in his hand. "A Commissaire Divisionnaire–rank tiepin. Serial number on the inside. One of only eight issued in the last few years. Yours, I believe, Commissaire Morbier." He said it with relish.

Morbier stared at the tiepin glinting under

the fluorescent light. Then he felt his tie. Gone.

"Looks like mine." Morbier nodded. Where had he dropped this?

"We discovered your tiepin in a muddy footprint close to the victim's body. I believe it will match the worn left heel on your shoe."

"What?" Morbier's jaw clamped tight.

Suffren pressed a button on his intercom. "We're ready."

Two white-coated technicians from the basement laboratory under the Quai des Orfèvres entered the office. He'd played cards with one of them, Desnos, the older and senior in rank, last Friday. Desnos still owed him a hundred francs.

"We're affording you privacy, of course, given your rank," said Suffren. "I'm sure you'll cooperate while they take an impression of your shoe. Undo your shoelaces, *s'il vous plaît.*"

Stunned, Morbier leaned forward.

Desnos averted his eyes and set down his metal box labeled PLASTER.

Morbier's jaw spasmed . . . he made himself speak . . . the words came from somewhere. "Under these circumstances —"

"From now on, Commissaire, I caution

69

you to speak only to the legal representative assigned by the Inspecteur Général," Suffren interrupted.

Inspection Générale des Services, Internal Affairs, *la Police des Polices.* Most called it *boeuf-et-carottes:* the stew of suspicion a *flic* simmered in while suspended.

Morbier could have sworn he saw a gleam in Suffren's small eyes.

"This is all wrong, Suffren. You don't really want to do this —"

"Escort him to IGS downstairs for interrogation, gentlemen. I believe it's on your way."

TUESDAY MORNING

Aimée woke up to the ringing of her cell phone, which was beside her on the duvet. Weak bands of sunlight slanted across the herringbone-patterned wood floor. Rubbing her eyes, she looked at the time. Eight A.M.

Morbier's number showed on caller ID. Finally. She sat up, took a breath, and clicked ANSWER.

"Leduc, why didn't you tell me?" Morbier's hoarse voice came over the line.

"I tried to." A pang of guilt stabbed her. "I'm so sorry, Morbier. When do you return from Lyon?"

She heard clanging noises in the background, like steel treads running over concrete. "I'm at the Préfecture."

"*Bon.* Won't take me ten minutes," she said, sitting up, grabbing her stovepipe jeans from the chair. "Just a moment." Awake now, she put the phone down, slipped her worn cashmere sweater over her head, put

71

the phone back to her ear. "I have things to tell you. Much better in person."

Pause. More clanging. "Not a good time."

"Why?"

Shouts, then a voice came over the line: "Time's up, Commissaire."

"I can't talk, Leduc."

"You're involved in an interrogation?"

"You could say that." Morbier's voice sounded different. Almost resigned.

That fast? "Look, something smelled last night. We need to talk —"

"A little difficult, Leduc," Morbier said. "Since I'm the suspect."

The Préfecture's vaulted stone holding cells oozed mildew and rot. Last remodeled during the Terror, if then, Aimée thought as she held Morbier's hand across the gouged wooden table. She felt his thick fingers, the moist ridges of his palm, and squeezed hard.

"Don't worry, Morbier, of course they'll release you at any moment," she said, managing a small smile. "Clear up this horrible mistake on top of —"

"I don't want you involved, Leduc." Stubble dotted Morbier's chin, lines were etched in his brow, and his drooping Basset-hound eyes were pools of pain.

"Xavierre loved you; there was no other

man." She squeezed his hand tighter. "She told me you met more than twenty years ago, *a coup de foudre*. You have to know that."

He nodded, but there was a lost look in his eyes. *"Merci."*

Her heart ached at seeing him like this. But they'd fix this mistake any moment. This terrible mistake.

She pushed the bag with a change of clothes and his shaving kit across the table. Handed him *un express* from the machine in a small white plastic cup. "I got this upstairs," she said.

He took a sip. Nodded. "The usual lukewarm brown piss."

His rumpled corduroy jacket and a food stain on the lapel caught her eye. The faint smell of mustard and defeat clung to him.

"We've only got fifteen minutes." She omitted telling him about the four hours it had taken to call his colleagues — numerous — and friends — not as numerous, it turned out — to wangle visitation for her in the *garde à vue*. No one had the "right connections" with Internal Affairs, they said. More likely they were head-in-the-sand afraid, she thought. It sickened her, knowing how Morbier had stuck his neck out for others. Favors oiled the system, her father always said, give and take, like currency but more valuable when your neck sat on the block. Favors conveniently forgotten if you became a pariah. Or had Morbier used up his favors?

In the end, she had opened the cell door by threatening to call the *Libération* journalist known for his recent exposé on police corruption.

"Xavierre was afraid," Aimée said; "your gut told you right. Someone was in the house. I saw blood outside on the gravel, heard a car take off, and found her . . . I'm so sorry, Morbier."

"Nice try, Leduc," he said. His shoulders sagged. "Proof puts me at the scene."

She shook her head in disbelief. "Proof? But you were in Lyon."

Dripping sounds in steady rhythm came from the corner. Morbier looked away. "I was watching Xavierre through the window. I couldn't help myself," he said. "A jealous old fool."

"I don't understand what you're saying." She let go of his hand.

"I was in the garden, Leduc." There was a faint hiss under his breath. "I left my footprints in the mud, and my tieclip."

This couldn't be happening. It didn't make sense.

"What?"

"I saw Xavierre arguing. Shouting, but I couldn't hear. She threw something at a figure. A man. But his back was turned."

She fought welling tears. There was a knot in her stomach.

"What do you mean?"

"Then cars pulled up with arriving guests and I left."

She took a breath. Tried to make sense of it. "Why didn't you tell me?"

"I hoped Xavierre would . . . what good did it do?" Remorse and grief cratered his face. He put his shaking head in his hands.

"*Mais* . . . wait, you'd gone to Xavierre's earlier?"

He nodded.

"What else, Morbier?" A growing doubt nauseated her.

"Don't get involved, Leduc. It's not safe." He looked up, then put his head back in his hands.

"What the hell does that mean, Morbier?" She stood up, took a step, sat down again hard in the chair. Calm, she had to act calm, and rational. Get answers. "What's really wrong, Morbier?"

"I'm too old for this," Morbier said. "Been too old for a long time. Xavierre's gone. Life's gone to hell."

Like a dog kicked too many times, the fight had gone out of him. "Tragic, yes, Morbier. So you spied on her. That doesn't mean anything. My god, *I* saw her alive after that. Your driver, the Lyon team will confirm." She snorted. "Why hasn't this idiotic investigation folded like a pack of cards hours ago?"

But he'd looked up, his gaze following the pipes snaking up the stone wall. An old-fashioned *robinet,* a metal-faced water spout, dripped, leaking a thin silver trickle into the grooved stone gutter. The whole place reeked of damp and wet. The continuous drip, drip got to her.

"That's leaked for twenty years," Morbier said, his voice lowered. "Time someone took care of it."

"Call the plumber," she said, irritated. Why had he given up? "Look, Morbier, you've got to fight this. You've given a lifetime to the force, lived and breathed your work. . . ." She stopped before she said *until Xavierre stepped into your life and gave you a shot at happiness.* Poor man, nothing to look forward to now. "So many years of service. High-profile investigations. Your retirement's coming up."

"All gone up in smoke, Leduc."

Her spine stiffened. "What are they holding over you?"

"Keep your friends close and your enemies closer, they say."

"Meaning?"

"*Désolé,* Leduc. My fault to have involved you." Morbier stood, nodded to the guard. "Forgive me."

Morbier asking *her* forgiveness. Had he ever in his life asked her that?

She jumped up and put her arms around him. Big solid Morbier, the one she depended on. She inhaled his musky scent mingled with tobacco, mustard, and worn corduroy and glanced at the guard. "Who's framing you, Morbier?" she whispered.

His brown eyes flickered. In his gaze, she saw the reflection of the silver pinpricks of dripping water.

"Stay out of this, Leduc. I don't want anything to happen to you." He kissed her on both cheeks, took his bag. "For once in your life, listen to me." Her last view of him was his stooped shoulders. Then he disappeared under the vaulted cell-block arch.

Aimée ran five flights upstairs and through the swinging doors into the Brigade Criminelle offices. Empty, apart from the cigarette smell and acrid odor of burnt coffee, not even a clerk to talk to. No one back from lunch, she figured.

Or all hands on deck for the investigation Thesset had mentioned? The *flic* killer?

Catching her breath at the far reception desk, where she'd finally found someone on duty, she asked, "When's Inspector Melac due back?"

"Melac's on personal leave." The female officer looked up. Her stiff blue cap, worn at the regulation angle, moved not a centimeter.

Merde! The one inspector who, as far as she knew, still respected Morbier. A rising workaholic detective in the mold of Morbier — albeit younger and better-looking. She pushed aside the memory of their night together last month, the brief interlude of phone tag. After that, he hadn't called back.

"Please ask him to ring me." Aimée handed her a card, knowing she needed to swallow her pride. "It's urgent."

"As I said, he's on leave. Incommunicado." The female officer, her lips gleaming with pink gloss, stuck it in a box labeled MELAC.

She trudged back down the drafty staircase, past officials with bulging files under their arms and strutting blue-uniformed *flics*. Everyone hurrying. Working. Like Morbier should be.

It tore her insides apart to see him so defeated, so lost and full of despair. No one else had lifted a pinkie. She would have to be the one to help him.

Her mind went to the blood spatters on the gravel, the figure watching from the window, the missing Mercedes. If things smelled bad last night, they stank today. Morbier's footprints, his tiepin. . . . Still, how could a case be mounted against him when he'd been in Lyon? Her hand paused on the smooth stone balustrade.

Had he gone to Lyon? But of course he had. He'd had a driver waiting.

When she asked him why the case hadn't folded, he'd changed the subject to the leaking *robinet.* A shudder went through her. So unlike him to make a trite comment like that. Not just "unlike": he *never* would.

That's leaked for twenty years. Time someone took care of it.

It bothered her. Was he telling her something? Knowing Morbier, there was more below the surface than he was letting on. And that protective "I don't want you hurt."

Her ringing cell phone interrupted her thoughts.

"Aimée, don't you ever answer your phone?" René said in a peeved tone. "I thought you were monitoring the account today."

"All handled," she said. "Early this morning, I set up the remote to record and store data."

"But you're where? We need to talk about —"

"At the Brigade Criminelle. *Un moment,*" she interrupted, running down the stairs to the courtyard. She stopped by a pillar, took a deep breath. "Morbier's devastated. He's in a cell downstairs. I'm worried."

Pause.

"Cell? I don't understand."

"An Internal Affairs investigation. It's not good," she said. "No one takes my calls."

A sharp intake of air came over the line. "But they can't think . . . Xavierre? That's impossible. We were there. *Mon Dieu,* the poor man. But what happened?"

"Like I know, René?" She leaned against the cold stone pillar.

"Can I help?" Pause. "You don't think . . . ?" René's words dangled over the line.

"That Morbier, who'd rediscovered the first love in his life after twenty years, strangled her?" A passing *flic* stared at her. She was shouting. "That he'd ruin his last chance at happiness? No, René, I don't. It smells like a setup."

The tinkle of a piano sounded in the background. "Meet you at the office later," René said, his voice now hushed. "Got to get back to the meeting."

"Some meeting, René."

But he'd hung up. She stared at the Préfecture's cobbled courtyard, recalling the times she'd met Morbier here and they'd grabbed a quick coffee at Le Soleil, the *flic* hangout around the corner. His shuffling gait on the uneven cobblestones, the sweater vest he wore against the cold, the stoop to his shoulders. How he'd aged. Their relationship, often problematic, seesawed over the years. Close during her childhood, he'd kept his distance after her father's death.

But the force he'd worked for all his life had now turned its back on him. No one would blacken their fingers to pull him from the fire. Or get scorched by association.

They'd done that to her father. Scapegoated him for a colleague's crime, she'd discovered years later. Years too late.

"But not this time," she said, looking up at the yawning gray Préfecture's windows. *Not this time.*

Aimée squeezed the handlebar brakes of her faded pink Vespa as she bumped over the uneven cobbles of the police laboratory courtyard. Weak slants of sunlight filtered through the sparse-leafed chestnut trees off rue de Dantzig. Five minutes later, she walked into the office of Viard, the crime-lab head. Viard and René's neighbor Michou, a transvestite performer in Les Halles, had just celebrated their three-year anniversary.

Misting his orchid collection, he looked up as Aimée set an orchid plant tied with a purple bow beside her shoes in the Baggie on his desk. "I could use your magic, Viard." She pointed to the signature red soles.

"Naughty, ruining a good pair of Louboutins," he said. "Walked over your latest conquest's chest in your high heels? You want a luminol test?"

She shook her head. "I'll settle for blood type, tissue samples, DNA. Tonight?"

"Dreamer." He raised his mister in mock protest. "Even the Interior Ministry DNA priority requests have a three-week backlog. Want to tell me why I'm more popular than the Préfecture lab?"

"Too in-house and you don't want to know," she said. Her hand trembled. "Look, I know you're busy, but. . . ."

"It's personal?"

Viard didn't miss a thing.

"Family." There, she'd said it. Morbier

was her family, her godfather.

She didn't trust the lab in the Préfecture basement. Her contacts there were Morbier's contacts and under tight rein from upstairs. Plus she didn't qualify for entry into the old-boy network.

"A career's at stake, Viard," she said. "A whole life."

"Stop. You're right: I don't want to know," he said. "We're booked solid, a time crunch." He paused. "But I do appreciate the orchid, Aimée. A beauty."

He dabbed the smooth leaf of the orchid she'd brought him with a linen handkerchief, then made a moue of distaste at the blinking red lights on his phone console. "See?"

She nodded, wondering what she could do, who she could ask, how in the hell. . . .

"You're shaking, Aimée. Sit down," said Viard.

She clasped her hands, took a breath. "It's all wrong. But no one lifts a finger, Viard," she said. "I need to prove that this blood belongs to the murderer. Not to him."

Viard stared at the lit-up phone console. Sighed. "Prelim blood typing, tissue analysis, if there's any. Say tomorrow morning at the earliest."

She kissed him on both cheeks. "I owe you."

"Just persuade René to roast a Bresse chicken in morel sauce," he said, donning a blue lab coat over his pink T-shirt. "We'll call it even."

Aimée knotted the wool scarf around her neck and popped the Vespa into first gear. She turned onto rue de Dantzig, gunning past the butterscotch-walled compound.

At the stoplight, she pulled out her cell and called Xavierre's house. The fourth time this afternoon. So far, there had been only busy signals.

"Allô?" said a woman's voice.

A horn blared behind her. She pulled over after the intersection to let a taxi whip by.

"Bonjour. Irati, s'il vous plaît."

"Who's this?"

"May I speak with her? I'm a friend of her mother's."

"Désolée, she's resting," the woman said. "Try later, Mademoiselle." The phone clicked off.

Avoiding phone calls was more like it.

But no time to waste. Back at the florist's on rue de Vaugirard where she'd bought Viard's orchid, she made a stop. Ten minutes later, she crossed under the arched metal supports of the Bir-Hakeim bridge into Passy.

In the pale afternoon light, Aimée buzzed the intercom set in the high stone wall of 40 rue Raynouard. A sense of déjà vu came over her. She wished she could turn back time. If only she'd. . . .

The buzzer sounded and she stepped inside.

Black cloth draped the front door, a mourning tradition she'd last seen in her grandmother's Auvergnat village long ago. Her gaze followed the driveway tunneling under the town house to the rear. A wisp of yellow crime-scene tape fluttered from the bushes.

Aimée heard leaves rustling and looked up. A middle-aged woman scrutinized her from a balcony trailing with vines. The woman beckoned. *"Viens."*

By the time Aimée arrived at the black-draped front door, it stood ajar. Instead of white chrysanthemums, the condolence arrangement *de rigueur,* she held a bouquet of gardenias — Xavierre's favorite, according to Morbier.

"Bonjour, Madame," Aimée said. "I'd like to pay my respects and offer condolences to Irati."

"Quelles belles fleurs," said the woman,

dressed in a shapeless black skirt and sweater. The maid? Late forties, no makeup, an unlined face, her black hair streaked with gray pulled into a bun.

So far the tactic had gotten her in the door.

"All this food I prepared!" The woman shook her head. "A waste. We can't even hold the memorial, much less the funeral." Her mouth tightened, her eyes brimming with tears. "They won't release my sister's body. No feelings for the family, I tell you. This tragedy, it's a crime."

In more ways than one, Aimée thought.

Butter smells came from the salon dining table, which was groaning with tarts and assorted pastries. Irati's wedding banner was gone, the mirror turned backward. An old village superstition, she remembered, so the departed wouldn't see their reflection and linger. It looked like the sister had turned her grief into a flurry of baking.

"How's Irati, Madame . . . ?"

"Madame Urioste. But you can call me Cybèle," she said. "The poor girl's gone mute. It's shock, I tell you."

Or fear. "I'm so sorry. May I give her these, offer support? Her mother's favorite, I believe."

Doubt darkened Cybèle's eyes. "The

86

police questioned her this morning. She's upset. The doctor's limiting visitors."

Frustrated, Aimée didn't know how to get around this. She needed to see Irati, to learn about this man Morbier had mentioned.

"Cybèle," she said, "during last night's party, Irati insisted that we talk. Told me it was urgent. And then. . . ."

"Last night? You're from Robbé's side of the family?" said Cybèle.

Wasn't everyone connected by six degrees of separation? She nodded, trying to ignore a twinge of guilt.

"Just a few moments, then."

Cybèle led her down a creaking hallway lined with paintings and motioned her to wait.

Aimée faced an arresting abstract of bright yellow punctuated by black lines. Alive, bright, and somehow disturbing. On the other wall, a sepia drawing of a factory in bold russet brown lines. Industrial and modernistic.

A door opened. Irati's aunt motioned her inside, then padded down the hallway.

A twentyish man with dark curly hair and thin black-framed glasses blocked the doorway. Weak-chinned and with a questioning look. "But I've never seen you before," he lisped: *hair on the tongue* was the old saying.

"Who are you?"

Robbé, the fiancé, stared at her, a mixture of alarm and irritation on his pale face.

"Some confusion. I'm sorry, Irati's aunt presumed I came from the family." She stepped forward. "We didn't meet last night. I'm Aimée Leduc."

"So *you're* the one!"

Whatever Robbé was implying didn't sound good.

"Irati's too shaken to see anyone now," he said, "as you can imagine." He turned toward the door.

"I'm sorry, of course. I understand."

He hesitated, a thaw in his voice. "But I'll mention that you came."

From what she'd seen of the ground floor layout, Xavierre would have used this hallway to reach the garden. So would the murderer.

She had to get information. No doubt he could shed some light.

"It's terrible, Robbé," she said. "Who would do this?"

"Talk to the *flics*," he said.

"Maybe you're unaware of the terrible allegation against Morbier. That he's a suspect. Can you tell me —"

"That's the *real* reason you're here, *non?*" he interrupted. "Not sympathy and flowers.

A tragedy, and you're asking questions?"

She hadn't expected this.

"He's the jealous type, I heard," Robbé said.

Anger flushed her cheeks. "Morbier was working in Lyon on a case."

Aimée heard footsteps, the creaking of the wooden floor. Irati — still in the red silk skirt, now wrinkled, her blouse half-unbuttoned — leaned against the door frame. For support, Aimée figured, given her vacant look and shaking fingers.

"Can I help, Irati? Why don't you lie down?" Aimée said. "We can talk. . . ."

"You told me so yourself," Irati said. "Jealous bastard. I hope he rots in hell."

Did she really believe that? Instead of being struck mute by tragedy, Irati's voice was edged with anger.

"But you know that's not true, Irati," she said. "Morbier loved your mother."

"Do I?" Her lip quivered. "I can't think any more," she said, clenching her fist. "I don't want to."

Robbé put his arm around Irati's shoulder. "Can't you see the strain you're putting on Irati? You'd better leave."

"Robbé, let me handle this," said Irati, shrugging him off.

"Someone was here, Irati. A man. You

must remember. The noises?"

"What?" Her legs wobbled.

Aimée reached to steady her, but Irati batted her arm away. Anger and fear suffused her pale face. Afraid to reveal what really went on? The bouquet fell, scattering gardenia petals over the Turkish carpet runner.

"*Je regrette,* I didn't mean to. . . ." Her voice was tinged with remorse.

Aimée sensed a chink in Irati's confusion. A chance to push for the truth.

"Did Xavierre's argument with this man get loud, so you shooed the guests away? Did you end the party early because of it?" she asked. "Did he threaten your mother, then you?"

"Who?"

"The man whose blood I found on the gravel."

Irati burst into sobs.

Robbé's hand clutched Aimée's arm and he pulled her down the hallway. "Look, last night we told the police everything," Robbé said. "And again today."

"Then you can explain. Who was he?"

"But there was a party, a house full of guests," Robbé said, his lisp more pronounced. "We've cooperated. They told us a suspect's in custody."

"Why can't you understand, Robbé?" she

90

asked, exasperated. "They've got the wrong person. Irati needs to tell the truth."

"Truth? As if we don't have enough to deal with right now? Canceling the wedding, relatives struck with grief, now we have to bury her. . . ."

Helplessness emanated from him.

"Overwhelming, I know. But . . ." She grabbed at a straw. ". . . I never saw a catering truck."

He blinked. "Now you're talking about caterers? You're crazy."

He edged away, shaking his head.

"What about the other Mercedes I saw parked in the driveway?"

"That's it. I'm getting a restraining order. Get out." He muttered something. A Basque curse by the sound of it. Slammed the door and locked it.

Closing ranks against outsiders. Again that smell of fear, like Irati.

She'd hit a stone wall. Played her cards and got nothing. She counted on Irati's aunt proving more helpful.

"Don't start with me, Mademoiselle," said Cybèle, hands on her hips in the dining room. "My husband's ill; I only arrived from Bayonne this morning," she said. "What do I know? Why should I be bothered about Irati's wedding? Xavierre, bless her soul" —

she paused, making the sign of the cross —
"I don't circulate in her chichi crowd.
Growing up, we never did either. We were
just sheepherding Basques."

A troubled look creased Cybèle's brow.
"The Basques say if you don't believe in a
law, don't break it; simply sidestep it." Cybèle shrugged. "I hadn't seen Xavierre for
months. But I tell you, all she talked about
was this wedding and that Morbier. What
we call *destino,* that fate meant them to
meet again."

She moved closer to Aimée. "Was it a
crime *passionnelle?* I'm not condoning it, I
tell you, but if it happened. . . ."

Aimée shook her head. "He's my godfather and I'd never seen him so happy. A
different person when they were together. I
saw them laughing, in love. . . ." she said.
"Morbier's devastated. He doesn't deserve
this."

"Who does? They say if the gods bless you
with a great passion once in your life, you
just endure the rest." A wistful look filled
Cybèle's eyes. "I discovered police instead
of wedding preparations," she said. "Did
anyone think to inform me?" A snort.

So she could tell Aimée little. Back to
zero: no one knew anything or would talk
to her.

"Not even Agustino's here." Cybèle sighed. "Always an empty stomach, that one." She gestured to an abstract on the wall, in a similar vein to the paintings in the hallway.

"This painter?"

"You know him?"

Aimée didn't, but nodded to keep her talking. The painting breathed life. Slashes of color, yet one could almost feel the heat, grit, and dust and hear the silver-green olive leaves rustle in a dry wind.

"Who'd have thought he'd become a Basque icon?" Cybèle expelled air from her mouth. "The old guard, Xavierre called him," she said, a tinge of disgust in her voice. "Just an aging *enfant terrible* who abhors politics now. Those old revolutionaries called themselves freedom fighters once."

Drawn to the painting, Aimée wondered at Cybèle's words. The mingled loss and despair in her voice. A brief hint of the past, something shared. Had there been more to their relationship?

"What do you mean, Cybèle?" she asked.

"That was another time, under Franco's dictatorship," she said. "We were young. Not that I helped much, stuck on the farm nursing my mother." A little smile. "Young, like you."

"So you're saying Agustino's sympathies —"

"Sympathies?" Cybèle interrupted. "The cause. Everyone wanted change, independence. Down in Bayonne, Xavierre, all the students, demonstrated to release Basque prisoners, protested the arrests in France. The daily arrests. Torture in Spanish police stations across the border. It was the times. We wanted to liberate the French Basque prisoners."

Now it made sense. ETA — *Euskadi Ta Askatasuna* — the Basque nationalist separatist group. Outlawed and regarded as terrorists by both France and Spain.

"You mean the ETA?"

"I never said that." Cybèle's jaw tightened. Her work-worn hands busied themselves on the table. "I've got no more to say."

Now she'd lost her.

"But such power in Agustino's work," she said, "such force. It's beautiful."

Cybèle gave a snort of disgust. "Agustino lives off fat commissions," she said, unable to resist one last dig. "A *très important* artist in residence at the Le Corbusier Foundation."

Aimée felt something warm being put into her hand. Caught the whiff of butter. Inside the blue cloth, tied up parcel-like, she saw the light brown crusted *gâteau* Basque. "You understand respect; you came to make proper condolences in your own way, Mademoiselle. I know that. And you, you're too thin."

Thin? She'd gained a kilo during her recuperation.

"Merci."

She shouldered her bag, scanning the room, the entry to the kitchen. No telephone. "My phone's out of battery," she said. "I'm late for an appointment. May I use yours?"

Cybèle gave her a piercing look, shrugged, then pulled a bronze metallic cell phone from the pocket of her skirt. "As if I remember how to use this."

"My colleague's got the same model." Aimée made a show of hitting buttons. "*Non,* I think to call out you push this." She kept the phone cupped in her hand while she scrolled down the contacts list until she found Irati's number.

"Busy." She clicked off. "*Merci,* Madame. I'll catch a taxi."

Outside on the path, she bent down to adjust her stocking. A green hose, coiled like a snake, dripped near the bushes. The damp butterscotch-colored limestone gravel crunched under her boots. The traces of the bloodstains from last night had been washed away.

Still, she scooped a handful into her pocket and with her black kohl eye pencil jotted Irati's number on her palm while she still remembered it. She shivered, but not from the cold. Irati stood in the upstairs window, a phone to her ear, watching her.

TUESDAY AFTERNOON

Agustino stroked the canvas with his horse-hair brush, leaving a swirl of dusky orange. He wiped the perspiration beading his neck, stepped back, and surveyed the tall canvas, his commission for the Guggenheim in Bilbao. A quiet sense of exhilaration ran through him. Ten hours of painting today in the studio already, and he could work five more.

Now in his mid-fifties, his wavy black hair threaded with gray, he carried a slight paunch and survived on cat naps. He felt alive, focused as always, when his work flowed. He'd almost captured the dance of light, evoked the tingling pine-resin scent, the indigo shadow tinting the Pyrénées valley.

More ochre, he decided.

He reached for his fine-point Kolonosky sable-hair brush, visualizing an arc for the curve. But his paint-encrusted fingertips came back with a brush tipped by hard-caked burnt sienna. The earth tones flaked over his palette. Ruined. His best brush, ruined! Jorge hadn't cleaned it.

Jorge was late, too. He'd sent him out for pigment hours ago. The nineteen-year-old slept in the atelier in return for doing errands and cleaning up. Frustrated, Agustino pushed aside the

dry jars, wanting to capture the line, to keep this rush. He searched behind the pestle where he ground dry pigments. Not there. He tried to remember where he'd stored his stock of brushes.

Where had he put them?

Shadows of fallen maple leaves on the glass-paned roof dappled the paint-spattered concrete floor. The odor of turpentine wafted from half-empty cans. Dustballs furred in the corners. He realized Jorge hadn't cleaned up in days. The atelier looked a mess. Pushing aside his irritation, he kept looking for the fine brush he needed for the crucial line.

The glass-walled atelier contained no closets, no storage; just southern exposure and light. Radiant light. When the clouds parted in the pearl-gray sky, he uttered inner thanks for the residency program. Not to mention the prestige, the commissions coming his way. Shoving easels aside, he found the trunks with supplies in the corner: charcoal sticks, tubes of Sennelier pigment, old frames he'd picked up at the flea market.

Somewhere . . . where had he put those brushes?

He tied back his paint-spattered shirttails and bent down behind an easel. Pulling open his grandfather's old leather trunk, he found his brushes strewn inside. His slow burn of anger notched higher. Why couldn't this boy respect materials? Agustino kept his tail sable-hair brushes, costing several hundred francs each, protected and ordered by size. With care, he gathered up the fine-tipped brushes.

Below were bulging navy blue canvas bags. Like postal sacks. IMPRIMERIE NATIONALE was stenciled on the blue canvas.

Startled, Agustino opened a bag. Hundreds of small official printed documents.

He leaned back on his haunches, stunned. Then looked closer.

French passports, vehicle-registration forms, identity cards. All freshly minted with official stamps, and without names. Blank.

Worth a fortune if authentic. And he had no doubt they were.

How had they gotten here? Besides himself, only Jorge and the half-senile concierge of the Arts Foundation complex had a key. Foreboding weighted his chest.

Jorge. He'd ignored the telltale signs, wanting to believe him, to give him another chance.

His heart sank.

The cell phone vibrated on the paint-stained table. Damn thing. He never answered it. But maybe he should . . . maybe. . . .

"Oui?"

"Finally you answered, Agustino." A snort of disgust. "I know you've ignored my messages." He recognized Cybèle's voice quavering with emotion. "You can't even come to mourn, ignoring our tradition. What kind of friend do you call yourself, eh? Xavierre's dead and Irati's beside herself. . . ."

Stunned, he gripped the phone.

"Dead?"

"Like you didn't know?" A sob. "Murdered."

Cybèle's sharp denial of Xavierre's involvement in ETA played in Aimée's head, along with doubts raised by Irati's reactions: anger, fear, and evasiveness. Aimée needed to discover the Basque angle and to talk to Agustino. If he'd been at the party last night, he'd provide answers.

A few streets away, Aimée reached the white sugar cube–like Le Corbusier Foundation buildings glowing in the afternoon light. The villas la Roche and Jeanneret, according to a sign, contained Le Corbusier's apartment and an exhibition space emblematic of the architect's modern style. Sleek, linear, and sparse: not her taste. More a revolt against Guimard's Art Nouveau swirls and curlicued noodles. Not her taste either. She felt glad she didn't live in this chic, sterile, residential *quartier* devoid of street life and cafés.

"The Foundation's closed this week." The

silver-haired concierge, glasses perched on his forehead, stood at the door eying Aimée's legs. "Opens next Monday."

"Of course, Monsieur," she said. "But the Foundation's artist in residence —"

"Can't you read?" He pointed to the wall plaque listing Le Corbusier's archives, library hours, and permanent exhibitions open to the public. "Not here."

The Foundation appeared to be devoted to architecture and Le Corbusier. Not to paintings like those she'd seen on Xavierre's walls, notable for bold lines and vibrant colors. But she wouldn't give up yet.

"But I've got an appointment with Monsieur Agustino, the Basque painter." She handed him a card from the collection in her bag. "Concerning a painting for my pied-à-terre."

He bent lower, adjusting his reading glasses under the loge light. Shook his head.

"Try the annex." He turned away.

"Where's that?"

"Rue Mallet-Stevens. Middle alley." The door shut in her face.

Another lane of white buildings, these attributed to the architect Robert Mallet-Stevens. Bright yellow, red, and chartreuse metal awnings gave a varied look to more luminous sugar cubes.

Not her taste either. And not promising in a deserted, shadowed street. Her hopes sank.

Ahead she made out a small sign reading FLC almost hidden behind a laurel tree. The Fondation Le Corbusier annex.

She turned into a lane, kept going, and found herself in a narrow parkway. Midway lay an eighteenth-century *hôtel particulier* — abandoned, from the look of the boarded-up doors. Beyond the trees were low buildings and ateliers backing the warren of apartment buildings. Gardens and greenery were set back in courtyards. Traces of the village it had been, she thought, like another world sheltered from the street. Hidden, discreet, exuding an old-fashioned charm.

Her boots crunched on the gravel and packed dirt. Also secluded, dark, and a perfect place to hide. A shiver went up her spine.

She felt a spreading dampness in her leather boots from the wet grass. Thick ribbons of light slanted over the dark green bushes. The source was a glass and metal-paned hothouse, an atrium resembling an old *jardin d'hiver* adjoining a building. Illuminated like a lighthouse, it shone with a blurred luminosity against the dark shadowy enclave.

On closer inspection, she saw canvases with orange-yellow splashes stacked against the glass. Frames around the larger canvases blocked her view of most of the interior. But by an easel she could make out a figure with his back to her. Heavy maroon draperies shielded the interior of the atelier against door drafts.

Her knuckles knocking on the glass made a brittle *ting.*

The curtains semi-parted. A man appeared, only his dark hair threaded with gray and a paint-spattered hand visible.

"Monsieur Agustino?" she said.

"What do you want?"

"Five minutes," she said. Her breath frosted in the cold air. All of a sudden, the interior light went out. "May I come inside?"

"I'm working." His head pulled back.

She couldn't lose this opportunity.

"It's important. Please," she said.

"Not the *facture* again?" He sighed. "Just a moment."

Facture? A bill? Before she could think of an answer, the glass door creaked open. A gnome-like man emerged. Looking closer, she noticed his physiognomy, a Basque prototype: solid, compact, olive-complected weathered skin, strong arms, muscular legs, long earlobes, prominent nose. The lines from his twinkling dark eyes radiated upward, giving the impression of perpetual wonder. She'd had a teacher once with the same visage; he'd never looked unhappy, even during lunch duty at her table when he'd been informed that his mother had died and tears had streamed down his face into the cassoulet.

"*Et alors,* tell the framing company we'll settle out of court," he said.

Thick brows furrowed his wide forehead. Black pinprick eyes darted over her outfit. The man pulsated with energy. Nervous energy.

He wanted to get rid of her.

Aimée smiled and handed him her card.

"A detective, eh?" A furtive look accompanied his shrug. "Insurance? One of my clients' paintings stolen? Not my problem."

No time for niceties or indirect questioning. Time to get to the point while she had his attention.

"I'm not from an insurance company," she said. "We're questioning the guests at the party last night —"

"You think I have time for parties?" he interrupted, rubbing his hands on his paint-spattered shirt. "I'm working on a commission for the Bilbao museum. On deadline."

She believed him.

"But whatever you can tell me about Xavierre d'Eslay, her past, a connection with ETA, could bear on the case."

That was stretching it.

"Why me?" He averted his eyes.

So he knew something.

"You're a family friend, from what I understand," she said, "from your student days as a Basque activist with Xavierre, according to her sister Cybèle —"

"Cybèle? Consider the source, eh?"

No love lost between him and Cybèle. "Meaning?"

"I *paint,* Mademoiselle. That's what I do. That's *all* I do. I'm not political," he said in a matter-of-fact tone. "Except in the sense that all art's political. My father fought in the Freedom Brigade against Franco. That was enough for me."

Au contraire, she thought: Franco's oppression spurred the Basques and Catalans to resist. And they hadn't stopped.

"Me, I have an appetite for life," he said. "Zest. You young people don't have it."

He spread his muscular arms as if invoking the weak sun. Hot-blooded, he didn't seem to mind the cold in his short-sleeved shirt. She rubbed the goose bumps on her arms, wishing she had worn another layer.

"Blame it on my little *nonna,*" he said, waxing poetic. "My grandmother raised ten children, then grandchildren. Never sick a day in her life. Every year butchered the pig, made blood sausage, salted the pork, took over sheepherding when my father lost his sight to Franco's fascists."

He was wound up now, his eyes alive. "Until I grew tall enough to climb over the pasture fences to guide the herd away from the cliffs. That gave me an eye for color, how things fit together, the economy of line in nature, nothing superfluous. The natural design, integrating use and design, utility and nature."

An articulate showman: he hit all the right notes, she imagined, for his clients. But she wasn't one.

"A room needs a painting and a view," he said. "That's all. Like our farmhouse."

Well-rehearsed in an earthy, Picasso-esque manner with a weather-beaten face to lend credibility. No wonder it brought him commissions. But he was hiding something.

"I'm French Basque, but you French complicate design with froufrou, rococo. Let the natural lines highlight the inner form, the beauty."

Forget the art lecture, she wanted to say. She wasn't in a classroom or about to write a check. And then it hit her: he was giving this speech to stall for time, or to avoid revealing his past connection with Xavierre.

"Monsieur Agustino, if you could listen for a moment —"

"*Non, you* must listen. Understand. It's life, how I breathe, my heritage that makes me —"

"Involved with ETA again?" she interrupted.

He shoved the card back into her hand. Glancing down, she noticed the stubbed flesh where his last two fingers would have been. Amazing that he could still paint masterpieces.

"Watch what you're saying." His voice lowered. "In the old prisons, I went back and carved memorials in the dripping walls, memorials to the fallen," he said. "To both sides — the Guardia Civil, ETA. My soul hurt, still does. For years my work has celebrated the Basque spirit, reconciliation, not violence."

His eyes bore into her. "How do you think I lost these?" He lifted his claw-like hand. "Xavierre knows . . . knew that."

Aimée nodded. "I saw your paintings. Breathing life, speaking to me."

"Then you know art touches more minds and spirits than bombs." His arm trembled. His showman side evaporated. "My heart mourns Xavierre. On the phone with her last night, all I could talk about was my commission. How I needed to paint. Our last words. Well, she said I was too caught up in my art like usual. I'll regret it all my life."

Guilt. But over that?

"But didn't you sense her fear? Did she tell you something?"

"Apart from how selfish I've become?" Agustino gave a small shrug. "The family, this big wedding, the home, it's a religion with Basques. Coward that I am, I can't face Irati now, or any of them."

"Who would murder her, Agustino?"

He made a sign of the cross. "God knows. But I broke our pact," he said. "You see, I failed her in the most important thing to her."

"What pact?"

"Made years ago. To be there for each other. I couldn't even do a simple thing, attend her party. And I'd promised to come." He looked away.

"Then this pact's deep, *non?*" she said, trying a guess. "What about the others from your student days in Bayonne? The protest-ors?"

He turned, his shoulders slumped. But he hadn't answered her question.

"Haven't you maintained the bonds you made with them?" she said. "Like with Xavierre."

"Time takes people away."

"Not the past," she said. "What if the past connects to Xavierre's murder?"

"All those people went to prison." A sigh frosted the air. "Like my brother."

"Look, I tried to talk to Xavierre last night," she said. "To find out if something was wrong. My turn to feel guilt. I couldn't even do that."

"You take your job to heart, Mademoiselle. I respect that."

"Not a job," she said. "A promise I made. A deep debt I owe to a person close to me."

If none of her other words got through to him, she sensed these would.

"You see, Agustino," she said, "I've already made one mistake. If I'd known the trouble Xavierre was in. . . ."

"Giving one's word. . . ." He spoke as if to himself, shaking his head. "But what if you gave it long ago and now it goes against everything you know is right, that you believe in?"

And she thought she understood. "Ask yourself this. Haven't hundreds of innocent people been killed in ETA actions? As you asked me yourself, will killing more people help the Basque movement?"

A flicker of his eyelid.

She pursued it. "There's ways to keep your word and yet help me without saying a thing."

Agustino stood dead still. A long moment passed. Then a little shake of his head.

He closed the door to his atelier. One light went on, a dim glow in the dark valley of green. Only afternoon sounds, the soft cooing of pigeons, a siren's distant wail, could be heard. Not only was he a sad man scarred by regrets, but he was also hiding something. She slipped her card back under the door.

Rubbing her cold hands together, Aimée shivered in the *allée* overhung with chestnut trees near Xavierre's high wall. She turned the corner. Xavierre's neighbor's window provided a view of the back garden and the driveway. This woman, Madame de Boucher — a busybody, according to the concierge — had been born in the building, had lived here eighty years. Aimée mounted the building staircase hoping for a font of information.

"My neighbor's comings and goings?" Madame de Boucher leaned on her ebony walking stick and gave a dismissive wave with her other blue-veined hand. "Ask the concierge."

"But I did, Madame, and she suggested I speak with you." Aimée gave a wide smile and flashed her PI license with the less-than-flattering photo. In the background she heard high-pitched singing and recognized "Leaves of Autumn," based on the Verlaine poem.

"I spoke to the *flics* already," the old woman said. "Told them like I'm telling you, I saw nothing, heard nothing. *C'est tout.*"

Aimée groaned inside. After Agustino, for the past two hours she'd questioned the lane's inhabitants: a retired professor, a musician, several cleaning women and maids, all of whom had said the same thing. People either hadn't been home last night or had drawn their shades. She'd hit another wall.

"A shame, Madame." Arms weary, she set her bag down. "The family's devastated that they can't even hold a service, but I thought —"

"Is that for me?" interrupted Madame de Boucher, staring at the *gâteau* Basque on top, which was emanating a fragrance of cherries.

Aimée saw a way in the door. "Of course, but let me heat it up. Seeing as you've got a. . . ." She paused. Was it a recital? Singing lessons? "There's plenty for your guest."

"Guest?" Then a look of understanding on the old woman's face, crinkling in a web of fine lines. "You mean Hector? I'm busy cleaning, Mademoiselle."

At her age? And in this *quartier* resplendent with hired help?

"Come back tomorrow, Mademoiselle."

She had to get inside in the door.

"But I can help and warm this for you in the kitchen."

"*Comme ça?* In that outfit?"

So her standby funeral suit, a flea-market-find black wool Givenchy, would go to the dry cleaners. "No problem, Madame."

Madame de Boucher tapped her stick on the newspapers piled on the threadbare hall carpet runner. Another wave of her hand. "Into the parlor, then, *s'il vous plaît.*"

Humor her, Aimée thought: she might know a detail, might have noticed something over the past few days. Aimée scooped up the rustling, yellowed newspapers and followed Madame de Boucher.

The cracked leather-bound volumes filling a wall of bookshelves and worn, brocaded Louis chairs couldn't mask the faded charm of the nineteenth-century parlor. A chandelier with missing crystals cast a dim glow on the high-ceilinged, carved-wood *boiseries* bordering the cream wood-paneled walls and dried flower arrangements under glass globes.

She felt like she'd entered a Proust novel. Except for the chrome high-tech medic alert remote-control device and the blue-and-yellow-plumed singing parrot perched near a matching cloisonné vase on a claw-footed table.

"Hector's particular, you know," Madame said, pointing to the dirty wire cage.

The parrot's repetitive singing grated on Aimée's ears. She set the *gâteau* Basque down on the table.

"He's my companion of twenty-five years now," she said.

Aimée's nose crinkled as she pulled out the birdcage tray clumped with bird feces dotted with feather fluff. Slants of light from the window lit the faded Turkish carpet, turning it a dull red, reminding her of old blood.

She changed the newspaper lining and

jerked her chin toward the window. "What a wonderful view over the garden." She paused, pretending to put it together. "That's Xavierre's garden, *non?*"

"They use it like a parking lot these days. Disgusting."

Aimée nodded. "Of course you notice the comings and goings. How can you miss seeing, eh? Especially last night, Irati's big party, the noise, guests. . . ."

"My stupid cousin widened the gate. In my grandfather's time it was just wide enough for a *fiacre.*"

A horse-drawn carriage from the last century.

"Nowadays they're garages," she continued.

"I suppose you knew Madame Xavierre?"

"What's it to you?" The old woman bristled, her tone changed.

Bad tactic. "Madame, I'm —"

"Snooping and asking questions, like they did," Madame de Boucher interrupted.

Aimée's ears perked up. The parrot's tone shrilled. She shoved the clean newspaper-lined tray back inside the cage and tried not to sneeze. If only the damned bird would shut up.

"Who do you mean, Madame?"

"I told them nothing, you understand.

Like always."

"But weren't you worried? Upset? Your neighbor's murdered in her garden almost outside your window?" She tried to keep her voice level.

"*Et alors,* I heard nothing." Madame de Boucher's mouth tightened.

"Help me understand the timeline, Madame," she said. "The report places the murder at seven forty-five. A Mercedes pulled out of that driveway minutes later. Did you hear —"

"The Bomb could drop while I listen to my program on Radio Classique and I wouldn't hear it," Madame de Boucher interrupted. "I knew the poor woman to say '*Bonjour*' in the morning, that's all."

Disappointed, Aimée knew she needed to change tactics. This woman, who'd lived here eighty years, had to know something. And didn't like the *flics.*

"But it's a person like you, Madame, who knows the *quartier,* the rhythm of life here, who can help me the most." She smiled, determined to ingratiate herself. "So quiet and peaceful here."

Madame de Boucher snorted. *"C'est un village ici."*

Aimée nodded. *"Bien sûr.* Maybe you noticed a person you hadn't seen before in the past few days?"

Madame de Boucher guided Hector, now perched on her ebony stick, into the cleaned cage. With one hand she covered the cage with a black flannel cloth, and the parrot quieted at once. She sighed, sinking into the armchair brocaded with fleurs-de-lis, setting her stick against the armrest.

"A detective?" said Madame de Boucher, her eyes hooded with suspicion, glaring at Aimée's suit. "Since when do the *flics* wear couture? Or do my taxes pay for that?"

Aimée didn't bother to enlighten Madame as to the fact that private detectives didn't work for the *flics.* And wished she had a tissue to wipe off the grit clinging to her hands.

"On my salary I shop at Réciproque, the *dépôt-vente* consignment shop, Madame." Aimée winked. That store was the *quartier*'s bargain-hunter mecca of gently worn couture from wives who cleaned out their closets every season.

"You're some special investigator?" she said, still suspicious.

Aimée sat down. The chair leg creaked under her. "Nothing so exciting, I'm afraid." She leaned forward as if in confidence. "You've heard of Internal Affairs?"

Madame de Boucher shook her head.

"*La police des polices.* We check irregularities in police investigations. But that's between you and me."

"You're all the same. Lists. Always lists," said Madame de Boucher, waving her hand. "We just follow the directives and go by the list, they said."

What did a list have to do with Xavierre's murder?

"Madame, what list?"

"Nineteen forty-three, the hottest July I can remember," she said. The old woman's gaze leveled somewhere in the distance. A past Aimée couldn't see.

"Beat the record," Madame said. "Humid like a steam room. Not even a breeze. I'd closed the shutters, but that didn't keep out the heat. At six A.M. they came pounding on the door. Within two hours they'd ransacked our building, looted every apartment."

Aimée opened her mouth to speak, but Madame de Boucher continued.

"The Milice, the French Gestapo, arrested my brother. Criminals, all of them. Felons released from prison to do the dirty work."

Madame gave a little shrug. "More Nazis lived here than in any other *quartier*. Six hundred ninety-two official German-requisitioned buildings, according to surviving records," she said. "They lusted after

118

the town houses, made the Hotel Majestic a *Kommandantur.* Forbade us calling them *boches,* preferred *Fritz.* Regardless of what we called them, *les Fritz* requisitioned whatever they wanted. Apartments, *hôtels particuliers,* garages, hotels, clinics, bars, restos, theaters. Four Gestapo bureaus, even a *soldatenheim* on the Champs-Elysées."

"But Madame," Aimée interrupted.

"They had taste, I'll say that for them." The old woman continued as if she hadn't heard. "After Liberation, I had to share this apartment with the family of a Milicien who took my brother. Can you imagine?"

Aimée shook her head, hoping this was leading somewhere.

"That too went according to a list. A housing-shortage list. I got a pittance after the war. A few pieces. That one."

She gestured to the blue-and-white cloisonné vase.

"The Milice forced my brother to work in the Bassano, a *hôtel particulier,* outfitted like a restoration studio but an internment camp," she said. "Just blocks away. Who knows now, eh? He restored the looted pianos stored under the Palais de Chaillot. Pleyels, Bechsteins, Steinways, all confiscated from Jewish apartments." A shuttered look crossed her eyes. "Took Madame Morgenstern's baby grand. She lived on the second floor. Later, they took her."

Impatient, Aimée wondered how this connected to Xavierre — or if it even did. Was it just another sad reminiscence of the war by an old woman who kept a parrot for company, death taking everything but her stories? Or had Xavierre's murder jogged loose the old stories, some with a parallel to the present? She had to draw Madame from the past, discover some detail from this eagle-eyed woman who, she suspected, didn't miss a thing.

"So the man, or men, you spoke to wore uniforms?"

"Uniforms?" The old woman shook her head. "They wanted to rent space for their car."

Aimée contained her frustration. The woman dipped back and forth in time. Not that this was leading anywhere. But she had to try.

"Was that before or after Xavierre's murder?"

"Everything's political, you know."

What did *that* mean? Aimée gritted her teeth. But she nodded, determined to persist.

"You're a Socialist, Madame?"

"Picasso said that. My father collected

some of his smaller works. All taken, *phhft*." She expelled air from her mouth. "A nasty little man, that Picasso, but I agree." Her tone dismissive. "So does Irati. It's those protests she attends."

Alert, Aimée leaned forward. A new angle to consider. "Protests? Irati doesn't strike me as political."

"*Phfft!* The young these days," Madame said, as if that explained it. "We met at the poll during the last election. We both voted Socialist. Irati joked that we're the only two Socialists in the *quartier*. Our mayor's a Taittinger, the Champagne seigneur; we're his fiefdom." Madame de Boucher's chignon loosened as she nodded. A strand of white hair fell, softening the contours of her thin face. "*C'est tout.* Then I get this! A mistake. No interest to me."

Aimée sat up.

"May I see?"

Madame de Boucher used an aluminum rod with pincers at the end to clutch some papers on the divan.

Aimée took the white paper, folded pamphlet-style, titled *Euskadi Action*. The Basque-language leaflet didn't make sense to her either. But an address on rue Duban and the date Sunday at 6:30 P.M., that

121

much she understood. The rest she'd find out.

Madame de Boucher nodded, staring at the *gâteau* Basque. "Aren't you going to cut me a slice?"

"Crime in our *quartier?*" Dubouchet, the on-duty sergeant in the Passy Commissariat, grinned, showing yellowed teeth. "Just the usual: rich teenagers thrill-shoplifting, *domestiques* stealing from their employer. What goes around comes around, eh?"

She'd come to check with Thesset about the Mercedes, but he'd gone off duty. "But on the *télé,* the news announced this crime of passion. . . ."

"I can't talk about ongoing investigations, Mademoiselle." Dubouchet's voice turned serious.

Great: now he'd clammed up. And Thesset, her source, was gone. The smell of hot printer toner wafted from behind her. An old-fashioned heater rumbled, sending out dribbles of heat.

"Zut!" Gandon, a middle-aged lieutenant sitting at a desk, ground out his cigarette in his demitasse saucer. "Dubouchet forgets the glory days, our unrivaled crimes." He opened a drawer, pulled out a thick stapled

manuscript with relish. "Bit of a history buff myself. My little opus, which I hope to publish next year, could enlighten you."

"Might want to finish writing the thing first, Gandon," Dubouchet said in a tired voice.

"Mademoiselle, our arrondissement encompasses two zip codes, with a Taittinger as reigning mayor. Despite our current *haut bourgeois* reputation, I recount our long history. It's fascinating reading." Gandon thumbed the pages, warming to his subject. "Eighteen seventy, the anti-Bonapartist Victor Noir's assassination by Napoleon III's nephew. A Républican hero. Legend goes women visit his tomb for fertility; go figure, but it adds glamour, eh, a footnote to history." Gandon winked.

She shifted her feet, hoping this would lead somewhere.

"The attempt on Clemenceau's life, 1919," he said. "I'll have you know we've even had our own serial killer, Dr. Marcel Petiot, a charmer who dismembered his patients, hid the bits in the courtyard well, then, copying his heroes the *boches,* incinerated them in his homemade crematorium. Of course, the real 'French Connection' heroin king, André Condemine, was gunned down not ten blocks from here."

Gandon's face was suffused with pride. Aimée unwound her silk scarf, wishing for an open window to ventilate the tepid, stale air.

"Who would have thought?" She hadn't bargained on an earful. But the eager Gandon knew his turf. "Anything interesting on the political front?"

"*Bien sûr,* we've had our share." Gandon thumbed the pages. "The 1980 synagogue bombing on rue Copernic, terrible. Four dead. I carried out what was left of the bodies." He shook his head. "We had political terrorists — Action Directe, who'd hooked up with Carlos the Jackal. Not to mention a cannibal." He looked up for Aimée's admiration. "Name me another *quartier* that had a Japanese student cut up his teacher and eat her, eh?"

Aimée tried to look impressed.

"Even René Bousquet couldn't hide his Vichy past. It caught up with him right in his doorway on Avenue Raphaël. Not two months ago, Princess Di departed on our patch too . . . don't forget that."

Gandon pulled out a map. "See, I color-coded and cross-referenced the crime locations on the chart below."

Not a book she'd pick from the bookstore shelf. "Amazing," she said, "such work and documentation."

"But I have more. . . ."

"Any action from the Basque Cultural center, your neighbor on rue Duban?" she smiled.

Gandon snorted. "Loud fêtes, noise-disturbance complaints. Unlike the eighties, when ETA came over the Pyrénées for sanctuary from Franco, robbed banks, bought guns." Gandon rifled under the papers on his desk, found a copy of the current *Le Parisien.* "A sea change. Look at this: a French Basque leader ready to broker peace negotiations!"

Aimée stared at the small article midway down the front page. *Basque referendum agreement . . . negotiations set for Bayonne area . . . military units pull back . . . celebrating a reception at Musée Marmottan.*

"*Merci,* Gandon," she said.

A sea change? She'd find out. It might mean nothing, but right now she had little else to go on.

She hit Morbier's cell phone number on her speed dial, praying he'd been released. Already late afternoon, and still no answer — nor any message from him on her phone.

In order to vindicate Morbier, she needed a suspect. Another angle. Minutes later, she headed down rue Duban, a narrow shop-lined street, feeding into the heart of the old village of Passy. Midway, she found the Basque Cultural Center in a courtyard near the rear staircase. After climbing the winding narrow stairs to the fourth floor, she knocked on the office door.

"Entrez," a voice said.

A young man wearing a T-shirt in red, white, and green, the Basque colors, and a wool cap sat behind a computer screen, humming to himself. Posters on the wall showed the picturesque harbor of Saint Jean de Luz and caramel stone castle fortresses in the Pyrénées, proclaiming LE PAYS BASQUE, VIVE LA DIFFÉRENCE.

"Bonjour, Monsieur." She smiled.

He pointed to the twilight descending over the jagged rooftops outside the window. "More like *bonsoir,* Mademoiselle." He gave her a big grin. "I'm Edrigu. You're here for tickets to the fête? We've got a special top DJ from Pau."

"I wish, but I'm out of town then," she said. "But my friend Irati. . . ."

"That's my daughter's middle name," he said. "Beautiful, eh? Means fern, you know."

"Vraiment? Then you know my friend?" she asked, hopeful. "She gave me this."

He shook his head. His brow creased as he perused the leaflet in Aimée's hand. Gave a snort. "Old news. The Euskadi Action?" He stood up from the computer, glanced at the time. "Haven't seen them for a while. We disagree with these protests. Not worth your while."

"But it lists your center. . . ."

"We pulled out," he said. "Those types ruin the dialogue, stop progress for Basque autonomy. We're progressive here."

"How's that?" she said.

"Simple. The referendum passed, and our consul Goikoetxea's brokering negotiations for a Basque peace settlement," he said. "Euskadi Action's staging a protest. So what? For once, the Progressives gained a majority. Almost a done deal. Goikoetxea's here to seal it."

She recalled the article in *Le Parisien.* But how did it involve Irati?

"So you're saying Goikoetxea's a force for peace —"

"And progress, modern thinking," he said. "Unlike ETA or the splinter group Euskadi Action. There's more to Basque nationalism than our famous Ixtapha cherries and bombs. He's making the official announcement of the new accord at the Marmottan reception."

Piped strains of tinny music drifted in from outside the window. The music of childhood. "Aahh, the *orgue de Barbarie,*" he said.

Down on the cobblestoned street, an older man was turning the handle of an organ barrel. A few children looked out their windows, pointing. Aimée reached in her bag and threw down a coin from the window, as she'd done as a child.

Edrigu shut down the computer and pulled on his windbreaker. "My daughter would love to see this. I've got to pick her up from *l'école maternelle.*" He paused at the door. "If you want to know more, ask the *mecs* at the bistro."

"Where's that?"

"On the corner."

For all the bistro's turn-of-the-century decor — pale nicotine-stained ceilings, an out-of-commission charcoal-burning stove with a flowerpot of asters crowning it, age-spotted mirrors above the red-and-white-checked tablecloths, lace curtains over faded lettering on fogged-up windows — the clientele surprised Aimée. Not the usual upscale wedge of the 16th outfitted in Hermès scarves, pearls, and tweeds.

Here the men at the bar wore flat black berets and loose suit jackets, and they perched over shot glasses of a pale yellow liquid. Everyone was smoking.

She'd kicked the habit. Three days and three hours short of a month. Not that she missed it.

To a man, they all turned, gave her a once-over that lasted a second, then turned back without a break in their conversation. A closed world, and she'd been noted as an outsider to their camaraderie. Her palms tingled; she felt as if she'd time traveled and been dropped into a Basque bistro in Bayonne. Complete with locals, pelota playing on the *télé,* and the aroma of something simmering in a red wine sauce.

At one of the tables, two older men — one wore a pinstriped suit, the other a cashmere overcoat — were selecting from a plate of green and black olives. The air lay thick with the tang of Gauloises and a dialect that she figured was Basque.

The only other female, a young woman in jeans and an apron, was sweeping the floor and didn't look up.

Still, Aimée had to concentrate, use this as a route to find out about the Euskadi Action group and its link to Irati.

If Irati was receiving flyers from a Basque group down the street that didn't meet any more, Aimée doubted it could be linked to Xavierre's murder. Yet Xavierre would be known in this Basque community. Hadn't René said that everything with the Basques was political? A peace announcement seemed to be imminent; little good that info did her. But right now she was clutching at straws, anything to point in a different direction regarding Xavierre's murder. Any suspect instead of Morbier.

"Something to chase the cold, Mademoiselle?" The barman gestured to a stool. "This gentleman offers to buy you a drink."

Time to learn whatever she could here. And a drink sounded good.

Aimée knocked back the shot of Izarra, the sweet Basque liqueur with its signature star on the bottle's label.

"Forty different herbs; good for the heart, the digestion, and the spirit," said the short white-haired man next to her.

More like forty proof. The herbal taste burned the back of her throat. He winked and pushed his beret farther up his flushed forehead. "Now, if I was forty years younger. . . ."

"But you're not, Citu," said a man from the table. "Quit boring the young lady."

The man at the table cocked his fist by his nose, the gesture meaning tipsy. Like most of the ones leaning on the bar, she'd noticed from their glazed eyes and high-octane breath. So far, they'd muttered in a Basque dialect and were more interested in the handball game than conversation.

"Some olives, Mademoiselle?"

But an idea sparked into her head. No doubt inspired by the Izarra.

"Why not?" She gave a big smile and sat down at their table. "Maybe you can advise me. The Basque center's closed. I wasted a trip here, but my niece wants to learn Basque," she said. "I promised her a visit to Bayonne. Irati suggested the Center might give classes. But is it safe?"

"You've never had an olive like these. Taste." Like a command, the man in the cashmere overcoat with a poker face rivaling film star Lino Ventura's pushed the bowl toward her. Wrinkled black and green olives glistening with oil. "From my cousin's grove in Navarre, aged, then cured high in the Alta Pyrénées."

She chewed, tasting a deep explosion of herbs, almost the warmth of the sun, the meaty olive.

"*Voilà,* look at her face. She understands." He gave a knowing look to his friend, jabbed him in the rib. Close-cropped white hair, rugged cheekbones, he let out a big laugh that splintered his face. "Ours is a language of the eyes. *Oui,* you already speak a little

Basque." Deep laughter erupted from his chest. "You Parisians don't know from olives, don't know from our country. Always worried, for what? Our people respect the land; we live with nature, not that old bloodshed."

She spit the pit into her palm, dropped it in the ashtray.

"Didn't I tell you, eh?" he said. "I'll leave some with the owner. Bring your niece. The girl must visit the Basque country. Learn our language, the oldest language in the world, our customs; not even the Romans ruled us. She'll never come back."

"You're from the tourist board?" She smiled. A high-powered broker of a sort, she figured, with his long black cashmere coat, well-cut suit underneath. A type to move in Xavierre's circles.

He jabbed his friend again. "I like her." He extended his hand, gripped Aimée's in a strong handshake. "Beñat. My friend Paulo."

"Aimée. But maybe you know my friend Irati," she said. "Irati's involved in the Euskadi Action, lives nearby."

Paulo shrugged. "We're here on business."

"Her mother Xavierre came from Bayonne," she said, lowering her eyes. "It was . . . terrible. It was on the news last night. Her murder."

"Aah, a tragedy. I heard." Paulo shook his head.

"My family knew hers, but years ago," Beñat said. "Who'd ever think this could happen? Mademoiselle, how can you worry about the Basque country when you've got murder here on the streets?"

Beñat erupted in a salvo of coughing and covered his mouth. Racking coughs came from deep in his chest. His eyes watered. *"Excusez-moi,"* he said when he recovered. "Chest cold. Can't seem to shake it."

She didn't know the man, but she felt sympathy.

"Has the doctor checked that out?"

"We have a deal, the doctors and I," he said. "I don't bother them; they don't bother me." He shot her a grin, dabbing his eyes with a handkerchief.

"You sound like my godfather," she said. Her shoulders tensed, thinking of Morbier in a cold cell in the damp, dripping underground.

"Tell him to try this. Puts the doctors out of business." He downed a shot glass of Izarra, waved to the barman. "We're late, Paulo." He stood, his chair scraping back over the mosaic tiles. He buttoned his coat. "Take your niece to Bayonne, Mademoiselle." He gave a brief bow. *"Enchanté."*

At the bar, Aimée caught the barman's attention. "What do I owe you?"

He waved her francs away. "Taken care of by the gentlemen."

"Great olives. May I order some?" she said, hoping to get more of a take on them. "That's their business, *non?*"

"And I'm Franco's bastard love child," he said, a current running in his voice. No amusement glittered in his eye. "Bayonne business bigwigs. Money coming out of their pores. Ones who moan that the Paris-to-Madrid high-speed train will carve up the Basque countryside, ruin the culture. That's until their lobbyists bribe planning commissions to build a station near their factory. Then they change their tune. Or ETA stops bombing the tracks."

"Sounds political."

"What isn't?" he said.

That phrase again.

"Or grist for business?"

"Like I said. . . ." He trailed off.

TUESDAY EARLY EVENING

Leaves scuffled outside the atelier. That detective again? Shaking, Agustino parted the maroon curtains.

Jorge, stoop-shouldered and rail-thin, in jeans and a brown hoodie, with a growth of a sparse reddish stubble on his long face, grinned, waved, and gave a thumbs-up from the brick-and-grass-tufted path.

"The color pops, Agustino." Jorge shut the studio's glass door, a Sennelier bag under his arm. "The painting jumps out from all the way —"

"Get out!" Agustino grabbed the Sennelier bag, the veins in his neck pulsing. "Take all this . . . you piece of shit!"

Jorge's face fell. His round brown eyes took in the open trunk. "You've got the wrong idea."

"Wrong idea? Think I'm blind, do you? And stupid?"

Agustino heaved out the blue sacks,

knocking the easel aside, sending it crashing against the wall. "*Putano,* you betrayed my trust. Again."

"I had no choice, Agustino." Jorge's eyes batted in fear; then he gave a pleading look. "I had to."

"Had to put me at risk: my commission, the residency, the Corbusier Foundation grant . . . stealing again!"

"But they'll kill me, Agustino." Jorge's shoulders shook. Sweat dotted his brow.

Agustino stepped back. What had his nephew gotten into now?

"Who?"

"No one knows; no one saw." Jorge's voice rose to a squeak. "I promise, Agustino."

Agustino shot a glance through the atelier's windows to the green lawn, the canopy of chestnut-tree branches wavering in the evening wind. The rear lighted windows of belle époque apartment buildings overlooked the park-like enclosure and the eighteenth-century *hôtel particulier* that somehow had escaped demolition. Fear coursed through Agustino. Who knew what eyes were lurking behind those windows?

"Don't you realize, you fool, stealing this, it means prison?" Agustino swallowed hard, imagining national security forces swooping into the atelier.

"Just until tonight, please," Jorge said. "The concierge's gone, everyone's still enjoying the long weekend at their *résidence secondaire*." He gave a little shrug. "Rich people."

"What do you know about that?" Agustino's eyes narrowed. "Or do you case their apartments, steal, and then fence what you've stolen?"

"That got me into trouble before," Jorge said.

At least he didn't deny it this time.

"Not now, I swear," Jorge said, a catch in his voice. "But that's how they found me."

"Liar." Agustino didn't believe a word. "Get out."

"*Maman* asked you to help me." He used that plea over and over.

Agustino's weak sister couldn't handle him, nor Jorge's worthless father, Agustino's brother-in-law. How many times had he bailed Jorge out of juvenile detention?

"You're in the big time, Jorge, stealing official documents. I can't help you now."

He rubbed his sweat-stained shirt, envisioning Jorge graduated to organized crime, the atelier as a depot for stolen goods to be sold on the Eastern European black market. Good god.

"But the *mec* followed me from the café."

"And just like that, he —"

"Stuck a gun in my ribs," Jorge interrupted. "Shoved me in the back of a van. Drove it right up to the rear entrance. But I wasn't going to involve you. . . ."

Agustino spit in disgust. "What kind of fantasy . . . ?"

"He knew about you." Jorge gulped. "If you got angry, he said to tell you *Remember '74.* That he was just a messenger, but you'd understand."

A cold vise clutched Agustino.

"Does he mean the time you lost your fingers in jail?" Jorge said in that trembling, innocent, lost voice of the little boy he'd once been.

Merde! It couldn't be. Xavierre, and now. . . .

Agustino's mind went back to the dank blood-smeared cell, moisture dripping from the stone. Twenty of them sweating, crowded inside with one chipped enamel pot to piss in. The gangrene blackening his fingers. But that had happened in another lifetime.

"A political action years ago? That's over. My life's changed, Jorge," he said. His throat caught, remembering that day: the hoarse shouts, the acrid black smoke winding through glazed silver leaves on the olive

138

trees, the thwack of police truncheons on the demonstrators. Xavierre's high-pitched screams. The policeman caught in the bombing. The mistake.

Jorge trembled. "He gave me no choice. I'm sorry, Agustino."

"But that's all over. My art celebrates peace, the cease-fire we're working to achieve, our Basque traditions."

"One thing never changes, Agustino. We're Basque."

One hell of a payback. Had Xavierre refused to cooperate and paid the price? From outside came the rustling of branches, the skitter of birds in bushes.

"If you dont . . ." Jorge swallowed, then looked down at his Adidas, ". . . he'll slit my throat, Agustino."

TUESDAY NIGHT

In the office of Leduc Detective, Aimée banked more juniper logs on the fire to combat the damp chill. Determined to catch up on work, she made *un express* on their office machine, then monitored the relay data feed from the suspect VP and filed a status report. All of which took her half an hour. Restless, she completed René's two security proposals and got a jump on their accounts. Working on a Tuesday evening, and it would still take an hour before she could make much of a dent in the work piled on her desk. But it didn't keep her mind off Xavierre's lifeless eyes. The questions.

She wished to god none of this had ever happened. That she hadn't failed Morbier. But wishing wouldn't bring Xavierre back or vindicate Morbier. Or do anything about the guilty feeling that she could have prevented it.

Somehow.

She took a roll of fax paper, unwound it, and taped it like a banner across the wall. Her mind worked better when she could see in black and white what made sense and what didn't. With a black marker, she drew a grid for a chart listing Xavierre, Irati, Robbé, Cybèle, Agustino, and Madame de Boucher, leaving blanks for guests. She sketched a rough map of Xavierre's street, the high-walled back lane; diagrammed the town house layout, the garden.

She drew a column for evidence, under which she taped pieces of gravel from her pocket, the Euskadi Action flyer, and the photo of Xavierre and Irati by the Mercedes. Under a question mark, she wrote *Heels at Lab, Footprint, Tiepin, Lyon Driver,* and *FRAMED?* in bold letters. Under unknowns she wrote *The Murderer.*

Things began to form a pattern, in a confused sort of way. The *flics,* calling this a crime of passion, hadn't been so far off the mark. Xavierre couldn't have been out of sight five minutes, if that. The attack reeked of desperation; she felt that too.

Something had gone very wrong.

Under *The Murderer* she wrote *Wounded? Man arguing, guests.* But she felt she'd missed something.

She raked her memory, pacing back and forth. If Irati blamed Morbier, what explained her almost palpable fear? Nothing added up.

Did Irati hold the key? But Irati wouldn't talk to her. Unless. . . .

Bon, then she'd listen. She checked her Rolodex, found a number she hadn't called in several years. Busy.

She tapped her high-heeled boot. Impatient, she checked the time, dialed again. Busy, always busy. She shut down her laptop.

In the rear armoire, she found her stone-washed suede leggings, warmest cashmere sweater, and red high-tops. She pulled on her faux fur to combat the cold.

Down on rue de Rivoli, her breath frosted in the night air. Before she turned the corner to her parked scooter, her cell phone vibrated in her bag.

Thesset with news of the Mercedes? Anxiously she hit ANSWER.

"Oui?" Her breath came out in puffs of frost. "You found it?"

"Found what? But perfect timing, Aimée."

She knew that voice. Her spine tingled, jolting her back to that evening haze of candlelight, the empty Champagne bottle, his clothes on the floor.

142

"Listen, my train's pulling into Gare Montparnasse," said Melac, the Brigade Criminelle inspector. "I still do takeout pretty well."

"But I need to talk to you about Morbier. Isn't that why —"

"And I'm hungry," Melac interrupted, his voice going low. "Dinner?"

Startled, she leaned against a peeling wine-auction poster on the damp wall. "I don't do *flics,* Melac."

"Then what do you call what we did at your place?"

Getting lost in his gray eyes. Weakness. The damn painkillers? "Taking advantage of me recuperating from injuries. Flat on my back, remember?"

"You on top: that's what I remember," Melac said, a huskiness in his voice. "Haven't gotten it out of my head. Not that I wanted to."

She blushed to the roots of her hair. After that night, they'd played phone tag until there was a big silence on his end. So now he assumed she'd be willing to rekindle a one-night stand? She had more important things to rekindle, like Morbier's alibi in this half-assed investigation.

"*Ça alors,* I don't get involved with *flics.* Never works."

Especially now.

"So, you speak from experience?"

Fat chance. "A lead homicide inspector in *La Crim* has no life outside work. That's if he's a good one."

"And you're one to talk?" Melac said. "Does your life separate from your career, like a yolk from the white of an egg? More like an omelette, I'd say."

These days, her life made one thin omelette. Taken aback, she tried to recover. "We're talking life in the force, Melac. I lived it."

Her father coming home at dawn, exhausted from all-night stakeouts. The dinners waiting for him on the stove that he never had time to eat. The paperwork, the reports piled up, waiting at the Commissariat. After school, doing her homework by the potted palm near his desk, hoping he'd finish on time. For once.

"Forget old school. Things change," he said. "Aimée, I'm just getting in from Brittany to meet with the *notaire* and settle the custody issue in my divorce."

Children. Commitments. Baggage she couldn't deal with. None of it hers.

"You know, we're not all macho misogynists incapable of a relationship," he said.

"That's good to hear," she said. "So just

forget the seventy-five percent of the force in a second marriage, twenty-five on their third. Reassuring."

"Where'd you get those stats?"

"My father's time. Have they gone up?"

Silence.

"I'm not your father."

"And that's not why I left you a message," she said, regaining her composure. "Morbier's in trouble."

"Who isn't, at one time or another?"

"*Boeuf-et-carottes* bad, Melac," she said. "He's rotting in a *garde à vue.*"

She heard an expulsion of air over the line, the clacking of train wheels.

"Gone awful quiet, Melac," she said. "You're going to desert him too?"

"*Tiens,* I had no idea. I've been on leave." Melac cleared his throat. "Put this in context, Aimée. If an investigation goes to Internal Affairs . . . *tant pis,* no one else touches it. Procedure."

"How convenient."

"Like you don't know the regulations? Don't even ask me. . . ."

"To listen to the trumped-up charges against Morbier?" she said. "Someone's framing him."

A sigh came over the line.

Frustrated, she wanted to kick something.

"*Bon,* I won't waste your time. Or mine."

"*Et alors,* let's talk over dinner."

"What's the point, Melac?" she said. "I'm helping Morbier. No one else will."

Pause. Leaves swirled in the overflowing gutter. Behind her came the groan of a garbage truck in the narrow street.

"What's the evidence?" Melac asked.

She gave him a brief account.

"From what you say, it sounds circumstantial. But I didn't say that," he said. "Anyway, what can I do?"

"A lot," she said. "Request the police dossier, find out who's been questioned, obtain copies of the lab results, the daughter Irati's statement, the statement of Morbier's driver who took him to Lyon. . . ."

"Aimée, all that's routed to Internal Affairs."

"As if you can't call in favors from the responding Police Judiciaire, suggest it links to a case you investigated. There's a million ways, Melac. Morbier says you're the best. Prove it."

"Look, I'm on leave. Think I'd complicate my own ongoing investigations?"

"*Non,* I thought you wanted to have dinner tonight," she said. "After you've dropped in at *La Crim,* chewed the fat, skimmed the file. I know you know how to do that. None of that's changed since my father's time, has it?"

"*Alors,* I go back to Brittany day after tomorrow. I just thought we could meet." He cleared his throat. "You do know that any outside interference could hurt Morbier's case?"

"Interference?" She tried to control her voice.

A woman bundled in a fur coat stared at her, then turned the corner.

"Morbier, my godfather, lost the woman he loves, could lose everything he's given his life to, the reputation he's earned, his honor, freedom," she said. "A lot more than just his retirement, Melac. It's all wrong. Tell me, could I live with myself if I didn't help? But look at it this way: What if you're in this situation some day? Who could you call?"

"You're just using me," Melac said, disappointed.

Her throat constricted. Was she using him? Wasn't she asking a favor for Morbier?

"Relationships don't work that way," said Melac.

Melac called a one-nighter and a brief bout of telephone tag a "relationship"?

"Aimee, I needed to wind up the divorce, work out the settlement," he said. "My ex is making it difficult. I wanted to settle custody arrangements before, well, getting back in touch with you."

Stunned, she wondered if she'd read him wrong.

"Morbier warned me you follow jungle rules like a feral cat," he continued.

What did she know? Her penchant for bad boys had racked up a miserable record. Feral cats did better.

In the background came the scrape of roller bags, the muffled arrival announcement. There was a pause. "I've been getting my life together, taking my daughter to piano lessons," he said. "Thinking a lot. Just hoped you wanted dinner. I'm sorry."

Score zero. Blown it again.

Dejected, she kicked at a pile of brown leaves. Soggy and damp, they clung to her heel. Like the guilt in her heart. "I understand," she said. "It's not fair to involve you. I just saw a broken man this morning. Not the man I know. Morbier's given up."

It tore her insides to see Morbier wrongly accused. In such pain. The arrival announcements boomed louder now.

She'd figure something out. Find another angle.

Somehow.

"Et alors," he exhaled. "I'm picking up

messages at *La Crim.* I'll test the waters. But no promises." Pause. "Still have that Champagne in your fridge?"

She envisioned the moldy Brie and Miles Davis's butcher's scraps in her otherwise empty refrigerator. Not smart to appear too easy. Her eye caught the lit maroon storefront of Nicolas, the wine shop, down the street.

"Let's say my office. Nine P.M." She hung up. Said a little prayer and looked at her Tintin watch. Two hours. Forget her scooter.

In the wine shop, she bought two bottles — a Veuve Clicquot and a Beaujolais Nouveau — on the owner's recommendation. At the tree-lined intersection, a taxi's blue light signaled that it was free. She waved her arm holding the bag and caught the driver's attention.

The young taxi driver threw her a knowing smile. "Clubbing, *Mam'selle?*"

"Not tonight. 11 rue Biot, near Théâtre L'Européen, *s'il vous plaît.*"

"A little culture in couture?" He grinned. "I should have known."

"Fifty francs if you get me there in ten minutes."

"How about nine?" He adjusted the laminated photo on his dashboard, hit the meter, and took off. "That's Lola, my daughter." The radio blared sixties ye-ye pop music, and the taxi filled with the driver's running commentary about his daughter's progress in beauty school. Her second day back at work, and it hadn't yet ended. Her feet ached; her hands jittered from the espresso.

The taxi sped up wide Avenue de Wagram into the 17th past dim-lit Place des Ternes and the darkened fun fair, along Boulevard de Courcelles and the gold-tipped fence under dark nodding trees bordering Parc Monceau, and over the rail lines crossed by rue de Rome.

At Place de Clichy, among a warren of narrow streets, she got off on the rain-dampened, cobbled rue Biot between Théatre L'Européen and an Indian restaurant. She buzzed the door. No answer. Her heart fell.

TUESDAY EVENING

"Never thought I'd put *les bracelets* on you," said Henri, the guard. He unlocked Morbier's handcuffs, shaking his head. Shouts and taunts issued from the cells and echoed off the walls of the low stone tunnel.

"Desnos at the Lab still owes me from Friday poker," Morbier said. "Tell him to pay me in cigarettes, *compris?*"

"Who the hell did you piss off, Morbier?"

"Who *haven't* I pissed off, Henri?"

He gestured Morbier into the cell. Morbier stooped to avoid the low crossbeam. "So you won't get lonely, you're sharing with an old friend."

The steel door clanged shut behind him. The key turned in the lock, metal grinding on metal. Near the barred oval window leaned Cheb DJ, whom he'd twice convicted of robbery and twice not convicted of murder. Morbier felt a tightness in his chest.

151

"Heard you killed your woman," said Cheb DJ in a thick Congolese accent. "Even I never done that, *mon vieux*." He emitted a little laugh. "You like the accommodation, the premier river view?"

"But you're the connoisseur, must have sampled them all," Morbier said. "How many times did I put you in here?"

Cheb DJ laughed. His front gold teeth glinted. "Lots to catch up on, *mon vieux*. 'Ruled by passion': didn't know that defense flew any more."

"To tell you the truth, passion's overrated."

"A *flic* like you do a stupid thing like that? Why not contract a hit man? Easy."

"But I didn't do it."

Cheb DJ shrugged. "You and everyone say that. Save it for *le Proc*."

All bravado gone, Morbier collapsed on the wood slat with a ragged blanket they called a cot. Dampness oozed from the corners, creeping up his legs. But the tremor in his jaw came from nerves.

"So you a jealous man, you flipped . . . ?"

The prospect of listening to Cheb DJ all night sickened Morbier. Worried him deep down. No doubt Cheb had worked a deal, a lesser charge for information. That's why they'd put them together. Cheb punched walls — and people — when irritated.

"I know the plan, Cheb. Used it myself. But did I beat or chain you up all night like my partner wanted after your holdup on rue des Capucines?"

"No disrespect, but you think I like it here, *mon vieux?*" Cheb's tone changed. "Give me something; my woman's pregnant; I need the deal."

"Eh, didn't I respect that poor mother of yours, in tears begging to see you? Arranged a visit, didn't I?"

Pause.

"Leave my mother out of it."

"So give *me* respect," Morbier said. "Screw the deal and shut up."

"I don't want them to hurt you, *mon vieux,*" he said. "They'll move in the next *mec* who's got no history with you. But us, we got history. Think about it."

Cheb DJ stretched out on the cot, pulled the blanket up, and was snoring minutes later.

Surprised that Cheb seemed to have given up so easily, Morbier stared at the bars, more on his mind. He didn't stand a chance without Laguardiere's testimony. And during the brief phone call, Laguardiere's wife had broken down in tears, saying Laguardiere might not live through tomorrow's surgery.

Morbier's *indicateur* — informer — might not either, if he didn't supply him protection and keep his word. But who could he trust? No one left to trust. No more favors left.

What did it matter any more? Why even care? Xavierre lay cold in the morgue.

He remembered the first time he saw her. That hot sticky August, under the lime-tree branches, the shadows dappling her luminous skin, her lips parted in a smile. The smile he'd never forgotten. The smile he saw now. Not the blue-tinged waxen face they'd pulled from the stainless-steel drawer.

The punch slammed him against the stone wall. There was a ringing pain in his head; sparks flared behind his eyes. Dizzied and disoriented, he felt the next punch in his chest: it knocked the air out of him. Gasping for breath, he rolled and kicked as hard as he could. A *thupt* as his shoe heel connected with Cheb's bulldog neck. Another kick. And again, until he heard the crunch of breaking bones.

Cheb sprawled half on the cot, half on the floor. Out of commission for a while, until he came to from the pain in his broken fingers.

Blood trickled down Morbier's cheek,

mixing with spittle on his chin. Too old, he was too old for this. The jaw tremor in his neck, his tingling shoulders. Shaking, he couldn't stop shaking, couldn't tolerate the pain in his ribs. And the shaking didn't stop after he'd slid onto the stone floor, doubling over in agony.

"Fell off the earth, Aimée?" Léo, a plump woman in her forties, frowned. "Four years. Not even a call." Léo, wearing a green tracksuit, spun the wheels of her wheelchair forward across the slick wood apartment floor. "Now you appear out of nowhere. Did I win the Keno pick?"

Aimée had kept her finger on the door buzzer a long five minutes. No wonder Léo appeared cranky.

"It's been a while," Aimée said. "I brought you something." She set the bottle of Beaujolais Nouveau on the counter. Léo, named after the opera singer Léontyne Price, ran her fingers through her short gray hair.

"Still think I'm easy, eh?"

"*Non,* the wine merchant said it's an excellent year. For once, a good vintage."

"I'll remember that for my next dinner party."

A cigarette smoldered in a filled ashtray; a

half-full demitasse of espresso sat by a lap-top screen. To the side, a bank of radio receivers, a set of headphones hanging off the end. Léo, a radio engineer before her accident, freelanced cell phone triangulation for select clients. Highly illegal and quite lucrative. Even the *flics* used her.

"Léo, I need your expertise. Morbier's —"

"So you work for the *flics* now?" she interrupted.

"*Moi?* Then the earth's flat."

"Too bad. Great benefits."

Aimée looked at her feet. "*Not* my strong suit, keeping in touch, Léo."

Léo made a *phfft* sound. "Like *tout le monde.* You're no different. I help out, then it's *adieu.*"

Stricken, Aimée realized how much it mattered to Léo, wheelchair-bound in the sixth floor walk-up, her only escape through the airwaves.

Glancing around the narrow L-shaped apartment, two rooms met her view. Clay pots with sprouting herbs lined the window-sill over the sink. "Quite a green thumb." She pointed, grinned nervously. "Look, I'm thoughtless."

"And I'm booked." Léo adjusted a black knob. She scratched her neck under the wool scarf wrapping her shoulders. "Could have saved yourself the trip."

Aimée's shoulders sagged.

"I contract GPS satellite tracking," Léo said. "It's going mainstream soon, commercial. Right now it's only a military tool, but not forever."

"You've got a military contract?"

"If I told you, I'd have to kill you," Léo said.

"Léo, for you this would be child's play," she said. "Only take you five minutes."

Orange and red lights blinked on the radio receivers. "No time, I told you."

"But Morbier's in custody," she said. "You're the only one who can help."

For the first time, Léo looked up with interest.

"So don't do this for *me,* do it for *him.* Please, you've known Morbier for years, *n'est-ce pas?*"

Léo put on the headphones. Sighed. "What do you want this time?"

Aimée wanted to hug her. But Léo wouldn't like that. Instead, she grabbed a pencil and the graph paper notepad on Léo's desk.

"Do that triangulation voodoo you do so well. Record the calls, pinpoint the cell phone location."

"National security involved?"

The lead pencil tip snapped. What if Léo had just hit it on the head? Militant French Basques? She'd think about that later. "Morbier's girlfriend was strangled. I found her. But someone else was in the house. Her daughter blames Morbier, but she's misguided."

"Misguided?"

But it felt more complicated than that.

"Either mistaken and looking for an easy answer or . . ." She hesitated. ". . . lying. I don't know."

"Never boring with you, Aimée." Léo typed in Irati's phone number. "Any idea of the transmission area?"

"In Passy, the 16th." Aimée pointed to the map covering the wall divided into arrondissements. "I figure the murderer will contact her."

"Doesn't sound like Morbier's type at all."

"She was Basque. I don't have anything else to go on."

"You think the murderer would call her daughter? Make a demand, more like it." Léo swiveled her chair and put on the reading glasses hanging from her neck.

"That's what I need to find out." Aimée winced. "Her daughter's not too happy with me right now."

"Doesn't do to piss people like that off.

But then tact's not your strong suit." Léo sucked in her breath. Shook her head.

Aimée shivered in the barely heated apartment.

She leaned on Léo's desk. "If I don't find the murderer, the evidence points to Morbier. It smells, Léo."

Léo paused. "And of course you don't want the *flics* involved."

"You got it, Léo." Aimée swallowed. "Blinded by love, Morbier wanted me to protect Xavierre. And I didn't."

Léo shook her head. "I'll input the phone's ESN and MIN code. When a call's made or received, my scanner will pick it up. Remember, the longer the call, the better the trace. For me to locate the phone, it needs to emit the roaming signal so the next nearby antenna tower picks it up. It's all about the towers."

"Don't all cell phones now do that continuously?"

"Not yet, but Big Brother's coming. Right now that feature's a military tool." Léo looked up. "Tracking depends on the signal strength of the antenna masts. This wind doesn't help. It scatters the electromagnetic waves like confetti. Say your prayers that the radio transmitter tower out there cooperates."

"Only one way to find out." Aimée dug her cell phone from her pocket and punched in the number.

Irati's number flashed on the screen. The halogen light cast a bluish glare on the window.

"Oui," Irati answered on the first ring. A breathy quality, as if she'd run to the phone.

"Any word, Irati?"

Pause. Glass clinked in the background. "Word?"

"On your mother's funeral? It's Aimée."

Disappointment and something else tinged her voice. "I told you —"

"I'm sorry for this afternoon," Aimée interrupted.

A click on Aimée's cell phone indicated another call. She ignored it.

Léo rolled one hand in a circular motion, mouthed, "Keep her on."

"Please listen: I want to help you," she said. "Do you understand, Irati?"

"L . . . leave me alone." Short shallow breaths.

But she hadn't hung up.

"*Enfin,* I lost my father in a bomb explosion. But the *flics* closed the file; the Ministry ignored my requests." That yawning hole inside opened, that need to know why, if it was a terrorist, an informer, a mistake. "I know the feeling. Afraid, alone. . . ."

A sob came over the line.

"Irati, you can talk to me," she said. "Whatever happened, I won't judge you. If you're in danger, you have my word, no *flics* involved."

Léo mouthed, "*Got* it."

"You haven't gone to the *flics* again, have you?" Irati's voice was a whisper.

A cold feeling hit the pit of Aimée's stomach. Why did Irati want to know? Léo pointed to the address that had popped up on her screen. 40 rue Raynouard. At least that proved that it worked and the towers in the area were functioning.

"Stay away, not safe to. . . ." Irati trailed off.

A creaking noise like a door opening, footsteps.

The phone buzzed. Dead.

The address disappeared from the screen.

"*Zut!* At least we established the trace. But it's more important to find out who calls her and their location. Not all that different, right?"

"In theory, if the call's active long enough, the towers cooperate, and her caller's not in a dead zone. But I'd need my second scanner free and operational to nail it. Takes two to tango." Léo gave her a pointed look.

"Your five minutes are up."

Aimée lingered, pulling her scarf tighter against the draft. "Let's say her caller was in close range, nearby, in the *quartier?*"

"That's a best-case scenario," Léo said. "Otherwise, compare it to the chances of finding a brown lentil in that." Léo jerked her thumb toward a 25-kilo sack of green lentils.

In the meantime, so much could go wrong.

A velvet-like fur brushed her leg. She looked down to see a svelte Siamese cat, turquoise-eyed, yawn, then stretch.

"Meet Marconi," Léo said. "He's hungry. His pâté's on the counter."

No proletarian, this cat. He ate better than Léo. But Aimée kept that observation to herself as she spooned the glistening pâté into a ceramic bowl glazed with the words CHAT LUNATIQUE.

Léo motioned from her wheelchair. "Irati's got a call."

Aimée rushed to see Irati's number on the screen. Her pulse raced. She glanced at the clock. "Can you pinpoint the location of who's calling her, their number?"

"Try patience, Aimée, and hope she stays on the line so I can track it."

Crackling noises. Beeping, a muffled

voice: ". . . a package. Got that?"

Irati's number disappeared again from the screen.

"What's wrong?"

"I'd say Irati's cell phone ran out of battery."

Merde.

Disappointed, she stared at the screen. "But you'll contact me if there's another call, right?"

A hooded look veiled Léo's face. "I shouldn't, but . . . seems like you and Morbier need all the help you can get."

On her way to the door, Aimée saw the soft curved mound, the cat's indentations on the duvet of Léo's hospital bed. At least Léo didn't sleep alone any more.

"*Merci,* Léo."

"Don't thank me yet," Léo said.

On rue du Louvre, Aimée handed the change back to the taxi driver. "Keep it." Her investment for rainy-night taxi karma.

"*Merci,* Mademoiselle."

The streetlight glowed yellow above the wet pavement. Quiet hovered for a brief moment as traffic paused at the rue de Rivoli intersection. The Louvre's lit limestone façade glowed like a misted pearl. Saddened, she thought of this spot last night when she'd met Morbier. His anguish, the slight tremor in his hand. Why hadn't she insisted he tell her more?

She tried to brush the guilt aside. Guilt, a luxury she didn't have time for. Plus it got her nowhere. Her phone beeped with a saved message. Thesset with news on the Mercedes?

She hit PLAY. Melac's voice: "Delayed. Don't wait for me."

Great! A bottle of Veuve Clicquot setting her back part of a paycheck, a cold office with a pile of work. No doubt with his career to consider, Melac had rethought testing the waters. She couldn't blame him. So he'd deserted Morbier too.

It was useless to go home; she knew she wouldn't be able to sleep. Might as well work. The wire cage elevator, circa 1910, shuddered up to the second floor. Stopped and refused to budge.

Par for the evening, she thought, opening the accordion metal doors and trudging up the next flight.

She unlocked Leduc Detective's frosted glass door, hung her coat up on the hook, and wedged several juniper logs in the grate. She blew until the coals burst into flame, pulled the mohair throw around her for warmth, and sat cross-legged on the floor.

The fax paper on the wood-paneled wall stared back at her.

Useless to try to work, too.

She heard the key turning in the lock. The door opened to a gust of cold air. For a moment, her hand trembled.

"Communing with the fire spirits, Aimée?" René asked, unwrapping his muffler. "Or sacrificing more logs to appease the god of fire?"

She turned to look at René, then back at the names on the paper flickering in the firelight.

"I think you've got something, René."

"I do?" He set down his cane, unzipped his judo bag, and took out a bottle of Evian. "Nice and toasty in here." He scanned the files on his desk, blinked in surprise. "All caught up too. A first. You even finished my proposals. *Merci.*"

"Not quite. Another pile to tackle." She pushed the mohair throw aside, picked up a marker. "But you might have hit the right nail. Maybe even on the right head. Gives me a scenario to work with."

"Care to explain? With a nice Veuve Clicquot getting warm?"

She'd forgotten. No reason to burden René, as usual, with her nonexistent love life. She wanted to pick his brain.

"Always good to have a spare bottle. On sale, too." Opening the double window, she breathed in the frigid air and stuck the bottle behind the window box of red geraniums. "Natural cooling."

She shut the window, latched it.

"Mind if I bounce an idea off you?"

"Now?" René glanced at the time. "Five minutes' worth."

She took the blue feather duster from the cupboard, pointed the tip at her map. "Say the wounded killer comes to Xavierre's for help." She pointed to the taped gravel, which she'd colored with red marker to indicate blood. "Bleeding, he leaves traces. After he gains entry to the rear bedroom, Xavierre tries to put him off: her guests, the party, she explains. Morbier, jealous, watches from the garden, leaving footprints, and loses his tiepin. He sees them argue."

"And you know this for a fact?" René sat back in his orthopedic chair.

She shrugged. "Morbier left his tiepin and his footprints."

"Quite an impressive state-of-the-art crime-scene reconstruction," he said.

"Homemade does the job," she said. "Just listen, René; see if it makes sense. Guests pull up, Morbier leaves. At the party, Xavierre pleads illness, some excuse. After a quick Champagne toast, Irati shoos the guests out. Meanwhile we show up, the old couple leaves. Remember?"

"The complaining geriatrics?" he said. "What about the caterers' noises in the kitchen?"

"We saw no van or truck, right?" she said. "What if those noises were coming from the impatient killer? Say they were, and we complicated matters, messing up his agenda. Xavierre needs us to leave."

"Why?" René said. "It would make more sense that she'd want us to stay, if she's in danger."

Aimée pointed the feather duster to the salon. "True. Let's say that at that juncture, she counted on being able to handle him. Using leverage, I don't know." Then she pointed to the rear bedroom. "But the argument escalates — say he demands that Xavierre find a doctor or let him stay. She refuses, threatens to expose him. She runs out the rear terrace doors; but, desperate, he catches her, strangles her." She jabbed the paper. "He has to prevent her from turning him in." Pointed to the Mercedes photo. "The killer hears you close the gate, assumes we've left. He runs back to her car, drives away. We know the rest."

"So if Irati confirms this, they'll release

Morbier?"

"That's the point. Morbier's the main suspect in a crime of passion, as the news termed it. Why?"

René shook his head. "But you're going to tell me, right?"

"If you were Irati, with your mother murdered almost before your eyes, would it make sense for you to lie? To corroborate Morbier's guilt?"

"You're going somewhere with this, right?" René stretched his short legs. Checked his watch.

Cool your handmade shoes, she wanted to say.

"Say this killer calls Irati, threatens that the same thing will happen to her if she exposes him to the *flics,*" she said. "Irati's hysterical: her mother's been murdered; she's threatened."

"A few issues you've neglected," René said. "The fiancé, this Robbé; the possibility that the killer was a guest who left and returned to meet Xavierre outside and then killed her."

Shadows flickered on the office walls.

"That could work. Still, it doesn't explain the kitchen noises, or why a wounded killer, who was bleeding outside, would attend the party. But Robbé's scared. Irati was calling the shots when I tried to talk to them. Both were eager to see the back of me."

"So the killer threatens Irati with her fiancé's death unless she cooperates," said René, nodding. "That might make me lie, to save the person I loved."

"Exactement." Aimée knelt down, adding a log to the now-sputtering fire. "Didn't you ask me if I was 'appeasing the fire god'? It fits, in a way. But you'll never appease your mother's murderer. Tonight Irati asked if I'd gone to the *flics* again, then said 'Stay away . . . not safe' before someone walked in the room and she hung up."

"But you're neglecting a simple scenario." René tented his fingers, interested now. "One you won't like. Say this blood has nothing to do with the killer or Xavierre. What if it's dog's blood?"

"Good point. But the lab results —"

"Will confirm or deny it," René interrupted. "So for argument's sake, say the blood has no bearing. The old couple borrowed the Mercedes, they're unfamiliar with the car so it takes them time to start it. Say Morbier, who'd asked for your help, has second thoughts en route to Lyon. Feels foolish, jealous, whatever. He instructs his driver to turn back. Or dismisses him. Either way, say Morbier returns, sees us inside, and is afraid Xavierre's revealing why she avoided his phone calls: she wants to break it off. She doesn't, of course, but what if she was afraid? But Morbier doesn't know that. He waits, lures her onto the terrace, accuses her . . . then. . . ."

Aimée dropped the duster, battling a seed of doubt. "How could you think Morbier . . . ?" Her throat caught.

"Not me." René's brow creased. "But I'm saying that's ten to one how the *flics* would look at this. His driver's his alibi. So why hasn't Morbier been released?"

She sank on the recamier. "I asked him that."

"Didn't answer, did he?" René averted his eye. "The facts don't look good. I'm sorry, Aimée."

"Morbier's no amateur. He knows the system. It doesn't make sense." She stared at René. "Unless. . . ."

"Give up, Aimée."

"The mustard stains on his suit."

"Eh?" René's eyes widened. "So he's hungry, stops at a *routier. Non,* not many of them any more. So a rest stop where the food's in plastic. He changes his mind and heads back to Paris."

"The first part's brilliant, René."

"All this from a mustard stain?" René

shook his head.

She remembered Morbier pacing on the wet pavement, the thrumming of the waiting car's engine, his black wool coat glistening with mist, open to his corduroy jacket.

"If anything, the timing could confirm his guilt," said René, his voice terse. "Look. Morbier's my friend too. This hurts. It's terrible. But right now, leave it alone. Don't pursue what guarantees his —"

"Innocence?" She picked up her cell phone, scrolled down her address list. Hit a number. "Inés? *Oui, ça va? Non,* I'm fine. Silly question, but does Emile still run Les Acacias? Retired? Of course . . . your son? Nice to keep it in the family. My number's the same, I'd appreciate if he could call me. You too."

She hung up. Rubbed her hands in front of the fire. Warmth crept up her arms.

"Why didn't I think of it?" She shook her head. "Emile's son runs the *routier* now, still a trucker stop with the best *frites* and *saucisson* on the A6 approach to Cachan."

"The A6 south to Lyon?"

"My father met his suburban *indicateurs* at Emile's. A lot of the *flics* did. The old-fashioned *routier,* good food, easy to blend in, and everyone's on their way somewhere. A quick getaway."

172

"Meaning?"

"Let's say Morbier met an *indicateur* there to get information on Lyon," she said. "He loves Emile's *saucisson* smothered in *moutarde de* Dijon."

"You're serious?" René's brow creased in thought. "But then why not. . . ."

"Reveal his informer?" She shook her head. "He'd never get another whisper."

How many times had she seen her father unearthing a lead, checking every detail cobble by painstaking cobble, finding it a dead end? Then came the one odd piece at the back of the file or discrepancy glossed over — or rechecked for the fourth time — that broke the case.

"Sounds far-fetched to me," said René. "You're reaching, Aimée."

"You'd drop your socks if you realized how much a *flic*'s work owes to an informer's tip," she said. "Like a slow-moving train gathering information — a name, the girlfriend's last address, bits and pieces that add up."

"Protecting a source, fair enough. But that goes both ways," René said.

"Depends on how deep the source goes, his cover, the connections, a lot of intangibles. Half of the *flic*'s work's done by listening to snitches; the other half, methodical plodding."

The reasons she hated criminal investigation.

"*Et alors,* say that's so, say the informer's related to Morbier's investigation in Lyon." René stood, did a neck roll. "My turn." He took the black marker, reached on his tiptoes, and circled Xavierre's name.

"What do you really know about her?"

Good question. Morbier had revealed little about his relationship until last night.

"Not much more than you," she said. "I'd only met her on the street once before. But she was in love."

René drew a column. "In love. *Voilà,* we also know she was *haute bourgeoise,* moneyed, lived in a chic *quartier;* she'd rekindled an old affair with Morbier —"

"But why her?" Aimée interrupted. "Why now, with her daughter's wedding, guests, the preparations?"

"Let me finish." He pointed the duster handle like a school-teacher. "Very important. We know she's Basque."

"True. Yet Xavierre and Irati don't fit the Basque Separatist profile in the headlines — hiding revolutionaries in safe houses after armed attacks and bombings."

She'd gotten nowhere with Agustino about Xavierre's past. But he had been hiding something. Cybèle had denied her sister's links with ETA. But Aimée wondered if Xavierre had supported the cause in other ways.

If it smelled, her father always said, track it down. Or it would bite your sinuses like ripe Port Salut.

Before she could pursue it, René's cell phone trilled on his desk. He glanced at the number, then reached for his judo bag.

"*Cherie?* Ready?"

Aimée looked up in surprise to see a wide smile on his face. He clicked off his phone and headed to the door.

"Hot date?"

"If that's what you call pot stickers with her parents at Chez Chun."

"The woman from the dojo? I call it progress," Aimée said. "Chinatown's perfect on a night like this."

She felt happy for René. It was time he met someone and it worked out.

He shook his head. "A Marais hole in the wall run by her uncle, near her family's wholesale luggage shop. Traditional types who think I should learn their Wenzhou dialect."

Aimée grinned. "And you're still here?"

He paused at the door. "What about you?"

She bit back her frustration, seeing the

names on the wall, the looming long evening alone. Stood and booted up her computer. "Work to catch up on."

He hesitated. His phone trilled again.

"Try and get her alone next time, René."

In the WC down the hall, Aimée splashed cold water on her face and leaned on the cracked porcelain sink. In the soap-speckled mirror, she studied a fine line under her eye. Expression lines, my foot, she thought. She squeezed the tube of Dior concealer. Empty. Like the evening ahead.

Emptier for Morbier in a cell. And a pity party would get her nowhere. She had work to do.

Back in Leduc Detective, she blew on the fire and sipped her espresso. Cold.

Until she discovered more about Xavierre, she was spinning her wheels. She had no suspects to point away from Morbier. She needed to know this woman: her family, her past, her secrets.

Everyone left traces; the hard part was finding the significant ones. Start with basics, what she knew. Xavierre's state-of-the-art kitchen would have required building permits.

Online, she entered the Ville de Paris Web site, searched *La Direction de l'aménagement urbain et de la construction,* and input Xavierre's address. The notation indicated the contractor's name, license, and renovation work totaling a year. All a matter of public record. A hefty sum for work that she figured should have taken four months at most. From there she dug deeper, from the city's approval to the renovation contract.

The approval form listed the owner as Xavierre D'Eslay *née* Contrexo. One bright star shone in the evening: now she had Xavierre's maiden name. Her tracking possibilities widened.

Morbier had met Xavierre Contrexo more than twenty years ago. At that time, post-Sorbonne riots, he'd been patrolling with Aimée's father on the beat. If Xavierre had been a student in Bayonne, had Morbier met her on holiday in the Basque country? According to Cybèle, her family herded sheep.

Or had he and Xavierre met in Paris, at a student demonstration? She let that simmer, sat back — and found it staring her right in the face: ask Cybèle. She tried immediately. No answer on her cell phone. She tried the house. No answer.

Determined now, she thought of the next family member, Cybèle's ill husband in Bayonne. A minute later, directory assistance

177

connected her.

A gruff voice. *"Allô?"*

"Monsieur Urioste?"

"Who's this, at this time of night?"

Nine P.M.? *"Excusez-moi,* Monsieur, but I'm calling from Paris regarding the investigation. . . ."

"You a journalist?" he said. "Call in the morning."

He'd given her the perfect opportunity. "Before the rumors reach epic proportions, we at *Le Parisien* wanted to confirm —"

"Rumors? You're all snakes." Pause. "What rumors?"

"Xavierre d'Eslay's link with the Basque ETA."

Instead of hearing the phone slammed down, she heard a clearing of his throat. "That old story?" A snort. "Happened years ago. My sister-in-law married money, didn't know us after that, changed her tune, believe me."

A dry laugh. She sensed he didn't hold warm feelings for his sister-in-law.

"I need more than that, Monsieur, for my article," she said. "That's if you want the *facts* presented, not distortions."

"Check with your kind, those rodents over at *Sud Ouest.*" *Sud Ouest* was the Bordeaux daily newspaper. "Talk to the archives and for once get your facts straight. And don't quote me." He hung up.

The *Sud Ouest* archives in Bordeaux didn't answer. But Martine, her best friend since the lycée and a journalist, could help.

"Aimée . . . hold on a moment," said Martine.

Singing, music, and laughter sounded loudly in the background. Martine lived with Gilles and his children in a huge flat overlooking the Bois de Boulogne. "Karaoke night for sixteen-year-olds," Martine shouted. "Like the old days, remember?"

"I'd like to forget them, Martine."

She heard a door shut, the flick of a lighter, a sharp inhalation. Martine smoked a pack a day. Aimée reached in her desk drawer for the strip of "stop smoking" patches. Empty.

"Now I can talk," Martine said. *"Ça va?"* Martine took another drag, not waiting for an answer. *"Bon,* I shouldn't say it but I'll say it anyway. A Tuesday night, and you're working late? You need a man."

Not this again.

Martine made it her perpetual mission to set Aimée up. Blind dates, dinner parties, discreet introductions at wine bar openings — all disasters.

"Buff. Strong, of course," Martine said.

"I'm thinking of Gilles's friend, career Navy and a champion diver, who commands the Naval underwater recovery unit in Toulon."

She meant GIGN, the military elite assault unit.

"Don't you have a weakness for men in Speedos?" Martine continued.

Speedos were one thing, career Navy another.

"Get back on shore, Martine," she said. "Do me a huge favor: tap into the vein at *Sud Ouest* archives for Xavierre d'Eslay *née* Contrexo, links to ETA."

Martine, a journalist, maintained an extensive network of contacts. *De rigueur* in her job.

"Now? But I'm jammed with my Radio France deadline, Aimée. Our four-part agribusiness program airs tomorrow."

"Can't the farmers wait an hour, Martine? They've waited this long."

"ETA's old news. *Passé.*" She exhaled. "No one's interested in explosions in vacant police stations or post offices. There's a cease-fire in the offing that they voted for in a referendum."

"But what if this bears somehow on the *haute bourgeoise* matron's murder —"

"The one on the *télé,* here in the 16th?" Martine coughed. "Near us?"

"Et voilà," Aimée said.

"See, we have a dark side. Haven't I likened our *quartier* to an elegant older aunt with a surprisingly hip and edgy side?"

Martine only lived there because Gilles had inherited a large flat in the building, comprising the whole floor. Fourteen-plus rooms overlooking the Bois de Boulogne.

"Think of your article explored from the angle of her past links to ETA," Aimée said, "her relationship with a Commissaire Divisionnaire, highlighting the skewed investigation based on circumstantial evidence?"

"Why do I feel . . . ? Wait, Morbier's new squeeze. That's her?"

"Was. Your nose should be twitching like a fox at the hunt, Martine."

A long inhale.

"Except that Morbier's investigating and doing his job, Aimée. What's it to you?"

"Au contraire: he's the *suspect."*

"Quoi! I don't believe it."

"Believe this." Aimée drained the demitasse of cold espresso and told her. "I need anything you can find."

"Let's see," Martine said. "One of the Radio France producers has a brother working at *Sud Ouest.* Used to. How far back?"

"Say twenty-five years," Aimée said. "And dig into the new generation of Basques," she said, trying to make her understand. "Euskadi Action demonstrations. The daughter's on their mailing list; she's afraid, too."

"Intriguing, Aimée." Pause. "But you'll join us for Gilles's birthday Sunday? An intimate dinner, close friends. Promise?"

Aimée groaned inside. Of course Martine needed another woman at the table — a date — for Gilles's naval commander diver. She hated to think of the long evening of underwater exploits.

"Gilles loves Veuve Clicquot, like you."

At least she had that covered. "You'll let me know what you hear, Martine?"

"Make that two bottles, Aimée." Martine hung up.

All this had taken time. She had an idea. It would cost her, and yet. . . . She sighed and grabbed a padded envelope. From René's drawer she chose a cell phone from their collection, checked the battery, and locked the office door.

She left her scooter and, still in high-tops, walked past the verdigris iron Métro entrance at Louvre-Rivoli. She needed to walk, to think, to contact Morbier. And she hoped her little plan would work.

She followed the dimly lit quai, pulling

her faux fur tighter. Under the cloud-filled night sky, she crossed Pont Neuf, the misted Seine gurgling below, and walked into shadowed Place Dauphine.

Ghosts everywhere, she thought, whispering in the wind, funneling past the damp corners, the skeletal trees, the seventeenth-century lawyers' quarters — long a bistro — that she'd frequented with Morbier.

Beyond lay the Tribunal, massive columns lost in shadow. A squirrel skittered over the gravel and disappeared behind a slatted bench. Otherwise, the triangular square lay deserted across from the lighted bistro. Her hopes rose after she turned onto quai de l'Horloge near the jail door. The same *flic* from this afternoon stood at his guard post. With luck, he'd remember her.

Better yet, allow her into the visiting area.

He guarded the Gothic thick-planked door dotted with square nail heads, leading to *le dépôt,* the jail under La Conciergerie, originally Jean the Good's medieval kitchen, often mistaken by tourists for the museum entrance to Marie Antoinette's cell.

"Long shift, eh?" She flashed a smile and her pass. "I'm back again. Anyone released from the *garde à vue* this afternoon?"

"Not through here." He stifled a yawn. "Visiting closed hours ago, too. Check with the bureau in the courtyard at eight A.M."

Her heart fell. Poor Morbier. And in this cold.

Time for her plan. She pulled out her checkbook, tore off a deposit slip, wrote MORBIER URGENT, and taped it to the padded envelope with the cell phone.

"Papers came from the lawyer." She smiled. "It would save me a trip tomorrow if you could leave this for Morbier with the duty sergeant." She racked her brain for his name. At one time she'd known most of them. During her childhood, half the force had played Friday-night poker at her kitchen table. "Sergeant Roche, that's the one. He knows me." She widened her smile. Debated a come-hither look.

"Never hurts to ask, Mademoiselle." He winked, then nodded to an arriving *flic*. "But I'm off duty."

She edged closer as he took out his keys. "But since you'll pass by Roche's desk . . . it would mean so much."

He hesitated.

"Look, Morbier's my godfather."

A hand shot out and he slipped the envelope into his pocket before the *flic* could see it.

"Flirting with flics? Nice, and after your

184

little sermon."

The hair rose on the back of her neck. She spun around to see Melac, his face just this side of craggy, defined by pale gray eyes with an unnerving focus. Arms crossed, he stood under the Resistance Memorial plaque on the Préfecture's wall.

"No law against that," she said.

The streetlight caught the pockmarks from bullet holes left by the Germans in 1944, the fresh flower remembrance for the fallen, and Melac's silver belt buckle.

"I remember you said that — before you broke a few last month," Melac said.

She felt his piercing vision going through her.

"All water under the bridge now." She pointed to the sluggish black water of the Seine. "But you canceled tonight, and now you're spying on me?"

"With this?" He lifted a gym bag. "Things got complicated upstairs."

"Most things do."

He stepped closer. A day's stubble shaded his chin. He wore black jeans, a black leather jacket, and a thick-ribbed blue wool scarf knotted at his neck.

"What's that saying? Don't give excuses, just apologize later?"

She hadn't remembered his eyes. How big

they were. Why did she feel twinges of guilt?

"Nice, Melac." She pointed to the pink hearts trimming his scarf's edge. "Your new look? Or from an admirer?"

"My daughter knitted this," he said. "Now she won't stop. I've got one in every color."

Aimée grinned.

And then he pulled her close in his warmth, his citrus scent. His lambskin leather jacket brushed her cheek.

"Look, Melac, I understand, ethics, compromising your work. It's not fair. . . ."

"I've missed you too, Aimée." He lifted her chin. His fingers traced her cheekbone. His warm fingers. Tiny beads of moisture clung to the black hair curling over his neck.

"What plan are you hatching in that mind of yours?" he said.

As if she'd tell him. He couldn't or wouldn't help. "I don't get it, Melac. Morbier's a respected Commissaire Divisionnaire, held on circumstantial evidence — as you pointed out — but you act like I'm subversive."

"Sabotaging Morbier's chances would be more accurate," he said, his finger resting on her cheekbone. "Politics are playing out behind the scenes. Don't you know that by now?"

"Morbier's navigated the waters and

survived this long. He's risen to the top," she said. And then it clicked: the fall guy.

Was that it? A shiver trailed her spine.

"You're saying it's too late?"

"I don't know," Melac said. "No one's talking upstairs. I tried. Everyone needs protection these days. Sometimes from themselves."

Was Melac holding something back? She'd get more if she listened and appeared to acquiesce.

Morbier's twenty-four hours in the *garde à vue* should end in the morning, barring discovery of concrete evidence of his guilt. She prayed Roche, the duty sergeant, would pass the cell phone to Morbier. She had to talk with him.

Melac drew a breath.

"But questions have been raised," he said. "There's an RG file. Not a place you should nose around in right now."

"An RG file exists?"

"The victim's got a dossier."

If Xavierre had a file from Renseignements Généraux, which handled threats to internal security, it meant one thing: ETA. The RG had prioritized ETA and their activities from the seventies to the early nineties, when a special military police unit had been formed to cover the Basque region.

Did hope exist for Morbier after all? But she kept these thoughts to herself.

"At least you tried. *Merci.*"

"They're stretched to the limit with events in Lyon, the *flic* killer in the *Imprimerie Nationale* heist," he said, rubbing his forehead. "Plus the continuing priority hunt for the phantom Fiat Uno speeding away from Princess Diana's crash. An ongoing headache."

A white-and-blue police car sped by, lights flashing, bathing the buildings and Melac's face in blue. Brakes squealed as it turned, bumping over the cobbles into the yawning entrance of the Préfecture.

"On top of that, my leave's canceled," he said. "Now I turn around, head back to Brittany, and explain to my daughter. Effective tomorrow night, I'm back at my desk."

He gave a little smile. "But we could have that drink. My train's later."

"*C'est dommage,* a shame the Champagne's chilling outside with the geraniums."

He gave a knowing nod. "Done that myself." He put his arm around her. "But the bar on Île Saint-Louis serves a decent *coupe* of Taittinger."

Chez Georges, around the corner from her place.

"Just one, Melac," she said. "That's all."

WEDNESDAY MORNING

Through a haze of sleep, Aimée heard beeping from the hallway. Struggling awake, she found her legs entangled by sheets, an arm around her shoulder. Soft warm breaths on her neck. The pale apricot rays of dawn wavered over the discarded clothes on the wood floor. And she remembered. Melac.

Her cell phone rang again. Miles Davis stirred on the floor, blinked his black eyes. Closed them.

She slipped from Melac's arms, grabbing her father's old flannel robe. She shivered at the cold floor. Good god, where had she left her phone? She found it at the bottom of her bag hanging from the coat hook.

A number she didn't recognize. Her feet were freezing on the creaking cold wood.

"Oui?"

"What's the emergency, Leduc?" Morbier's disjointed voice was broken up by static.

"Morbier, are you all right?" she asked.

Her knuckles clenching the phone whitened.

The flush of a toilet. "I've been better. Make it quick, Leduc."

"The RG have a file on Xavierre."

"That's it? But there's a file on everybody," he said, irritated. "Thick as phone books."

"Everybody was in ETA? How was she involved? How did you meet her?"

Pause. "I'm an old fool." She heard the catch in his throat. "No one ever came close to her, Leduc."

"I understand. But tell me, Morbier."

Shouts and clanging metal. "We met at a demonstration in the early seventies near the Champs-Elysées, typical pot-au-feu, troublemakers, students. She was part of a trio from Bayonne, just students. . . ." His voice faded.

She thought of Irati's involvement with Euskadi Action: like mother, like daughter?

"En route to Lyon, you stopped at Emile's *routier*, right? That's your alibi?"

"Don't go there, Leduc," he said, anger vibrating in the static.

"But your driver. . . ."

Coughing. "Told him to go home. You know the rules of the *routier*. Solo."

Bad to worse. The informer his only alibi. She thought fast. "But couldn't Melac talk to your informer on the quiet?"

"*Merde!*" She heard the gush of water, a squeaking, like a faucet turned off. "Leave it alone."

"Why?"

"Listen," he said.

She heard dripping water.

"*Compris,* Leduc?"

"A leaky faucet," she said, exasperated. "Give me something to work with, Morbier. Anything."

"I did." Pause. "Think."

Her shoulders tensed. "A leak. You're investigating a leak. . . ."

"Trust no one, Leduc. No one."

The phone went dead. The floor creaked behind her and she jumped.

"Who's that, so early?" Melac said, his warm arms encircling her waist.

"The plumber." She said the first thing that came into her head and shoved the phone into her robe pocket. "He wants to finish work on our floor. At this hour, too!"

He pulled her closer, nuzzled her neck. "But you're shaking. Your hand's like ice."

Trust no one, Morbier said.

"Poor circulation." She managed a smile, steeled herself not to pull away. "Coffee before your train?"

His eyebrow lifted. "That call shook you

192

up, I can tell."

And I can't trust you, she thought, even after last night. Had he overheard her talking on the phone?

She exhaled, shrugged. Miles Davis whined at the door. "Our concierge neglects things. It's not the first time." She made a fist and cocked it to indicate drinking. "The woman's got a vendetta against me, leaves messages. . . ."

"But I can block those calls, if the number. . . ."

Why had he turned so curious? She needed to quit rambling, quit these lies before she messed up. She needed him out of here.

She nestled under his shoulder, steered him toward the kitchen. "How about *un express* before Miles Davis waters the trees and I walk you to the Métro?"

Aimée parked her scooter in the viaduct under the elevated Métro at Passy. Light drizzle beaded the curling white bark of the birch trees, and her eyelashes. She wished she'd worn rain gear instead of a leather coat over her ruffled silk blouse and black denim pencil skirt.

She found the café nestled at the bottom of the steps. At the crowded café counter, she wedged in the back among the horse-race bettors. Wisps of blue smoke spiraled to the nicotine-stained ceiling. She almost didn't hear her phone ring amid the whooshing of the milk steamer.

"Aimée?" Martine's voice whipped in the wind. "Where are you?"

Aimée peered over the shoulder of the man shouting at the horses on the *télé* mounted in the wall. "In the back."

Martine waved from the window.

"*Voilà,* I see you now."

A man slapped his PMU — *Pari Mutuel Urbain,* the racing association betting slip — on the counter. He shouldered his way through the three-deep crowd toward the cashier. The fetid air resulting from too many bodies, wet wool, and smoke filled the café.

"Trying your luck on the horses, Aimée?" Martine said, raising her voice over the din of the *télé* and the shouts of the patrons. "Nice and quiet, too."

"*Désolée,* the only place I remembered near Radio France."

Martine smiled at the bearded man behind the counter and ordered. *"Un thé à la men-the."*

"You found something, Martine?" Aimée set down her espresso.

194

"Yes and no."

Hope pounded in Aimée's chest.

Martine dipped the tea bag in the steaming cup of water. "Don't get me started, Aimée."

Startled, she looked sideways at Martine. "What's that look on your face mean?"

"It's not good."

"The Basques?"

Martine opened a pack of Muratti Ambassadors, tapped a filter on the zinc countertop, and flicked her orange lighter. She blew a stream of smoke over her shoulder. "Did I tell you about the hoopla? A madhouse at Radio France." Martine made a moue of distaste. "They cut my agribusiness feature in half. Assigned me to cover tonight's Basque referendum reception, minor royalty — a Spanish princess — in attendance. To highlight the historical and cultural implications of 'new' Franco-Spanish relations. Boring. We're becoming as royalty-mad as the BBC."

Aimée leaned her arms on the counter. "I'm more interested in your *Sud Ouest* connection. Don't you have things to show me?"

Martine, in a checked black-and-white wool suit, reached into her matching soft leather briefcase. She set two folders of printouts next to the ashtray and flicked ash from her cigarette. "Makes for interesting reading. I culled the highlights. My contact ran a search up to the present. Thin, but all they had."

She pointed to the other file with her red-lacquered nail. "Euskadi Action. Not a group a mother wants her daughter involved with, according to my source. A radical offshoot faction of ETA. But I didn't have time to read it."

Aimée picked the cigarette from Martine's fingers, took a deep drag. The nicotine jolt went right to her head.

Martine took back her cigarette. "You quit."

"I'm always quitting." Aimée tapped her heeled boots.

Martine exhaled a stream of blue smoke. "Prada boots. Nice."

"Borrowed them from you, remember?"

"No wonder." Martine leaned back, cocked her head. "Who is he?"

Aimée sighed. She could never keep anything from Martine. "That obvious?"

"You're glowing." Martine grinned. "For once, you're following my advice. In a way. Knowing you, *une aventure,* the one-night kind?"

"The *flic.*"

"Lean over: time for a spanking," Martine said, crushing out her cigarette. "Never learn, do you?" But Aimée saw the wheels spinning in Martine's head; a job, possible advancement. "So he was good, eh, like last time?"

A pang went through her. Too good. "I don't trust him."

"He's married?"

"In divorce proceedings, custody issues." She took a cigarette from Martine's pack of Murattis. "But that's not why."

Martine lit her cigarette. "I'm listening."

So she told her. Everything. Like she had since they were sixteen.

"Sounds like Melac's watching his back, wants to keep his job, make alimony payments." Martine shrugged. "So either keep it physical or ignore his calls."

"Morbier said trust no one."

"He's right," Martine said. "In his situation, I'd say the same."

Once a leak sprang, it watered everything. But she had an idea. "How's your sister's husband's cousin?"

Martine glanced at her watch, set some francs on the counter. "The half-deaf one with the hots for you? Florent?"

"That's him. I forgot his name."

"Still half-deaf, still has the hots for you,"

she said. "As usual, he asked after you last Sunday at dinner. Promoted, I think."

Even better. Florent worked in an administrative branch of the RG. She couldn't remember which one. "Then I should take him out to lunch."

"Don't play with him, Aimée. He's naïve."

"And he's forty-five years old, a grown man still living with his mother."

"I know what you're thinking." Martine's eyes narrowed. "You'd use him to find what the RG has on this woman's involvement with ETA?"

"Put that way, no. I couldn't." She averted her eyes. "But the woman Morbier loved was murdered and he's the suspect; who knows what they've done to him. He's protecting his informer, something to do with his case in Lyon, so he's got no alibi. I need to find her murderer."

"Makes a kind of logic," Martine said. "But the ETA connection's a stretch. A twenty-year stretch."

"Somewhere to start, Martine."

"Somewhere to dead-end, quick." Martine picked up her bag. "See for yourself tonight. Join me. As I said, I'm covering the Basque minister's announcement of the agreement. You'd get to see a princess and find out how defused ETA's become. ETA's bombings alienated their old power base; people want no more violence. Meet the man, listen; he'll tell you."

Out on the windswept street, the drizzle had stopped. The Métro thundered by overhead. Martine checked her much-used Vuitton agenda. "Time for my news feature. All seven minutes of it."

Martine gestured to the distant sphere-like aluminum-coated Radio France building, referred to by all as the Camembert. "Awful, *non?* Five kilometers of snaking corridors and half the time I'm lost. See you tonight, Musée Marmottan, six-thirty."

Now she could check out Euskadi Action's demonstration at the same time.

Martine hurried over the cobbles and turned the corner. The wind picked up, scattering shriveled leaves from the gutter. The roar of the Métro receded as it crossed the Seine.

A few low dark clouds threatened rain. Aimée left her scooter protected under the arched metal Métro supports and climbed the steep, narrow Passage des Eaux, pinched in a deep groove between tall limestone buildings. Wide enough for two-legged creatures. Just. A lone glass lantern on a curled metal rod hung like a stubborn raindrop determined not to fall. She looked beyond the deep butterscotch walls in the crackling, hard autumn light paling on the roof tiles.

Stupid to sleep with Melac. And to like it. She wanted to kick herself. Panting, she reached the last step and stood atop Passy. Beyond the passage summit loomed the Trocadéro hill on the right. Below lay two-story buildings and flashes of green: back courtyards and streets threading the old village, widening in places and reverting to the original horse-cart dimensions. No hint of the stone vaulted cellars and passages underneath, honeycombing ancient quarry tunnels. Hidden, covered, like everything else so far.

The sky opened and she ran for shelter.

In the room the Balzac museum pamphlet described as his "study," Aimée paused at Balzac's simple wood writing desk. At least the place was dry, the heater worked, and quiet reigned until the next tour of this labyrinthine series of small rooms — a strange place where one entered on the third floor, then descended a corkscrew staircase to the first. Like entering the neck of wine bottle.

But a place in which to think. Figure out Melac's angle. At *La Crim,* she'd seen his empty desk. The receptionist confirmed he'd taken leave. But a leave of two days, as he'd said? Or two weeks? She couldn't be sure. There was no guarantee in the sweet talk of this man who'd put her under investigation last month.

Morbier's cryptic comment about the leaking robinet in the jail's visiting room made sense now. A leak. A leak in the force.

Knowing Morbier, he was keeping something close to his chest. He could have been putting on a show for watching eyes in the visiting room. Just like him.

Her mind went to the secrets he was keeping from her, hinted at by a gesture, a word when he was unaware. This gray past buried deep. As if she didn't know. Didn't suspect what had really happened to her father. Or her mother. Every time she'd asked, his answer had been to tell her to leave the past alone.

She paused by the window overlooking the narrow, walled back lane. The heater hissed, emitting puffs of warmth. In the terracotta vase, an arrangement of burnt orange-red maple leaves glowed in the light. But the maple leaves provided no answers.

Nor did the bust of Balzac with his opaque marble stare. A debt-ridden Balzac had rented rooms here in Passy, then a village outside Paris. Hounded by creditors, he'd often had to escape out the back door and down the lane. In spite of this, he'd written much of his early nineteenth-century saga, the many-volumed *Comédie Humaine,* and drunk fifty cups of coffee a day at this gouged wooden desk. She could relate to that.

She chewed her lip, trying to face the fear that was making her insides shiver. She kept reliving Melac's appearance in the hallway, his nuzzled kisses along her neck, his insistence on knowing her feelings, his curiosity about the phone call. The probing of his gray eyes.

She didn't do *flics.* Simple. She'd ignore the way he'd made her feel, his warm legs entwined with hers under the sheets, this talk of a "relationship."

No mistaking the veiled panic in Morbier's voice. He needed her help. The little he'd given her — a leak, an informer he couldn't name — didn't point her to Xavierre's murderer. Unless a bent *flic* had murdered her to put blame on Morbier and derail his investigation. She doubted that. But this Lyon case, this leak? She put that aside for now.

She had to concentrate on the info Martine had given her on Xavierre's background. Find a link, figure out if it led anywhere. Her father had always said think like the perp; if you don't know the perp, go to the suspect; no suspect, back to basics — the victim.

In the Balzac museum's narrow reading room, she opened Xavierre's file. Reading from the faxed newspaper articles dating from 1974, a whole other aspect of Xavierre Contrexo emerged. Student ETA activist and supporter, implicated in a bombing in Navarre that claimed a policeman's life. Along with two other students: Timo Baptista, and a man simply referred to in the newspaper as Agustino.

The painter. No wonder he regretted the past and devoted himself to painting and making peace his life's work now.

She sat back, wondering if this Timo Baptista had taken the oath, too, and served time in prison. Morbier's words rang in her head. The trio from Bayonne. Had he known of Xavierre's ETA past?

According to the next article, also dated 1974, Xavierre's lawyer, d'Eslay, bright and from a wealthy family, had found mitigating circumstances, and there was a retrial. Xavierre had served seven months in total. A later article mentioned they had married and had one daughter. Then the only mentions were of the Basque cultural and art society fund-raisers and society events over the years, of Bayonne and Paris charity functions. A divorce. His last year's obituary in *Sud Ouest.*

A wild youth, then a 180-degree turnaround to patroness of the arts, of Basque culture. From all appearances, Xavierre had changed and led a different life.

Not much progress or an arrow pointing to a tie-in with ETA today. Yet Agustino, Xavierre's old compadre, hadn't told her the whole story. Why not?

Right away, she'd sensed he was hiding something. His reluctance, admitted "cowardice," causing him to avoid facing Irati, stuck in the back of her mind.

She'd question Agustino again. Still, no tie-in to Xavierre's murder.

Next she phoned Florent at the RG. After two calls, she reached his office. "Monsieur Florent's attending the Strasbourg conference, Mademoiselle," the saccharine-voiced secretary told her.

"Until when?"

"Monsieur Florent's on holiday after that. Returns middle of the month, Mademoiselle. A cruise."

With his mother, no doubt.

She left her number just in case he returned.

Her arrows hit no targets, no return calls with respect to the Mercedes or Irati's triangulated cell phone line. She sat back in the chair, shoulders slumped, rubbing her neck.

So far she'd left messages and learned Xavierre had been involved with ETA years ago and had an RG file. And she'd slept with Melac, whom she didn't trust. His citrus scent was still in her hair. Thank god Balzac's bust was the only witness.

The second file on Euskadi Action contained stapled articles and clippings. One printout dated two months ago from the Basque Watch security newsletter got her attention.

Bylined in the article was ETA's motto *Bietan jarrai*, "Keep up on both," illustrated by ETA's trademark symbol of a snake — representing politics — wrapped around an ax — representing armed fight. A little shudder ran through her. Headlined FRENCH BASQUE *ETTARAS* AFFILIATED WITH ETA, the article pointed to a logistical network of *ettara* in France using a pool of mostly youths scattered across the Pays Basque who were willing to engage in missions under ETA's political guise.

French and Spanish police seek to reduce ETA's capability by banning the political wing of the movement, which seeks an independent, autonomous Basque state. The logic to banning the political wing, which has operated for the last decade under different names — Euskadi Action the most recent — is that both wings are inextricably linked.

Banning the political branch, authorities hope, would reduce the flow of funds and support to the militant units or *ettaras* of Euskadi Action. Yet other authorities disagree, arguing a ban would stimulate robberies used to fund ETA operations along with "revolutionary taxes" exacted on local businesses under the guise of protection.

No one knows just how far the covert organization extends. Authorities estimate the *ettara* active in France using false passports and identities — members who are trained to kill and who work in cells of four people — could number a hundred youths.

Not a comforting thought. Her mind went to the *Imprimerie Nationale* heist, figuring it was connected. After all, to travel, to operate, one needed ID. Hard to find hundreds of clean passports for an activist group any other way. And profit by selling the surplus to fund operations.

She scanned the next article, from January 1992, focused on GAL, the dirty war. The article gave background on France's vaunted tradition of a haven, an asylum for political dissidents, citing Lenin, Trotsky, and the Ayatollah Khomeini. Notably, since the Spanish Civil War in the thirties, it had been a sanctuary for refugees from Franco's dictatorship, and the tradition continued into the eighties of providing political-refugee status for ETA militants, even refusing Spanish extradition demands.

But things changed, she noted, with the "dirty war."

From 1983 through 1987 forty attacks on French soil by GAL, Grupos Antiterroristas de Liberación, mercenaries hired by high Spanish officials, shot, kidnapped and blew up ETA members and innocent French bystanders. Responsibility extended to the highest offices in Madrid's ministry. GAL mercenaries crossed the French border to wage war on refugee ETA members, and on French civilians thought to collude.

More than ten years later, with new disclosures and impending GAL trials of high military officials, ETA violence renewed with *ettaras* enlisted from disaffected youths. Known activities include sabotaging rail lines for a new high speed train from France to Spain. The planned route, a Y shape with 80% of the rail lines underground, runs aboveground the rest of the way through the Basque countryside. Authorities dismiss the sabotage as tactics by local business, under the cloak of ETA, to reroute commerce to their area.

The next article, dated the previous week, a stilted translation, led further:

This year in continuing reverberations from the revelations of high-placed security officials on trial suspected of organized vigilantism under the auspices of GAL, the dirty war, ETA's attacks have escalated.

The airing of the state-sponsored GAL, "dirty war," scheme in the early 1990s led to a political scandal in Spain.

Reactions to those attacks have caused an ideological split within ETA between those who refuse to condone violence and those who support armed struggle. The shift from general support for ETA showed during the election of former ETA sympathizing with Goikoetxea, a French Basque

assemblyman from Navarre, who engi-
neered the referendum recently passed by
a narrow margin.

So Goikoetxea's formal announcement
tonight of the referendum agreement had
faced dissent in broken ranks. Serious
enough to spur the *ettaras?*

If Martine had had the time to read this,
her tune would have changed.

Still, what did that have to do with Xavierre's murder? Why now, on the eve of her
daughter's wedding?

But Irati's connection, slim if anything,
existed. Covert operations required money.
A network needed funds to operate safe
houses, to purchase arms. Irati, with the
town house in the 16th and her inheritance
from a successful, rich father, represented a
small fortune.

Could Irati have sympathized with Euskadi Action, attended meetings, even
donated, been put on the mailing list? An
unwitting accomplice? Forced by . . . by
what?

"In the next room, we see Balzac's genea-
logical chart of *La Comédie Humaine,*" said
a guide leading a group of middle-aged
couples, educated retirees by the look of
their culture-vulture guidebooks and high-

end anoraks. Part of a culture tour, so popular with active retirees who boned up on history for educational dinners with their grandchildren or to impress their belote playing partners.

"On this chart, illustrated by Balzac himself, he outlines the saga's chronology, with an amazing and detailed fictional character family tree. The interrelatedness by marriage, dalliances, friendships, village and clan ties, love triangles, tied by oaths, connecting . . ." the guide droned on.

Aimée looked up. Tied by oath. Agustino's words.

Her cell vibrated in her pocket. *"Allô?"*

"Irati's on the phone," Léo said. "She's on the move, too."

At last. Aimée scooped up the printouts and slipped them in her bag.

"No cell phones allowed, *shhh*." Poking her head around the corner, the guide, a white-haired, pert-nosed woman with frameless designer glasses, frowned. She pointed to the sign. "You're disturbing our tour."

Aimée nodded, rushing to the stairs. "Can I listen, Léo?"

"My equipment's not hooked up for second-party relay," Léo said. "But I'd say she's in a car."

"What's she saying, Léo?"

"Too much interference, fading in and out of dead zones. Doesn't sound French."

Aimée stiffened. "Basque?"

"Sounds Greek to me. But I can give you her geographic coordinates."

High-pitched bleeping noises punctuated by intermittent blips sounded in the background.

"Hold on, Léo."

With the phone to her ear, she took the narrow stairs two at time, crossed the tree-lined courtyard, and went up more stairs to rue Raynouard. Not two blocks from Xavierre's, yet still several blocks from her parked scooter.

"Her tracking signal's emitting on rue de Passy."

"Cross street?"

"Looks like Boulainvilliers Métro."

Merde! Blocks away.

"Keep talking, Léo." A biting wind hit her cheekbones. She wrapped her scarf tighter around her neck, plugged in her earbuds, stuck the phone in her pocket, and ran.

By the time she reached her scooter, she was out of breath. She pulled the scooter off its kickstand and keyed the ignition.

"I'm at Passy Métro. Which way?"

"Go north to Trocadéro."

She gunned the scooter, the wheels bumping over the cobbled street.

After climbing the Trocadéro hill, she saw the bland white wall of the Passy cemetery. "I'm at Trocadéro . . . the Passy cemetery?"

"The signal's moving down rue de la Pompe."

Aimée turned left, shifted into second gear. She wove among the buses, faster now, flying over the zebra-striped crosswalks.

"She's passing Lycée Janson de Sailly."

The elite Catholic high school was several blocks ahead. Aimée swerved to avoid a sweeping street cleaner. Aimée tried to think where she was headed: Shop? A market? "What's nearby, Léo?" A gust of leaves swirled by her feet from the gutter. Horns blared.

"On the map, Marché Saint-Didier," Léo said.

"Can't you pinpoint her caller's location, the number?" Aimée asked, breathless.

"If she stays on long enough," Léo said. "All my other scanners are monitoring work-related contracts right now."

In other words, the military. And Léo needed another scanner to pinpoint Irati's caller's number and location.

Irati would be driving a Mercedes, the other dark-colored one from the driveway.

But that described every other car in this neighborhood. Straining now, her breath vaporous in the chill mid-morning air, she veered right onto rue Saint-Didier.

A block down, she saw the rose-brick–covered Marché Saint-Didier. Locals with string bags clogged the pavement. A Mercedes was backing up into a crosswalk. Aimée braked, hopped off, and pulled her scooter near the lamp post.

A gray Renault came to an abrupt stop on her left. Two men jumped out. From the look of their short hair, nondescript dark blue windbreakers, and thick-soled black shoes, undercover *flics.* Or a special forces terrorist branch.

Aimée didn't have time to figure this out, much less to speculate about how they'd known and gotten here so fast. She had to warn Irati, use this chance to get information from her.

Irati, wearing a long dark chocolate wool coat and boots, carrying a full Printemps shopping bag, hurried across the narrow street and into the crowd. Morning shoppers thronged the entrance.

Aimée followed her; she had to reach Irati before these men got to her. The playing field had shifted, but she didn't know how.

"No signal, Aimée."

"Got her, Léo. *Merci.*"

Aimée lowered her head and followed. The two men split up, and Aimée reached for the phone in her pocket.

She hit Irati's number.

"Two men followed you, Irati," Aimée said. "They're entering the market."

"You again? Leave me alone." Pause. "You're lying."

"Turn around. See the one in the blue windbreaker?"

A gasp of air. She'd seen him. "You had me followed . . . why?"

"No, not me," she said. "You're being watched."

"But who are they?" Irati's voice quavered.

"*Flics,* special forces, who knows? But before you find out," she said, "tell me where you're meeting the Basques."

"But you. . . ." Irati stumbled. "How in the world . . . ?" she caught herself.

But not in time. She hadn't denied she was meeting the Basques.

"Trust me, Irati," she said. "I'm trying to help you, to find out who murdered your mother. What do they want?"

The line buzzed. Irati had hung up.

Aimée ran past counters of hanging red string sausages, lifeless beady-eyed rabbits suspended upside down, and displays of winter melons. Milling shoppers lined the aisles in the cavernous iron-strutted market hall. Shouts of "fresh Bresse chicken" came from a butcher in a bloodstained apron, along with scents of rosemary and fennel from the herb counter.

No Irati.

Think. Given the phone call, a "meet" set up in a crowded market, Irati's options narrowed. Damned if she didn't meet their demands, damned if she led the *flics* to them. In Irati's position, she'd get the hell out.

One of the blue windbreakers stood by the cheese counter, the other near the sample segments of glistening orange clementines behind an iron column. They were ignoring the first rule of shadowing, the rules her father had taught her: never attempt to hide. No doubt they'd break the others too: keep behind the suspect, act naturally no matter what, and never meet the suspect's eye. But she wasn't going to wait to find out.

Aimée walked backward in the crowd, mingling in the stream to avoid attention. At the entrance, she turned and hurried like everyone else. A rear side entrance exited on rue Mesnil. In the distance she saw the back of Irati's coat, already three quarters of the way to Place Victor Hugo. Almost a block ahead.

Aimée took off, her boot heels echoing off the tall limestone buildings lining the street. The sharp wind made tears form in her eyes. And then Irati had turned the corner.

Aimée pumped her legs. Ran as fast as she could. A minute later, she rounded the corner. Place Victor Hugo shone in the weak sunlight, a roundabout with ten streets radiating from it like the spokes of bicycle wheels. And no Irati.

WEDNESDAY MIDDAY

In the humid vaulted visiting room, Morbier wiped his neck with a stained handkerchief.

"Life's a tightwire, high above the circus crowd: any moment, you risk falling," said Lucard, the *juge d'instruction*. "But I don't need to tell you that, Morbier."

Lucard tented his slim fingers, trained his beady black eyes on the ceiling, and emitted a sigh.

Lucard had always reminded Morbier of a crow, scanning for shiny bright things in the gutter. After all, that was his job, so why shouldn't he resemble a scavenger?

"The IGS insists on extending your time in the *garde à vue*. They asked for my opinion," Lucard said. "A formality, of course."

Another twenty-four hours in this hellhole. No chance of reaching Laguardiere, or finding Xavierre's killer. A shame, too, since he'd worked with Lucard, a tough, thorough examining magistrate despite his youth, stylishly tousled hair, and Grandes Écoles bearing. He'd turned out to be just another lackey, a pinstripe suit in the system.

"Think I'm a flight risk, Lucard?"

"Liken it to the balancing act between the past and present," said Lucard. "Keeping to the tightrope analogy, you reach the wire by practicing, preparing. Above the crowd, it all depends on using what you've learned, drawing on your skill. This expertise gets you to the other side. To success, Morbier. Worry too much about the height, the past, and it weighs you to one side. If you don't focus and balance, you plunge."

The less-than-veiled analogy meant "back off." Forget the corruption investigation assigned him by Laguardiere. Turn over the source he'd met en route to Lyon.

The reigning powers assumed that a smart *flic* would wish to maintain the *esprit de corps* of his men, exit his lifetime of service with some dignity. Have a retirement to enjoy. Especially if they could dangle the carrot of a reduced murder charge.

No one except Laguardiere remained to watch his backside. Morbier's stitches itched, two in his scalp tugging on his hair;

a dull pain thudded in his side. He needed more painkillers.

"Anything wrong, Lucard? Wrong enough that twenty-four hours makes a difference, eh?" Morbier wiped his brow. "Or did the photographer raise ripples in the IGS sea?"

Last night, light-headed, he'd keeled over during transport to the sixth-floor prisoners' clinic of Hôtel Dieu. At the elevator, a freelance photographer had snapped his fall. Almost a bit of luck. He'd known the photographer, a strident Communist, for years. But, if they hadn't confiscated the photographer's camera already, they'd get to him.

No doubt his "incident" had necessitated a hurried meeting to defuse a scandal. No one could know the *flics* allowed their own to suffer what they did to other prisoners. They'd sent Lucard to make nice before the ax. Cover their judicial asses. As always. He'd been a fool to think he'd be able to nail corruption this deep.

"But I can make this go easier." Lucard smiled. "I want a name, Morbier."

Reveal his informer and sign the man's death warrant?

"Pierrot *le fou.* Jacques Chirac. Take your pick."

"Don't waste my time, Morbier," Lucard

219

said, his black eyes squinting in frustration. "The IGS consulted your team, assembled your investigation reports and notes. You've got no alibi. It's a done deal. You know how this works. Make it easier for yourself. Co-operate. You've commanded respect in a long career. You don't have to throw it all away."

Morbier swallowed, his throat dry. What he wouldn't give for a glass of water.

"Then think of the men you work with," Lucard said. "What about your team? I promise to do what I can. You know I keep my word, Morbier. I've worked deals for your cases before, haven't I?"

Tired, Morbier wanted all this to end. Had no stamina for it any more, apart from Cheb DJ's broken fingers. A nagging part of him longed to pick up his last paycheck, get incoherent in his apartment with a crate of half-decent Bordeaux, and maybe Xavierre's face would go away. For a little while.

"Five years for a crime *passionnel*," said Lucard, gauging his reaction. "But I can suggest health issues to the IGS and sentencing judge, knocking it down to three. A private cell, *télé,* the protected wing in La Santé."

All *flics* served their sentences in the protected wing; they wouldn't last five minutes in the general prison population.

"The IGS, unofficially of course and pending their investigation," Lucard said, "recommends you retire effective today so your pension remains intact."

They'd thought of everything.

"But I need a name, Morbier. You owe your partners, your team; time you came through on this."

Lucard had hit home. Morbier thought of his relationships made in the force. Like those friends and enemies formed on the school playground, they never went away. Did the past ever go away?

Fresh from the police academy, he'd entered the Commissariat boy's club — a camaraderie of brothers — they joked. Formed bonds with his partner, his team. The ones watching his back, his life, when he faced the street. Depending on each other. Trusting the code that kept each other alive to the end of their shift.

Like war, he imagined: only those who'd lived it understood. The good ones, like his first partner, operated that way. Had all his life. He'd made closer bonds with Jean-Claude Leduc than his own daughter or her mother.

But they were dead. Gone. And Aimée? A stab of guilt hit him. He'd made provisions in his will: his reduced retirement pension would keep Leduc Detective afloat for a while. But he'd have to do what he'd avoided for years and in all conscience should have done a long time ago: give her the key to the safe deposit box holding the letters, her mother's things. Tell her the truth. The whole truth. And she'd spit in his eye, walk away, and never see him again.

Not that he'd blame her.

Et alors, in the end, the men he'd worked with were all he had.

"You're mulling it over, I can see. That's good. Think of your men, this tight unit who look up to you, Morbier. It's your only recourse."

Morbier took a deep breath. Pain sliced his ribs. He clenched his teeth, feeling the tremor in his jaw, the shaking of his hands.

"We want to oil the wheels for the IGS, make it a formality, don't we?" Lucard leaned forward, pushing a water bottle that had materialized from his pocket toward Morbier. "Water?"

"Eat shit, Lucard." He leaned on the table. "And make sure to quote me."

Drumming her fingers on the round marble-top table of the café overlooking Place Victor Hugo, Aimée watched for Irati. The outdoor rattan café chairs gleamed like copper in the mid-afternoon light. Sparse brown-leafed plane trees encircled the spurting fountain. Opposite stood Saint Honoré d'Eylau, a narrow toffee-colored stone church. Hemingway married one of his wives here, the story went. She had a clear view of the three streets Irati might use to return to her car.

A traffic light shone green above the PIETONS ATTENTION sign as a rush of pedestrians crossed the zebra crosswalk.

She answered her phone on the first ring. *"Allô?"*

"Aimée, have you seen *L'Humanité?*" René said.

Since when did René read that Communist rag?

"Not your style, René."

"Look at the latest edition, the last page."

"Hold on." She found the newspaper rack on the café wall, took the wood roll, and scanned *L'Humanité's* back page. Her breath caught when she saw the photo of a bruised, kneeling Morbier clutching his stomach.

"My god, they're torturing him."

"Gets worse. Read the caption. 'Untold story of a bent Commissaire Divisionnaire.' " Concern vibrated in René's voice. "The article accuses Morbier of beating up a fellow *flic* who discovered irregularities in a Lyon investigation."

Her heart fell. "Lies!" she shouted. The waiter looked up.

"A trumped-up charge," she said, lowering her voice.

"You don't know that, Aimée," he said. "What the hell's going on?"

"Confined in jail, bruises? They beat people up, that's what they do, to make them talk," she said. "Maybe I'm ruining his chances after all."

"What do you mean?"

A flicker of dark brown passed the window. She leaned forward, her gaze traveling over the passersby, alert. She bit her lip. Only a blonde pulling a shopping cart.

"There's a leak in the force."

224

A long expulsion of air from René. "So now you're going to take on the Préfecture?"

"Not by myself."

She couldn't trust the *flics,* Melac most of all. Aimée slid a ten-franc note under her demitasse saucer in case she had to leave in a hurry.

"Xavierre's murderer's my priority," she said. "Irati almost let something slip. Call it instinct, but I know it links to Euskadi Action, the separatist Basques."

"And I have a bad feeling, Aimée."

She had to reassure René. "Listen, I called in a favor so patrols are on the alert for that Mercedes."

René said, "With a high-end car like that, they change the plates. That's the first thing they do."

"You sound well informed." Aimée's finger ran over the calcium deposits streaking in her water glass. A wind rose, like a sigh, shivering the yellow and brown leaves.

"I should." He sounded miffed. "My car's been stolen two times."

She heard clicking in the background. "I'm on a break at the symposium. Lots of interest in the security proposal you finished for me last night. Two potential clients already."

How could she have forgotten the two-day Data Encryption symposium René was participating in at La Villette?

"Brilliant, René."

"Of course, you're monitoring the data sniffer feed," he said. "You know, working?"

She'd set alerts, customized the feed, and prepared it to continuously download to her laptop. Automatic, but René didn't know.

"Of course."

Pause.

"Why do I think you're keeping something back, Aimée?"

She couldn't get him more involved. More compromised. And she couldn't tell him that, or he'd protest.

"I'll finish the report. You concentrate on the symposium. Those potential clients." She picked up her bag and buttoned her coat, wondering if Irati had taken the long route instead of the closest.

"The *juge d'instruction*'s mentioned here, a Lucard," René said. "His reputation's solid. Distinguished record. Trust him to get the truth," René said. "Now I wish I hadn't told you."

Trust the system? The *flics?* René hadn't grown up with them like she had.

"Didn't you insist on driving me to Xavi-

226

erre's, René? Saying you're Morbier's friend too?"

"And I'm not?" René inhaled. "This makes me sick. I don't understand what's going on or why. But what if your interference backfires — on him?" René hesitated. "Or on you?"

She shuddered, remembering Melac's fingers tracing her cheekbone.

"Right now, that worry is at the bottom of the list, René. Talk to you later."

The espresso machine grumbled in the background. The white-aproned waiter set down Aimée's change on the round marble table.

"Don't suppose you've seen my friend?" She gave a little sigh. "I could swear she meant this café. Petite, long dark brown coat, carrying a Printemps shopping bag, shoulder-length black hair, early twenties?"

The waiter jerked his thumb toward the zinc counter. "Just them."

A group of men wearing blue work jackets with the EAU DE PARIS water company logo on the back stood at the counter drinking beers with a chaser of red wine.

"*Le quotidien,* their daily dose, same time every day." The waiter spread his hands. Not good tippers, she figured. "Seems like there are always more of them."

He wiped a towel over the table. Paused. Gray-haired, sturdy black shoes with rolled-up toes that spoke of wear. Bad feet? But the talkative type, old school, proud of his métier, she could tell.

"Nice that they keep your gutters sparkling clean," she said to the waiter, cocking her head toward the workmen, her gaze still scanning the pavement.

"Not the gutters." He shrugged. "We've got the most picturesque reservoir in *la ville.*"

"Here?" Aimée asked, engaging his conversation, darting her eyes over pavement. "Not the one in Belleville?"

He shrugged. "Passy reservoir's a well-kept secret. *Caché,* hidden above ground, too."

Sounded familiar. Had she learned that in school?

"It's like a private pool with a view of the Eiffel Tower, like going on a holiday." He re-wiped the table with a towel. "The *Carlingue* liked the view."

Carlingue, a phrase she hadn't heard since her grandfather's day. Most referred to them as Gestapistes, the French auxiliary of the Gestapo. Run by Lafont, the convicted criminal, and Bonny, the former policeman. Her eyes widened.

He caught her look. "So much so," he continued, "that they reserved the tunnels under the reservoir for torture chambers. Convenient, right across from their offices."

"Offices? You mean rue Lauriston?"

He nodded.

Madame de Boucher's account of her brother came back to her. Even today, rue Lauriston meant one thing.

"The right address on the wrong side of history."

A philosopher too, this waiter.

Just the street name sent shivers up the older generation's spine. Few talked about it or about French collaboration. Few had survived.

After twenty more minutes in the café, Aimée returned to the Marché Saint-Didier. Irati's Mercedes windshield held a parking ticket. From the corner of her eye she saw four men sitting in the Renault, the gray Renault she'd seen before.

She took clear black-framed glasses from her bag, put on a wool cap, pushed her scooter down the street, and knocked on the car window.

"*Pardonnez-moi,* messieurs," she said, affecting a singsong Breton accent.

The man in the passenger seat ignored

her. Most Parisians regarded Bretons as crêpe-eating provincials, seacoast simpletons.

She knocked again, put her face to the window, and pointed to her tire. "Don't mean to bother you."

The window rolled down. *"Oui?"* A curt voice.

"My tire's leaking air. Don't suppose you noticed a garage nearby?" She gave a vacuous smile. Blinked, but not before she'd scanned the interior hi-tech radio and computer console visible under a jacket on a seat. "I'm new in the *quartier.*"

"New, eh? Me too, *Mam'selle.*" The one in the passenger seat, tan and muscular, started to roll up the window.

"I'm lost, too," she said. "Can't find Avenue Foch."

"Back there," he said, eager to get rid of her. "Past the roundabout."

"You mean over there?"

His eyes narrowed. "You're a *domestique, non?*"

She shrugged. "My madame doesn't like it when I'm late for work."

Since the turn of the century, Bretons had immigrated to Paris, settling near Montparnasse, the station where they arrived. Many worked as housemaids in the 16th. Like Bécassine, in the comics her grandmother had read to her. Bécassine was always depicted as a bumbling Breton maid without a mouth, in clogs, who stumbled on adventures.

She'd seen enough. *"Merci."* Waved, then walked her scooter, noting the Renault's license plate number. Undercover special forces were noted for driving late-model Renaults. The high-tech console in the car could spell GIGN, *Groupement d'Intervention de la Gendarmerie Nationale,* the well-funded elite military unit of the Gendarmerie. Or RAID, *Recherche Assistance Intervention Dissuasion,* the police version of the assault unit. They were in competition with each other.

Interesting. Why was a terrorist special elite force — whichever one they were — following Irati unless she was involved with Euskadi Action? Time to find out what the hell Irati was up to.

At least she was one up on the watchers. Her scooter's wheels crunched over piled leaves. She punched in Léo's number.

"She got away, Léo," she said. "Any more activity on her phone?"

"Time's up. I'm booked solid on a project, Aimée," Léo said. "You're not the only one

231

I'm helping. Right now my paying clients take priority."

"And I appreciate it. Morbier's —"

"Par for the 16th, eh?" Léo interrupted, disgust in her voice. "Born with pearls up their backsides."

Little rankled the Parisian in a cramped apartment more than the 16th arrondissement's wide leafy boulevards and huge apartments with rents higher than the Eiffel Tower. Or the conservative trappings of the old-moneyed inhabitants.

"Bet she wears a quilted Chanel headband, too. Typical."

Something had ruffled Léo's proletariat feathers. "Hold on. What's bothering you, Léo?"

"Partying so soon after her mother's murder! Should I be feeling sorry for this Irati?"

"Party?" The murky outlines emerged, then cleared. "Do you mean the reception tonight at the Marmottan museum?"

A sigh. "I only did this for Morbier, you understand?"

"Me too, Léo."

Aimée's mind reeled as she wove the scooter between vehicles on rue de Passy. Special-forces involvement pointed to terrorists, extremists like Euskadi Action.

No doubt if Irati's meeting at the market had been aborted, the fallback was at the Basque Spanish Marmottan reception tonight.

At Xavierre's house on rue Raynouard, her repeated buzzing elicited no answer. Nor were her calls on the house phone answered. She stepped back, looked over the wall, and saw the shuttered windows.

No luck here. She glanced at her Tintin watch. The Marmottan reception would begin soon.

Her unease heightened. With Morbier in the *garde à vue,* Irati and her fiancé blaming Morbier didn't look good. If Irati knew something, wouldn't it make sense to tell the *flics?* Why shield her mother's murderer?

Again her mind went back to René's words. Protecting one you loved would make you lie.

She powered her cell phone back on. One message from a blocked number. She hit LISTEN. Only a rustling, low cough, a hang up.

Morbier? She'd missed him, couldn't call back. Stupid.

She buttoned her coat against the rising wind. A taste of moisture settled the air. Like the *orage* in the south when hot

Mediterranean currents hit humidity from the Atlantic. A storm was brewing.

Her phone trilled. She answered on the first ring.

"Meet me," said Agustino, his voice terse. "Twenty minutes, Jardin du Ranelagh."

Surprised, she cupped her phone closer to her ear. A change of heart? Guilt? she wondered.

"I'll make it in ten," she said, reaching for her scooter key. "You know who murdered Xavierre?"

"No *flics,*" he said. "Can I trust you?"

A frisson went up her spine.

"Count on it. But wait, Agustino. You know who —"

"The documents, Xavierre, it's all linked," he interrupted. "They'll stop the accord. Wait for me."

"What documents? What do you mean?"

"Not now." He hung up.

She angled her bag over her shoulder, revved her scooter, and took off.

She sat on the green slatted benches, her coat pulled tight around her, in the Jardin du Ranelagh near the pony stand. Despite the wind, bundled-up toddlers escorted by designer-clad governesses took pony rides led by a red-cheeked old man. A fur-coated grandmother or two watched from the sidelines. Another world, Aimée thought. The pampered upper middle class. Balzac's refuge had yielded to old-fashioned refinement for the protected few with a leavening of *commerçants,* workers, and boutiques.

Too bourgeois for her.

Mansions, all equipped with surveillance cameras, studded Avenue du Ranelagh. Nestled in the ivy-covered walls, their frames poked out from above the intercoms. So the rich protected themselves. Nothing new. Behind her lay the Musée Marmottan, a *belle époque* mansion housing the Monet collection donated by his family. The clouds had parted; late-afternoon light hit the ornate metal scrollwork above the doors.

Agustino's terse words nagged at her. What did he mean by documents? Why didn't he hurry up?

The ponies circled a worn dirt path. Their snorting breaths misted in the air. Aimée turned around and stared at the museum's limestone façade and tall windows, the cameras trained on the low, blue grilled fence. This was the site of the Basque accords announcement reception to be held in an hour.

Twenty minutes became forty. No Agustino. Unease prickled from her black-stockinged calves to her scarved neck.

She pulled out her LeClerc compact, touched up her face, and angled the mirror to reflect the Marmottan's façade: only surveillance cameras and the blue grille fence.

Was Agustino hovering somewhere, afraid she'd alerted the *flics?* Or had his courage deserted him? Tension knotted her stomach.

She'd give him another ten minutes before going to the entrance around the corner. She applied Chanel red to her lips and stood. After a few steps, she paused and scanned the park. Twilight had long since dusted the limestone mansions facing the square; sunset's orange ribbon faded from the Marmottan museum's slanted rooftops. The pony stand stood shut and dark in the park opposite.

More than an hour now. And she'd be late to meet Martine. Maybe he'd entered already? Brown leaves scattered over the toffee-colored gravel.

She turned the corner. Light glimmered in the Marmottan's upper floors, framing the ground floor ablaze with lights. She imagined a gauntlet of security and a guest list check-in. No doubt a formal receiving line inside the reception.

But instead of Euskadi Action protestors,

valets stepped forward to open the doors of limos depositing evening-gowned and tuxedoed guests. She saw Martine's blond head, visible beyond the tall doors. A clap of thunder, the first sprinkles of rain, and she ran inside.

"*Encore,* Mademoiselle?"

Maria, Princesse de Villargoza, fifteenth in line to the Spanish throne if her aunt, the Infanta, renounced the succession, shook her head.

"Non, merci." Maria smiled at the balding thirty-something man at the resto's bar. Too old. "Dinner reservations."

The man set the empty wine glass onto the gleaming bar, stood, and left for the lounge. No fun, that one, Maria thought. She caught her reflection in the gold-framed mirror and adjusted her spaghetti shoulder strap.

Maria sipped her white wine and winked at the barman, who was tall and muscular under his black vest. He ignored her. Pretentious, the place a crashing bore, she thought. No way to treat royalty, even, as her father reminded her, one with obligations. At home in Madrid, the bouncers recognized her, ushered her past the club line, undid the velvet rope. There were five trendier places no farther than a finger touch on her speed dial where her ID wasn't questioned or even looked at.

Snobisme, typical, as her friend would say. And where was she? Stupid to insist on meeting here. Weren't they going clubbing? As a Madrileña, her first rule was to avoid places such as this with the fossilized upper crust. Five more minutes, that's all, then she'd leave. The ceiling of the cavernous room swayed a bit, an old train station converted into a "chic" resto. More like dead space, as hip as her toenail and full of bland couples oozing self-importance.

Like the ambassador and his wife. So eager to present her at one of their *rallyes* — the interminable parties where old money and the titled ensured that their offspring and their money stayed together. *Rallyes* organized by mothers with lists of eligible bachelors of the same class; *cinq à neuf* for the young, *six à minuit* the teens, and then *le bat* as they got older. Four or five years of parties within the same milieu. She hated it, had refused to take part any more this year.

No one would know where she was after begging off from the reception. Another yawn-stifling affair. Escape and enjoy freedom for a few short hours. Maria's silver-buckled Birkin bag tumbled off the adjoining stool as she reached for a cigarette. One drink too many?

"I'd hang on to this if I were you."

In the dim bar, lit by butterfly-like halogen lights, a man on a nearby stool set the bag in her lap. "Wouldn't want it to get ideas."

Not bad, this *mec.* All in black, tall and not that old. He gestured to the glass-roofed ceiling. A startled wren fluttered high up.

"They like sparkling things."

"And I'm not?"

He gave a little grin. Glanced at his watch. "Not your kind of place, I'd say. Or mine either."

"Going to a club, but my friend's late." She flicked her lighter, inhaled, watching him from the corner of her eye. Definite possibility, this one.

"Rouge-Bleu?"

She shrugged. "Her call. I don't know."

"Hot. The only place. She'll know it." He checked his phone. "The valet brought my car. First stop for me, then the rave later. See you there?"

Rave? Her friend was half an hour late. What if she didn't show up? She'd face a grilling from the ambassador's wife, recriminations over preparations for tomorrow's official duties. It sickened her half the time; the rest of the time it scared her. The endless round of charity functions at retirement homes with drooling seniors bent with age. So many vacant-faced old people with translucent paper-thin skin. The helpless feeling at the sadness and old-people smell trailing in their hobbled wake.

"Let me ask her." She hit her speed dial. Just voicemail.

Irritated, she twirled a wisp of her black hair, spoke into the phone, and left a message, crossing her fishnet-clad legs. Thank god she'd changed from her "uniform" of the pastel pink wool suit to the black chemise-like mini.

"Mind giving me a ride?"

She smiled, knowing she looked older than eighteen, but figuring this *mec* could smooth his way past any bouncer anyway.

"Finish your drink," he said. "Won't your friend come here?"

She drained her glass. "I've taken care of that. Let's go."

Maria liked Rouge-Bleu: packed, celebrity-studded, crowded red sofas, filtered blue rays of light, the signature red-and-blue sapphire vodka cocktail fizzing with raspberries. A throbbing techno DJ mix. But the

walls sagged and the lights blended now;
sweat dotted her brow on the dance floor.
The heat, the bending, twisting floor. She
grabbed him. Lucas . . . wasn't that his
name? But a girl shook her hands off,
laughed, and danced away. Where had he
gone?

She staggered toward the pillars. Lucas
took her hand. "Need some air?"

Lucas guided her around the red sofas and
into the clear night . . . and the cobbled
pavement rose to meet her flushed face.

She came to, alerted by beeping near her
ear.

Where was he? Dark shadows, a musty
smell. Her hands and feet felt heavy, constricted.

"Lucas?"

"Over here." A red-orange light flickered
over his face. Another club? Or the rave?

She tried to get up. Her head swum. Then
a happy warmness rippled over her.

"Ooops." She hiccuped and laughed. "Got
to get back." She'd slip in the embassy's
rear entrance. Sneak in like last night. But
she couldn't move her legs.

Duct tape wrapped her ankles, her wrists.

"I don't think so," he said, putting a hood
over her head.

WEDNESDAY EARLY EVENING

At the reception, Aimée accepted the flute of Kir Royale from Martine. The rose gold fizzed down her throat like raw silk, the hue matching the Monet beside her. "To think," Martine said, pointing to the framed oil painting, a sunrise glinting on the river, "Monet's critics dismissed this as 'Impressionism,' unworthy of even wallpaper. Ironic, eh, later they named the art movement after this painting."

Aimée preferred the small oil by Berthe Morisot, two women and a small girl gazing from the hill at Trocadéro. The painting communicated an intimacy, a fleeting glimpse of a long-gone time, moments captured in fluid brush strokes of light and color.

She'd hadn't sighted Agustino or Irati. Just a roomful of Impressionists, heavy on Monet, and security everywhere. No way to prevent this accord announcement, as far as she could tell.

"When's Goikoetxea's announcement, Martine?" she said. "Do you see him?"

Martine handed Aimée her Champagne. "Not yet. I'll find out."

Feeling out of place, Aimée glanced at the designer-dressed crowd milling in the circular exhibition room. Felt the undercurrent of excitement from the media, an expectant buzz in the low conversations, the clink of glasses.

Martine nodded to a group of journalists taking advantage of the well-stocked hors d'oeuvre table. Beyond the Marmottan's tall doors, sheets of rain pelted the glistening grassy courtyard. Rumbling peals of thunder sounded. The flickering lantern light caught the water dripping from the scrolled metal balconies, the mossy limestone building foundation.

Martine put her arm on the Spanish military attaché's elbow, guided him toward Aimée. "Carlos, it's been too long." The drill-bit–thin man in a black suit smiled. A professional smile below a thin black moustache. "What's the holdup? Anything for me, off the record?"

"Martine." He pecked her on both cheeks. "Of course," he said. "Goikoetxea canceled."

Canceled? Aimée's shoulders stiffened. Martine shot her a keep-your-mouth-shut look.

"Trouble?" Martine said. "Stalled negotiations?"

"Let's say the no-show of the party-girl princess impacted matters. A spoiled brat. Trying to launch her modeling career. Not the first time she's pulled a disappearance."

"You're treating this like a stunt, then?" Martine said. "Carlos, what aren't you telling me?"

"On the surface." He shrugged then leaned closer. "And I never said this," he said, his voice lowered, "but we're keeping things under wraps for now. Possible kidnapping, but on a low alert. For now. You will remember: off the record."

Aimée froze.

Another professional smile, and Carlos leaned closer. "We're expecting a quick resolution and a positive slant, like always, from you."

Martine nodded. "But I fail to see the connection to Goikoetxea's announcement," Martine said. "Wasn't the princess just window-dressing?"

"Her father's furious, knows she'll turn up, press in tow, describing her escape from terrorists and get an *Elle* cover."

Martine's eyes narrowed. "Terrorists kidnapped the princess? You mean she's leverage preventing the Basque announcement? That's what you can't say?"

Aimée's heart quickened. Agustino knew. But how? Foreboding filled her.

"If the kidnapping becomes official, her father refuses to cooperate," said Carlos. "He insists on handling the Euskadi Action demands via his own channels. Goikoetxea's livid, insists we're playing into their hands, but we've been told to cooperate. If her father fails, we expect the terrorist demands to be made public within three hours. But if that happens. . . ." He shrugged. "Might as well forget it. And I didn't say that."

"Of course you didn't," Martine purred. "I protect my sources."

Given the attaché's attitude, no one was treating this as a priority. Or could. They were just going through the motions for now.

"Meet my friend Aimée. She didn't hear that either," Martine said, turning.

But Aimée had melted into the crowd.

At the cloakroom, she reclaimed her coat. She had to find Agustino and confront him.

At least the downpour had abated. Fresh

damp smells of vegetation greeted her; moonlight illuminated the droplets on the plastic covering her scooter.

"Aimée, wait." Under the dripping tree branches, Martine, coatless, hurried toward her, a cell phone to her ear. "Word's come down, via the ambassador's aide. The whole negotiation was tetchy from the start."

"Didn't I tell you, Martine? Agustino warned me they'd stop the agreement. This connects to Xavierre's murder, and I've got to find out how."

"What do you mean?"

"When I know —"

"I need another slant for my story," Martine interrupted.

"What story?"

"So far it's unofficial, but Euskadi Action demands the release of French Basque prisoners and to put Goikoetxea's peace referendum to a 'lawful unrigged election' — their words — or Princesse Maria, who was to appear tonight, will never appear again."

So that was the plan. A sinking feeling in her stomach told her Irati was part of it. But her own mother . . . ?

"Aimée, the princess's father's advisory to the prison board," Martine said. "No one has much hope, since those prisoners got life for school bus bombings, a rash of them several years ago. Dicey."

René's cousin? she wondered.

"I'll get you more, Martine," she said. "Information to get Morbier released. I just need to —"

"Mademoiselle?" She heard the muted thump of approaching footsteps on the damp pavement. "We'd like a word," said a bland-faced man with short cropped hair stepping into view. Several more like him fanned out, encircling her and Martine, their gazes boring into her.

A Citroën four-door with blackened windows pulled up with a screeching of brakes.

"This way." He gestured to her, then Martine. "Guess she'll need to come with us too."

"Why?"

One of the bland-faced crew hulked over her. She couldn't read his eyes and didn't relish a ride and questioning. "Don't you know this woman, Mademoiselle?"

"Soon everyone will," Aimée said, thinking fast, prodding Martine. "Show him your press card, Martine."

"I'm a journalist covering this event." Martine flashed her press badge. "Radio France."

"I can read," he said.

"Any comment?" Martine said, pulling out a small notebook. "Like which branch you work for and why you want to take my friend and me for questioning?"

No one had ever asked him that before, Aimée could tell. Assault teams were trained to act, follow procedure, not deal with the press. Or think. Their bosses did that. His right eyelid quivered.

"I ask the questions here."

"Bon." Aimée smiled. *"Détective privé."* She displayed her card. "Let's try for polite. Your turn. Show ID."

A thin wire trailed from an earpiece to his collar.

"In this situation, we're not required. . . ." He paused, barked a short *"Oui"* into a microphone tucked under his jacket collar, and turned. The others joined ranks around him as he spoke into a cell phone.

Great. She pictured hours of questioning. And hoped to god they hadn't recognized her from the market.

Martine slipped her ID back into her purse. Her hands shook. "This charade can go on only so long, Aimée. My boss —"

"For you," the bland face interrupted. He held his thin silver cell phone out to Aimée.

"Who wants to speak to me? Why?"

"My patron." He gestured her away from

Martine. "In private."

Her throat caught. What choice did she have?

"Oui?" she managed.

"For once, wouldn't you prefer to get paid for investigating, Mademoiselle Leduc? Colonel Valois speaking." A crisp man's voice spoke. Was he with GIGN, who operated under the Gendarmerie, a military branch under the Ministry of Defense? Or with RAID, their rival police equivalent out of Les Invalides?

"Quite a few of us in the Gendarmerie have a police background and training," the voice continued. "I had occasion to liaise with your father on several incidents."

Stunned, the slick phone slipped in her moist palm. She gripped it before it fell.

"Meaning?"

"Think of it as eyes on the ground in a consultant role," Colonel Valois's voice continued. "Mademoiselle Leduc, it's kept quiet, but we employ people such as yourself in that capacity. Think of working for us as an occasional sideline, a supplement to your income. On a case-by-case basis, of course, and no worry about paperwork. Direct payment into a special account. Untraceable."

She gasped. Had her father worked with this man?

"I don't understand," she said, trying to catch Martine's gaze.

"But I think you do." Pause. "Let's just say an active splinter ETA organization came to EPIGN's attention in the last month."

EPIGN — the elite military sub-unit, rarely in the news. A skilled special-operations group operating within the better-known GIGN. The men in the car at the market. Her spine tingled.

"Our branch would appreciate your co-operation."

Meaning they were as desperate and clue-less as she was?

"My father never mentioned you," she said, stalling, thinking of the implications. Morbier's words played in her head: "Trust no one." Had they screwed her father? And were about to do the same to Morbier?

"Think about it, Mademoiselle Leduc," he said. "I'll be in touch. Don't worry, I can always find you."

She tried to control her shaking hands as she passed back the phone. The man's bland expression didn't change.

The men piled into the car. She watched until the brake lights turned the corner.

"Whatever you said . . ." Martine swal-lowed. ". . . worked."

"The EPIGN wants to recruit me."

Martine blinked.

"He asked me to think about it," she said.

An hour, a day? she wondered.

"Rumor goes they make it impossible for you to refuse."

Like her father? "Not my thing, Martine."

"Think of it this way, Aimée," Martine said. "The EPIGN's active in Basque territory. Even have a HALO detachment specializing in VIP protection." Martine shot her a look. "But it was sloppy work allowing the kidnapping. Matter of fact, they blew it. Figures. All that training on emergency response goes to their head. Now they need you."

"But I screwed up, Martine," she said. "I didn't protect Xavierre. Her murder's connected. She's the link. Now the princess."

"Put it in perspective," Martine said. "ETA needs to prove the princess is alive. That's the first step in any negotiation. This could take days, make for a nice long feature."

Aimée didn't return Martine's grin.

"It's your *derrière* you need to watch." Martine handed Aimée a tissue. "Clean up your mascara: you've got raccoon eyes."

Aimée wet the tissue with her tongue and dabbed under her eyes. And the wheels clicked. The museum surveillance cameras. She scanned the museum's entrance, but the cameras were obscured by hanging branches. Another look revealed that the town house cameras opposite were trained in other directions.

"But the cameras would have caught the kidnapping."

Martine shrugged. "The princess was a no-show. Nothing on tape."

Merde. She'd wasted time already, and she needed backup. She pulled out her phone and spoke to her cousin Sebastian, arranging to meet in twenty minutes.

She keyed her scooter's ignition.

"The ambassador agreed to sign a vaguely worded promise," Martine said. "But no way can he or the girl's father authorize a prison release just like that. Or snap their fingers and hold a new election."

Martine lit a cigarette. Smoke hovered, dissipating under the bare branches like mist. "Aimée, find me another angle to this kidnapping."

"Doesn't sit right, does it?" Aimée pulled on her Blue Fever helmet. Oil-slicked rainbow puddles bled into the cracks between the uneven cobbles.

Martine nodded. "If this Basque agreement ties somehow to Xavierre's murder, and Agustino knew . . . ?"

"Martine, he knows something, but —"

"He's a small fish," Martine interrupted. "I want the big fish. Trust me," she said. "That *mec,* by the way, the charmer without expression?"

Aimée nodded. Monsieur Blandface.

"Warned me off the story." Martine ground the cigarette out with her toe. "Thinks he can muzzle the press? Not me. But you're on to something: there's more to this. The way I write this up . . . well, if you find me ammunition, I'll load it Morbier's way. But I need proof, *compris?* Why should those boys have their sick fun?"

Aimée wished that made her feel better. She revved the engine, popped into first, and took off into the night.

Maria struggled, trying to see through the grainy darkness of the burlap bag over her head. Cold dampness sent shivers up her arms, bare but for her spaghetti-strap silk mini. She strained to hear, listening for traffic or voices, but heard only the echoing of footsteps. Hers and another.

Then a low, short toot. The recognizable whistle of a barge. The smell of algae. They were by the Seine.

She tripped on metal pipes, losing her balance and sending them clanging and rolling. Hands jerked her bound wrists behind her.

"Get up!"

Trussed and bound like a pig, she couldn't move sideways. Or yell with her mouth duct-taped shut. She kicked out her foot and hit a pipe.

Sharp pain shot up her leg. And the terror she'd tried to fight took over. Hot, panicked breaths from her nose filled the bag with warm suffocating air. She couldn't breathe. Couldn't open her mouth.

She felt herself rolled over, pulled upright, leaned against wet freezing metal. The bag was pulled off her head.

Water dripped from a broken pipe, and puddles reflected the sputtering glow of a kerosene lamp. The reek of kerosene and mildew was everywhere. A man leaned over the lamp, adjusted the flame brighter. She gasped at his face. Silhouetted against the darkness, a blood-soaked bandage covered his eye.

She felt a searing stinging as he ripped the duct tape from her mouth. Her lips were raw, and chunks of her black hair had been pulled out. Her eyes teared and her body shook with cold.

"Where's Lucas . . . where am I?"

No answer.

"Let's pretend this didn't happen. Take my bag." She turned her face away. "I didn't see you. I don't know you."

"But you already have." She heard the accent, the Basque way of saying *b* for a *t,* the *r* turning into *err.* He squatted next to her on the flaking rusted pipes. "Be a good girl. Do what I say."

"You've got to let me go." Her voice rose.

This wasn't happening. Couldn't happen. "The ambassador will raise hell if I'm not back. I won't say anything."

He took a pistol from his brown leather jacket pocket. "Do I have to use this?"

She gulped. Shaking, she couldn't stop shaking, or her teeth from chattering. She'd lost her shoes, her stockings were ripped, and her bare feet were going numb from the cold.

"What do you want?"

He turned away.

"Don't you understand they're expecting me? I'll get in trouble."

Like the last time.

He gave a small smile. "You don't call this trouble?"

She let out a scream. Screamed again and again. Only the piercing echoes from the steel rafters responded.

"No one can hear you," he said. "Quit moving."

"I c-c-can't, too cold."

"Call this cold?" He snorted. "Try living a winter in the mountains. Wind like ice cutting over the Pyrénées, through the valley, and only boiled snow to drink."

A Basque. That didn't stop her shaking. Her memories of the Basque country came from summers in her friend's mother's village. Pine branches heavy with rain, their crisp scent wafting over the whitewashed farmhouses and red-tiled roofs bordering the green sheep meadows. Not this bone-chilling, damp-permeated, rusting warehouse.

He was a fine one to talk. He wore a jacket, boots, and wool scarf. Her dress was soaked, a copper-tinged reeking mess. What did he expect? She was without a coat.

"B-b-but you've got warm clothes."

"Complaining?"

At the look on his face, she tried to make herself small. Fear coursed through her veins. *"Non."*

"Prove it. Can you?"

She nodded.

He unzipped his jacket, threw it on her shaking bare legs. "You sew?"

Nonplussed, she stared, shivering.

He unwound the blood-soaked bandage covering his eye. Pulled the kerosene lantern closer. She gasped. Clotted blood surrounded his bruised left eye, which was swollen shut. His shirt collar was stained dark with blood.

He reached over and untied her hands. She inhaled a metallic whiff of blood, his perspiration.

"Use this." He handed her a travel-sized

sewing kit. A small bottle of liqueur, airplane-sized, and a white embroidered towel. "Clean it right."

She didn't want to touch him.

"Or I use this."

One hand held the gun; the other pulled back the matted black hair from his temple.

She winced. "Bring the light closer so I can see."

The kerosene lantern scraped over the stained concrete floor.

Black slivers studded his eyelid; deep red cuts scored the edge of his eye. She sucked in air. "I need tweezers."

"Eh? Just clean and sew it up."

"But there are pieces of something in there. If you don't take them out, you'll get an infection. Now if I had my bag with twee . . . zers. . . ." Her teeth chattered again.

He reached over, took her vanilla leather Birkin bag, and dumped out the contents: her new Vuitton wallet, agenda, checkbook, receipts, key ring, and cell phone tumbled on the rust flakes.

Her cell phone.

Her hopes lifted. A chance now. She'd help him, gain his confidence, and call for help.

"Check the side pocket for the tweezers,"

she said. "Beside my lipstick."

She pulled his jacket around her legs, glanced up. Giant tarnished metal cranes loomed over them, suspended in the air, like giraffes caught in flight. A slanted industrial glass roof above what looked like an assembly line. Wheels and rubber conveyor belts strewn on the floor. A familiar insignia with an *R* molded into one of the iron pillars.

R for Renault. She realized they were in the derelict Renault auto works on Île Seguin. The old production plant on the outskirts covered the island in the Seine. It had been abandoned for years. She'd gone by the plant countless times on the way to school when her father was posted to the Paris embassy. As a little girl she'd watched the finished cars loaded onto barges, fascinated.

She had to get her phone. Give the location. Grab a taxi and slip in the embassy back door, no one the wiser.

She poured the liqueur on the tweezers and over his cheekbone. He made a light intake of breath. Considering the blood he'd lost, he should be ready to pass out.

He grabbed the bottle, took a long drink. Then another.

If he passed out drunk, even better.

"Hurry up."

She got to work. Instead of clubbing, she found herself in a freezing abandoned auto works swabbing a terrorist's wound. But she had a plan.

"My friend's mother's people come from Basse Navarre," she said, chewing the thread off with her teeth, determined to make conversation, relax him and lull him to carelessness. "Know it?"

"Why?" His chest muscles flexed. Hard. He grabbed her hair.

"Oww . . . your accent's like her uncle's. That's all."

"Rich brat, what do you know?" He relaxed the grip on her hair. "What's this?" He picked up papers from her bag, her student card mired in the puddle. He stared at it. "You study?"

"No, I'm just a spoiled brat shopping and lunching with my girlfriends." Anger flushed her cheeks. "I take design courses. Function in architecture. Model a bit on the side. Not. . . ." She stopped before she said "a kidnapper like you."

"Impressive. Maybe you'll give me design tips."

He nudged her with the gun.

Feeling more confident now, she tried to keep the conversation going. "I'm moving

261

in with my boyfriend next year."

"Does your father know?"

"My boyfriend's a photographer," she said. "An artist."

"Art's political."

What did that mean? Art went on the wall. "Ready?" She probed deep with the tweezers.

He squinted, closing his eyes, his teeth grinding.

Her pink phone gleamed in the beams of kerosene light just a reach away. She edged toward it.

His left hand grabbed hers in a grip like steel.

"What's this?" Her tweezers held a blackened sliver of sharp metal.

"Shrapnel." The lines in his brow relaxed. "Take it all out." He drank more.

"Shrapnel . . . you mean from a bullet?"

Horrified, she dropped the tweezers, which clattered on the wet cement.

"Did you kill someone?"

He leaned back, still pointing the gun at her. "Struggle has to be seen within the political context," he said. "There are people who choose nonviolent struggle; and then us, who have another vision and use other tactics."

He'd never before said so many words in

a sentence. He reminded her of her friend's uncle, a stocky farmer with long ears who was short on conversation.

"The government outlaws the Basques' right to decide our future," he said. "No one wants violence. But struggle demands sacrifice."

She'd seen the bombings on the *télé*. The rehearsed speeches and demands by men in ski masks with guns. Like him.

"But deep down, you can't mean you'd shoot —"

"Ask the seven hundred prisoners held in Spanish jails, the corrupt French *flics* who rule Basse Navarre," he interrupted, letting out a deep breath. "Or ask my brother. Tortured. My father. A cripple for life."

She didn't know what to say.

"But the law . . . ?"

"Welcome to the real world," he said sarcastically. "It gets down and dirty outside the palace."

"What palace? My father works. So does my mother."

An awful fear filled her. What if Lucas and these terrorists meant to hold her for ransom?

"Take the pieces of shrapnel out. Now." He held the gun, his fingers looser. His Adam's apple bobbed. She rubbed her hands in the cold. Trying not to look at her phone. So close. How with one little reach . . . maybe with her toe. . . .

He growled. "What are you waiting for?"

She hid her disgust. Coating crime with politics got no sympathy from her. Just a renegade, like all the bandits, those smugglers high in the Basse Navarre. A Basque stronghold. Since time immemorial, holing up in remote villages, banding together, spitting in the eye of authority and the government. Robbing pilgrims, the innocent, the desperate, whether they were fleeing from the Inquisition, the Bourbons, or the Nazis along the ancient paths and escape routes through the Pyrénées.

"Pull more splinters out, understand?" he said, gasping in pain.

Her breaths frosted in the air. She edged her numb foot forward. Further. Her big toe touched the pink casing.

Loud crashing noises. Then the tramp of boots.

"Why the hell didn't you answer?" asked a gravel-voiced man in a black ski mask.

Terror gripped her. Another man leaned down, riffling through the strewn contents of her bag. Grabbed her cell phone. "Pink?"

Mud rimmed his boots. The mixed smell of earth and algae as he kicked the bloody bandages. "Letting her play doctor, Joxi?" he said. "And messy. I don't like messy."

The gravel-voiced one gestured to the *mec.* "Pick this up. All of it."

Panic sliced across her like a blade.

Joxi groaned and fell back.

"Time for a real doctor." His black eyes glittered behind the eyeholes in the mask. "Tape her back up. Put her in the van."

"W-wh-where?" Her voice chattered with cold.

He looked at her, back at the other *mec,* and just laughed.

WEDNESDAY EVENING

Mist hovered low over the hedgerows, silent and damp. A gust of wind stirred the dead leaves. Not even a twitter came from the bushes. A wave of relief passed over her as she saw Sebastian's secondhand van, a Berlingo, at the curb.

She switched off the scooter's ignition, pulled off her helmet, and noticed a run in her black stockings. A new pair, too.

"Tool set, like you ordered, all loaded in back," Sebastian said.

Sebastian, her younger cousin, stood a head taller than Aimée. He sported a wool cap over his dark blond hair, jeans and a hand-knit fisherman's sweater accentuating his lean frame. A former junkie, he'd been clean for several years.

"You've put on weight, Sebastian," she said.

A good sign.

"Blame it on Regula's fondue, and the

raclette."

His new girlfriend Regula, Swiss and steady, cooked with the *chefs collectifs,* which put on roving underground gourmet events. Exclusive and only by word of mouth.

"The framing shop business good?"

Sebastian had expanded his framing business to a third shop. She'd cosigned the loan. He owed her.

"Orders and more orders." He grinned. "I've only got an hour."

"No problem." She squeezed his arm. "I'm happy for you."

She helped him load her scooter into the back of his van. "Ready. You remember how to dust for prints?"

"There's a Web site, Aimée."

Like for everything now.

At Agustino's she didn't know what they'd find. But they'd find something.

He gunned his van down Avenue Mozart. Skeleton-branched chestnut trees shuddered in the wind.

"All over this *quartier* you see neo-Cubist architecture fighting the flourishes of Art Nouveau," Sebastian said. "Neo-Cubism speaks to the Bauhaus and Gropius influence." He pointed out his open window, respect in his voice. "Between the wars, 'the style international' was the hit at the Decorative Arts Exposition in 1925."

She stared at Sebastian. "My little cousin knows Bauhaus from a *boudin* sausage?"

"Courtesy of my client on neighboring rue de l'Assomption," Sebastian replied. "When I called Bauhaus a *très* cool DJ, he set me straight. He's a real Mallet-Stevens buff."

Aimée pointed to a spot in the lane. "Park it here."

She grabbed two flashlights and handed him one. "Let's go."

She retraced her steps from yesterday past the almost-hidden Fondation Le Corbusier annex sign.

Sebastian's work boots crunched on the gravel and packed dirt. Secluded darkness, a perfect place to hide. She shivered.

The damp bushes trembled in the gentle wind. A quiet breeze rippled the sparse carpet of brown leaves. The derelict *hôtel particulier* was a dark shadow in the background. Ahead, Agustino's lit atelier was like a beacon.

She wished she'd worn wool socks and Doc Martens like Sebastian, instead of high-heeled Prada boots. Skittering noises and thumping came from the tree branches overhead.

Sebastian hissed. "Over there."

Something darted in the glistening wet hedgerow. A shadow moved on the white stone wall separating the atelier from the garden. Startled, she felt Sebastian grab her arm, shove her down in the wet grass.

Maria shivered in the bone-chilling cold. The jacket over her torn silk chemise offered little protection from the dampness. She couldn't distinguish night or day in the stone-vaulted cavern. She knew she was underground somewhere, her purse and phone gone. Periodic pumping sounds came from above, punctuated by the whine of a bell. Hours ago she'd heard ducks quacking, caught the odor of water, before the men herded her, with the bag over her head, down a sloping ramp.

Now she saw a line of electric lights receding down the long tunnel, shadows in cell-like caverns like the one she huddled in now, chained to the metal pipe.

Voices murmured in a mixture of Basque and French. She could pick out words, part of a phrase, but they were speaking a rural dialect.

"You worry too much" came from one

with a gravelly, grating voice. "The Gestapistes used it. No one heard the screams down here."

Her heart thumped, looking around at the blackened stone. A Gestapo torture chamber? She didn't doubt it.

Her bare feet skittered on the loose pebbles and crumbling plaster. How could she escape? What had happened to the wounded one they called Joxi?

"Fascinating, eh, the underground." The *mec* wearing blue trousers and work jacket stood still in his ski mask. "Historic. Like the caves in my valley." He handed her a rag, acting solicitous. "Wipe those eyes, eh. Cooperate and you go home."

Her chained hands reached for the rag.

He tore the duct tape off her mouth with a loud rip. Her eyes blinked, tearing with pain from her raw skin.

"You'll let me go?"

"Behave, or it goes back on."

It would anyway. But they needed her alive.

"What . . . what do you want?"

"Read this. Word for word." He thrust the card at her.

She shivered. "Did anyone . . . get killed?"

"Not yet."

Liar.

He checked the time. Pulled out a small tape recorder.

"Read just what it says."

Garbage. Lies. She spit and it landed on his sleeve.

"Full of spirit, eh? Better speak better than you aim."

He wiped his arm. Reached for a hunting knife with a bone handle and ran the tip along her chin. "That's if you want to live."

She struggled to kick her feet, but her ankles were taped.

"Read it, Princess, a simple thing. Then you're free, back home like you never left."

"Bombing buildings, shootings . . . all that violence goes nowhere," she said, gasping for breath. "Didn't you learn that in the eighties? That's *passé* . . . the Basques I know want peace —"

"*Et alors,* you're a patriot," he interrupted. "Like us." Only his dark eyes were visible behind the ski mask. "But if you don't read, you die, others die. What will that prove?"

Her shoulders shook. Fear rippled her insides.

"So, Princess?" The cold knife tip touched her chin bone.

A steady drip, drip, drip came from the corner. She took a breath and read: "I support and advocate the autonomy of the

Basque region. And ask my father to do the same." Her throat caught. He pressed the knife tip harder against her chin. Somehow she made herself keep reading. "Not only should there be cultural centers teaching Basque history and language, but there must be the release of all Basque prisoners, and a new referendum."

She stifled a sob.

He hit STOP, rubbed his neck, impatient now. "Keep reading. Convince your father." He moved the knife blade to the jugular vein in her bare white throat. "Talk."

He hit RECORD.

She stumbled a few times but continued to the end.

"You think I'm a bargaining chip, a means to some end?" Her lip trembled. "Kidnapping me won't give Basques autonomy. Don't you understand?"

He stuck the duct tape back on her sore, bleeding mouth.

"Just squirrels, Sebastian." Aimée pulled herself up from the wet ground, brushed herself off. A run in her stocking, now a mud-coated sleeve, grass clinging to her mascara. Picture-perfect.

In Sebastian's flashlight beam, a quartet of arched squirrel tails disappeared up the linden tree trunk. "Quit scaring the marrow from my bones."

She heard strains of baroque music drift from Agustino's atelier. "Ready?"

Not waiting for his answer, she knocked on the glass door.

A split second passed before Agustino opened the door.

"You stood me up, Agustino —"

He clapped his thick paint-spattered hand over her mouth. Shoved her outside, down the path.

"Go away. Now." His words didn't hide the fear vibrating in his voice. "Forget what

I said. Leave."

Had the terrorists coerced him?

"Not until you tell me who murdered Xavierre. How you knew the referendum —"

"Who's he?" His grip tightened on her arm. She saw a nervous shift in his thick shoulders.

Sebastian shifted from leg to leg behind the bushes. A telltale sign. "My cousin. He needs to pee. The cold does that to him. Can he use your —"

"With a night sky like this and all the bushes you could want?" Agustino shook his head. "Over there."

She jerked her chin toward his atelier and mouthed, "The princess?"

Agustino stood dead still. A long moment passed. Then came a little shake of his head. Then he pointed to her watch, showed ten fingers.

"Ten o'clock?" she whispered.

He shook his head. Sebastian returned from watering the bushes and shot Aimée a look.

"Here? They'll bring the princess here?"

"I don't know, I swear," he whispered. The volume of the melancholy string music rose. Agustino's shoulders twitched. "I have to go."

"Did Xavierre's murderer kidnap the princess?"

"Give me time to get away," Agustino said, "ten minutes."

"Why? What's going on?"

"Please, do this for me. Wait before you alert the *flics*."

A cell phone trilled from his pocket. He answered, muttered a brief *"Oui,"* then hung up.

"They're almost here. Just ten minutes."

He backed up, but not before she caught his arm. "Not until you tell me —"

"They call him Txili."

"I want his real name, Agustino."

"His *nom de guerre,* that's all I know." Agustino shot a nervous look at the atelier, held up ten fingers, and then was gone.

Sebastian took out an Indonesian cigarette. Lit it. The pungent clove-spiced smoke caught in her nose.

"Saw something while you were watering the bushes, Sebastian?"

He shook his head. "But I heard noises over the music." He pursed his lips. "Like scraping, pulling something heavy over the floor."

She took a drag from his cigarette. The smoke seared her windpipe and she choked.

Cloves were for pork roasts, not inhaling.

Light glimmered above the atelier drapery, rimming the canvases blocking the view inside.

"You believe him?" Sebastian asked.

Did she? Did she owe him time to get away? But get away from what?

"He didn't know about the princess," she said. "I believe that."

And it bothered her. Besides Sebastian with his tool kit, she had no other backup. Why hadn't she brought her Beretta? Stupid.

A yell pierced the night air. The lights went out in the atelier. Her shoulders stiffened. "Front door, Sebastian," she said. "Hurry."

From his tool kit, Sebastian pulled out his lock-picking set. She shone her penlight at the door. *"Merde,"* he said, "three dead bolts."

By the time he picked the last dead bolt, five minutes later, she could forget the element of surprise.

Once inside, she parted the floor-length velvet drapery. The atelier was dark except for the moonlight filtering through the glass roof, tracing the outlines of stacked canvases and paintbrushes littering the floor.

Her foot hit a can, knocking it over:

splashing sounds, and she caught the whiff of turpentine.

Sebastian hit the switch. Light flooded the atelier, illuminating a canvas with bold, dusky orange and burnt umber strokes on an easel. Behind stacks of canvases, Agustino sat straddling a chair, his head slumped, facing away.

"Agustino?"

No answer.

Running around the canvases, she noted his half-open vacant eyes. Had he suffered a stroke? Her heels skidded on the slippery floor. She grabbed at the easel, catching herself before she landed in the dark puddle on the floor. That smell . . . copper mixed with dry paint. Righting herself, it took a moment before she registered the wide red slash across his neck, his severed carotid artery. And the slow dripping from his blood-soaked shirt to the puddle.

She stepped back in horror.

"Mon Dieu!" Sebastian's screwdriver clanged on the floor. He pointed to a pair of blood-spattered Adidas poking from an oilcloth.

The princess? She gasped in horror. Forcing herself to move her shaking hands, she parted the oilcloth to reveal a slumped figure against the wall. Blood clotted the matted hair, protruding bone, and pinkish gristle of what had once been a young man's jawbone.

"But who . . . ?" The copper-tinged smell of blood overpowered her. The bile rose up in her stomach.

Sebastian's booted toe pushed the papers scattered from a wallet on the floor. "Jorge Gustati. Nineteen, I'd say, according to these juvenile parole papers. Agustino's nephew."

Of course. Agustino had tried to protect him. Failed. She looked around, willing her nausea down. Fought the sadness, the fear. Canvases, paints, and boards filled every corner of the atelier. No cupboards, no closets. No sign of duct tape or rope to hold the princess. Let alone space.

And then she saw an open antique chest. But it contained a scatter of paintbrushes. Nothing else.

She kicked it, frustrated, jarring the chest to the side, turned around, and noticed Agustino's paint-spattered palette. The slight bulge underneath it. She shoved it aside. Underneath lay a navy blue passport of the République française embossed with gold on the cover, inside blank. A blank *carte d'identité*.

The *Imprimerie Nationale* heist. Her pulse

raced. That's what Agustino had wanted to tell her. The Basques had been waiting inside to pick up the stashed documents. But she and Sebastian had disturbed Agustino during the pickup. Had Agustino put up a fight and . . . ?

The *thupt* of a helicopter came from overhead. A sharp whine emanated from the rotor blades over the glass roof as strong gusts blew leaves in through the open door. *Merde!* The EPIGN were right on top of them.

Not for long, if she could help it.

"Hit the lights, Sebastian."

Sebastian's tool set dropped, spattering the paint-clotted brushes. She grabbed it. "Quick. The back door. Move."

The *salauds!* They'd tracked her and let her do the dirty work. But it hadn't saved Agustino. Or the kid.

And she still hadn't found the murderer.

Sickened, she made her feet move, feeling her way along the frames of the damp canvases, and found the back door. She heard Sebastian's shoulder ram the frame, the wood splintering. Then they were in a dark, wet walkway that ran along the building. Trailing ivy from the high walls caught on her shoulders and hair.

"Isn't this when we run like hell?" Sebastian panted.

"First we hop inside your van, keeping the lights off until we find the first covered parking garage," she said. "Then we run like hell."

Morbier's heavy eyelids closed. The throbbing pain ebbed; he drifted and was back on a Wednesday evening years ago. Late, he was late. Hurrying down the Marais alley, hearing piano chords coming from an open window, followed by the teacher's voice: "Heels against the wall. Breathe. Now arms outstretched and *pliez. Excellent. Encore, mesdemoiselles,* again on the count of three."

Ballet lessons.

A chorus of little girls' voices. *"Un, deux, trois. . . ."*

Jean-Claude, his former partner, embroiled in a stakeout, had begged him to fetch Aimée from ballet. Feed her dinner. But what did he know about taking care of little girls?

Morbier remembered the row of pink and white tutus reflected in the mirrors, the patter of leather-soled slippers in Madame

282

Olympe's ballet studio. Later, of course, the ballet recitals that he and Jean-Claude attended without fail, sticking out among the bourgeois mothers and fathers in the audience. But it hadn't mattered to Aimée then.

Or so he thought. Until that evening when, with her tutu stuck among the leeks in his shopping bag, she took his hand.

"I picked out my birthday present," she said.

"About time, too. I'm on duty this weekend and it's next week, so. . . ."

She'd smiled. "Only you can give me the present. Papa won't."

"Not that puppy business again. . . ." He pulled his hand away. "Your papa's told you. . . ."

She tugged his arm, pulled him down as if the narrow high shadowed walls could hear, and whispered in his ear. "All I want for my birthday is *Maman* to come to my recital. You know, like the other ballerinas."

Struck dumb, he wondered for a moment if he should he tell her. But Jean-Claude had avoided all mention of Aimée's American mother Sidonie from the day she abandoned them. He treated Sidonie as if she hadn't existed. His pain shut him up like an oyster.

"I know we're not supposed to talk about

Maman. But it's different if *you* talk to her, *non?* Can't she come to the recital? Papa won't know. We'll keep it secret. I promise I won't talk to her."

"But that's . . . I don't where she is."

"You're a bad liar, Morbier."

He'd felt his cheeks redden. "So you're a good liar?"

"I don't get all red in the face."

He'd clutched the shopping bag handle tighter, took her hand.

"*Bon,* I'll remember that," he said. "Hurry, the *fromagerie's* closing."

That night she refused to eat the dinner he'd spent an hour cooking. He knew nothing about little girls. For the tenth time that evening, he wished he'd told Jean-Claude he'd be busy.

"Hunger strike, eh?" he said, at his wit's end. "Think of all the children starving in China. Children who have no dinner."

"But they have a *maman.*" She sat in the corner, pouting.

"It's a crime to waste food, you understand," he said, feeling helpless. "During the war, we caught pigeons to eat."

"I wouldn't eat a pigeon even it was war; they're rats with wings."

He'd raised his hand to slap her, something he'd never done, and caught himself.

Tears brimmed in her eyes. Her little shoulders heaved, her fist clenched over her mouth, determined not to cry.

He sighed, sat down, and poured himself a glass of red. "It's like the *boulangerie* and *fromagerie.* One sells bread, the other cheese, you need them both, but you don't buy them in the same shop."

"I know that." She removed her fist. Her lip trembled. "So?"

"*Bon.* A ballet recital and who attends, well, it's not the same thing. Yet the ballerinas need the audience and the audience needs . . . *alors,* wants to see the ballerinas." He took another sip of red. "Eating dinner makes you strong so you can perform. . . ." Where had he been going with this? How could he make her understand?

"Like you said." She wiped her eyes. "The audience wants to see the ballerinas. I know *Maman* wants to see me. So even though she must have been very bad and promised Papa not to meet me again, it's not meeting, is it?"

Smart. Why had he forgotten that? She'd figured this all out. The church bell from Saint Antoine pealed outside the window. "I can't do it, Aimée," he said at last. "Can't break my promise. You don't want to hurt your papa, do you?"

285

"Never." Her eyes serious. "That's why I don't talk about *Maman*. But you won't break your promise. You're different. Because you're just letting her know. And if she comes, you're giving me the best birthday present ever. The only one I want."

The clock chimed the hour. "Your papa's due soon. He's going to wonder why his little princess didn't eat her dinner."

"And if I tell him, he'll get sad." Her lip quivered. "I always tell Papa the truth."

Morbier shrugged. "They call this blackmail, you know. But I've never before gotten it from a nine-year-old."

She took his hand, her fingers reaching his knuckles. Squeezed it and put her head on his shoulder. Light as a bird. What could he do?

"Will you eat your dinner?"

At the ballet recital, Jean-Claude was oblivious to all but his princess's pliés. Sidonie, if she came, stayed out of sight. But Aimée glowed during her final curtsy. The only hint of her that Morbier noticed came from the rear of the studio: a flash of black hat, the swish of air from the closing door.

After that, he told Aimée that she didn't keep in contact. Later, that she'd left the country. The lies.

286

Until, years later, Jean-Claude's death in the explosion demanded new lies to cover up the Ministry's involvement. His role. Guilt overcame him.

He'd avoided Jean-Claude's funeral, made a perfunctory appearance at the wake, unable to meet Aimée's eyes. Her questioning. Avoided her for several years. Until she came to him for help and he couldn't refuse. Or any time after that.

But he didn't read Sidonie's letters any more. Hadn't answered them. Like a coward, he'd put them in the safety deposit box to be opened upon his death.

All the truths he couldn't face telling Aimée while he was alive.

Aimée's shoulders heaved as Sebastian dialed the digicode on the keypad. A click. The Art Nouveau iridescent glass-framed door opened.

"Fourth floor." He gestured to the metal-stemmed froth of leaves and tulip-shaped wire cage. An Art Nouveau elevator.

"It's like going into the Métro," Aimée said, catching her breath. "Or a museum."

The accordion gates creaked closed and they jerked upward. "That's what my client would like to make this. An homage to Guimard. Here in one of the few remaining preserved Guimard buildings." The cage shuddered to a halt. "But he's got three more apartments to buy before that happens."

Sebastian took the key ring from his jeans pocket and inserted a long-necked, old-fashioned key. *"Voilà."* He grinned. "Hide-outs don't get more *classique* than this."

A well-preserved 1898 Art Nouveau apartment intact to the wood parquet floors, elongated water lilies on sage green wallpaper, swirling carved moldings, stained-glass panels of peacock feathers, and Tiffany lamp.

"Impressive." She hurried to peer out the floor-to-ceiling paned window. "When does he return?"

"End of the month sometime," said Sebastian, setting his tool box on newspaper. "The independently wealthy run on different calendars from you and me."

The helicopter's sweeping white searchlight illuminated the grass swath and greenery of the Fondation Le Corbusier annex not three blocks away.

"So he gave me the keys to finish restoring the frames," Sebastian said. "Likes them to stay put. Worth more than the paintings."

Sebastian gestured to two frames propped against the wall on clear plastic. Concoctions of smooth, curved maple wood. Exquisite. "I'll walk on eggshells," she said, worried she'd break something.

Sebastian had parked his van in Garage Moderne, a block behind on the next street. To make sure they weren't followed, they entered the Métro and left by the other exit. No one would ever think to look here.

She needed clothes and her laptop. And to get the picture of Agustino's slit throat, the puddle of his blood, out of her mind. Figure out what he hadn't told her. How to find Txili.

"Help yourself to food, the computer," Sebastian said. "Even Art Nouveau heated towel racks."

"So he's your architectural expert?"

"He's taken me under his wing, taught me all I know." Sebastian looked at his watch.

"No doubt he appreciates your fine craftsmanship," she said. "Sorry to get you involved, Sebastian."

He shrugged. "It's what you do, Aimée."

A twinge of guilt passed through her.

"But like René, you think I should leave this alone, take care of my life, my business, don't you?" she said. "Afraid it's a little difficult now."

"Did I say that?" Sebastian shrugged again. "That's how you're wired. I even understood why you didn't follow Uncle, you know, become a *flic*. But what I don't understand. . . ." He hesitated. "Giving up criminal work, that never made sense to me."

"What do you mean?" she asked, surprised.

"Why not get hired and paid for this, that's all."

Sebastian too? But he had a point.

"You're not the only one who says that," she said.

At this rate, she might have to.

Sebastian wiped the tulip-shaped table with his sleeve, set the duplicate key down. An odd look in his eye. "Would you be upset if. . . ."

Another loan? "You're expanding, need me to cosign?"

". . . if Regula and I got married?"

She burst into laughter. "You?" She covered her mouth. "Sorry, I mean I thought you didn't believe in that."

"Regula's traditional." He stepped closer. "I mean it. Would it bother you?"

She hugged him tight. "Only if I can't wear something outrageous in chiffon."

Relief flooded his face.

"Why would you think it would bother me?"

"*Tiens,* I'm younger," he said, "getting married first, and it's Saint Catherine's day tomorrow."

"The patron saint feast of unmarried women, celebrated by wearing silly hats and parading to her statue? Do people still do that?"

"The couturiers keep it alive. Regula's friend sews for Chanel. Every year, Lagerfeld gives his *'midinette'* seamstresses a party."

The *thupt* of the helicopter hovering in the distance. At the door she hugged him again. "I've got more to worry about than silly hats."

But after Sebastian left, she sat down on the intricately inlaid wood floor, peering out the window. She clasped her knees, rocked back and forth, thinking of Melac's words. *Relationships don't work that way. . . .* Well, how *did* they work?

Did she go for bad boys, as Martine insisted, to avoid commitment? Afraid to settle down, and would end up an old maid wearing a silly hat?

The helicopter's sweeping searchlight grazed the roof tiles opposite. Her breath caught. Seconds later it swept on.

She pushed that aside. Right now, proof from the *Imprimerie Nationale* heist — the blank passport recovered from Agustino's — sat in her bag, and she had the murderer's *nom de guerre*. Txili.

If only Agustino had revealed more. If only the terrible events hadn't happened. But she couldn't waste time wishing. Play with the hand you're dealt, her grandfather had said once; that's the only way you survive.

In view of the Euskadi Action's impossible demands, the girl — the princess — would die. Like Agustino. She couldn't let that happen.

She knew the pieces led to Xavierre's murderer. Knew that in her bones.

In the adjoining salon, she found the owner's high-end laptop. No problem to run a program to connect to her office network, monitor the surveillance, and ask René to hack into . . . no, she couldn't involve him. She'd do it herself. She booted up the sleek laptop and, in two tries, figured out his password: GUIMARD. Looked up the Spanish princess and saw the *Hola* magazine articles.

Party girl all right.

She felt a pang seeing the paparazzi photo of the girl caught outside a Madrid club, early morning bleary-eyed, mascara-run raccoon eyes, looking fourteen instead of eighteen. Vulnerable, lost, pathetic. Sad. A kid with too much money and privilege.

And her problem now. Agustino had given her the name of Xavierre's murderer, Txili, who was also the kidnapper. She had to find her. Him. And to vindicate Morbier.

With the EPIGN on her tail, how in the hell would she manage within three hours? How to find her if the EPIGN couldn't? Should she even venture to leave this apartment?

In the stainless-steel state-of-the-art fridge, at odds with the deco apartment, she found half a baguette. Rock-hard. A frozen *crème brûlée* from Picard. She opted for the latter and heated it up. Sitting on the floor, she cracked the caramelized topping with a spoon and ate the *crème brûlée,* observing the crime-scene van pull up in front of the atelier. A unit was patrolling the grounds and area. The helicopter was gone now.

She wanted to kick something. She was stuck. Then her cell phone vibrated.

About to answer, she stopped, her finger on the ANSWER button. The EPIGN would dump Agustino's cell phone, trace all the numbers he'd called. Hers.

Or what if ETA had taken Agustino's cell phone?

She copied the number calling her. Picked up the thirties-style apartment phone, a black behemoth rotary-dial model with the old Passy prefix, and dialed.

"Commissariat de Passy, *oui?*" answered Thesset.

Thank god.

"Thesset, it's Aimée," she said. "You called?"

"Five minutes ago a license plate, reported stolen last night, showed up on a traffic report," Thesset's terse voice erupted.

René's comment about how car thieves stole plates to disguise vehicles came back to her. "On a Mercedes?"

"A maroon Mercedes coupe matching your description down to the custom fog lamps."

At last.

Thesset gave the location, just off Place Victor Hugo.

"I've instructed officers to leave the vehicle in place for six hours. Counting on the boyfriend to return this on the quiet," he said. "I don't want to know any more. Call me crazy for sticking my neck out, eh. Do I have your word?"

"*Absolument,* Thesset." Her spine tingled.

Her one lead. Correction: a possibility. Thesset had come through. At least Morbier had one ally. For now.

She had to move fast. But with her description in circulation and patrols combing the lanes, she wouldn't get far. Best to avoid them and stay here. Safer to curl up in a luxurious hole and watch Morbier convicted from the sidelines?

She tossed the remains of the *crème brûlée* in the trash. In the black marble bathroom she scrubbed off her makeup with lavender-scented soap, praying that Sebastian's patron's style sense extended to his armoire.

She hadn't bargained on him having only one arm.

A flesh-colored arm, down to the lifelike latex rubber fingers, leaned inside. Along with shirts, all colors, seamed at the elbow. Not much good to her, except for the one full-sleeved tailored white dress shirt. Silver cuff links attached, and formal black tie ready with one snap. About her size. No reason to dress it down when she discovered a velvet *le smoking* — a man's tuxedo jacket with quilted lapels. Or matching satin side-seamed black-cuffed trousers. She notched the lizard belt in the last hole so it rode on her hips, and stared at herself in the tall beveled deco mirror.

Big problem.

She removed one diamond stud earring and put it in her pocket. No time to peroxide her hair, so she reached for a broad-brimmed fedora, slipped on the soft vicuna silk-lined long coat. Turned to look in the mirror.

She could probably pass for a man at a distance.

She rolled down the trouser cuffs to cover Martine's Prada boots. Using the apartment phone, she called a G7 taxi, the reservation-only service. Seven minutes later, she descended in the creaking elevator and, head down, entered the taxi waiting out front.

The taxi driver turned and raised an eyebrow. "You booked an hour, 'Monsieur'?"

"For now." She sat back. "Place Victor Hugo. Wait in front of the café Midi."

For ten minutes she checked the dark street radiating east from Place Victor Hugo. A high stone wall ran down one side of the canyon-like rue Lauriston near the former French Gestapo headquarters. She located the maroon Mercedes parked on rue Copernic. A few leaves clustered under the windshield wipers.

She felt the engine hood. Warm. Driven recently. Inside, on the leather passenger seat, was a street guide of Paris. Wedged between the gearshift panel and seat were the edges of something dull gold and narrow. She wiped the window with her sleeve, shone her penlight in, and recognized the red-diamond–pattern Ormond insignia on the rectangular cigarillo box. A slender six-pack pocket-size box of Meccarillos.

Where had she last seen a cigarillo? She racked her brain as she scanned the street.

Given the block of apartment buildings, inner courtyards connecting to inner court-yards, the man or men could be in any of these — or on another street altogether. Hundreds of people inhabited this block.

Prepare for the unexpected, her father always said; think of another scenario before it surprises you.

It came back to her — the acrid burning smell of the cigarillo near the plate of *gâteau* Basque at Xavierre's on Monday night. Of course. The man had left his cigarillo, still burning. She imagined him wounded, stanching the blood, a heated argument, him grabbing Xavierre's scarf to strangle her.

Given the effort he'd taken in stealing the plates, she figured he planned on using the car again. But when?

She couldn't waste this chance. Or stand in a dark cold doorway without being noticed. Think. Use what you have, her father had also said.

She rooted in her bag for the camera René had purchased as backup for their under-cover computer-surveillance contract. Just the thing. Still in the box. A mini wireless camera with a built-in transmitter. More suited for a nanny-cam, the camera fit in her palm and had a visibility range of up to twenty meters away, restricted to line of sight. It transmitted video to a small receiver.

She prayed to god it worked outdoors in dim light as well as indoors.

The tiny camera was powered by a nine-volt battery and could run for up to fifteen hours. Enough for what she needed, she hoped.

She scanned the limestone buildings, the high stone wall opposite, for a location in which to install the camera. Rue Copernic was a one-way street. For a moment, sheltered from the night wind by the wall and buildings, streetlight filtering over the crosshatched metal tree grille, she heard a faint rushing of water.

Opposite, the EAU DE PARIS sign on the wall indicated the reservoir, the one the café waiter had mentioned. The wall must support the aboveground pools. No need for a *sorcière* with a witch-hazel branch to locate water here.

No time to memorize the street and building locations. On the back of her checkbook she sketched the street and the car's location, using the wide, dark green door of the Eau de Paris as a landmark. Given the camera's short range and the darkness, it was impossible to view the whole street, but the microphone would catch the sound of approaching footsteps and guide her.

So she'd attach the camera to the car. If it pulled away, the camera would film the route. She ran her fingers along the rooftop, felt the sunroof lip curve, a space. For now it would work.

She pulled a stick of cassis-flavored gum from the bottom of her bag, chewed it, then attached the gum to the sunroof lip and positioned the camera over it. She activated the camera, clicked the transmitter ON, then checked the receiver.

A woman pushing a stroller emerged from the apartment door behind her. She pulled a blanket over the infant inside and smiled at Aimée. Aimée smiled back, took a few steps, and lifted the receiver to her ear as if talking on her cell phone. The woman stopped a few steps away, putting the brakes on the stroller to converse with a man emerging from an apartment.

A watcher? Lookouts? Surveilling the car?

Aimée hit MUTE on her cell phone, just in case, nodding and pretending to listen to the receiver crooked between her neck and shoulder.

By the time she'd walked halfway down

the street, she'd slid the receiver into her coat pocket. With this wireless model, she'd have the car in sight if it kept within fifteen kilometers of her. More than she needed. Unless, with the stash of stolen blank documents and the princess, they left Paris en route to the border. But she couldn't do anything about that right now.

At the end of the street, she checked the monitor in her pocket. The red light blinked in transmission mode. The dark outlines of the Mercedes roof glinted with raindrops.

But she needed a clean cell phone, to hook up to her laptop and record the feed. She needed René's help.

At Place Victor Hugo, the lit fountain sprayed and the taxi waited. She slid into the back seat. "Rue de la Reynie, *s'il vous plaît.*" She passed a twenty-franc bill over the leather backrest.

"Eh, you pay at the end," he said, tired eyes under his brown-gray grizzled hair.

"My battery's dead. Mind if I use your cell phone? Local call."

"Then I'd have to give you change and. . . ."

"Keep it."

She used the taxi driver's phone and punched in René's number.

"Oui?" said René.

301

"It's Aimée. Has anyone asked about me? Called?"

René cleared his throat. "*Oui,* Madame. Matter of fact, even more than that."

She heard conversations in the background. She shivered. "The EPIGN's at the office, aren't they? Big man, bland face."

"I'd say so," he said.

"Then you haven't heard from me. You're going home, it's late, closing the office," she said. "Bring me a fresh cell phone, too. Leave. Matter of fact, why are you there?"

"Some people need to work, Madame. To pay bills."

As if she didn't?

"I'll meet you in your garage. Ten minutes."

Within ten minutes, the taxi crawled up narrow medieval streets leading to Beaubourg. The soot-stained spires of Saint-Merri loomed, highlighted against the space-age red-and-blue–tubed Centre Pompidou behind it. Her hands shook.

The taxi pulled over under a streetlight. "Monsieur, I'd like to book another hour. Can you wait here?"

"Pas de problème."

She kept to the walls on narrow rue Quincampoix, entering the back door of René's garage. The automatic garage door opened and René's DS Citroën rolled in. She waited behind the dustbins until the aluminum shuttered door rolled back down.

Darkness.

Then she felt a gun in her ribs.

Wednesday Night

Out of breath and shaking, Maria scraped a twisted wire into the crumbling concrete surrounding the iron rung holding her leg chain. At this rate, it would take hours to dislodge the rusted iron. Hours she didn't have. She prayed that her father was cooperating with their demands. But for the life of her, she didn't know if he would — after last time. Or if he could.

Only the steady drip of water accompanied Joxi's moans. His tossing and turning raised the goose bumps on her arms. The man was in pain, his condition worsening. And the others had left.

They were alone. Her stomach gnawed with hunger. No food.

His moaning escalated.

Unnerved, she set down the wire, held the chain, and crept over to him. Joxi was covered by a rough blanket, and his sweat-beaded face was flushed. Broken red blood vessels marked a path from his swollen eye; the blood-soaked bandaging crisscrossed his inflamed cheek. Sour smells of sweat emanated from him.

His vise-like grip encircled her wrist. "Ur . . . ur."

A moan, or the Basque word for water? In a stone niche, she saw bottled water among the strewn contents of her bag. She scrabbled her fingers through the objects. No cell phone. Her agenda containing addresses, phone numbers was gone. Fodder for ransom demands?

But she couldn't stand Joxi's moans. Or understand how they'd leave their wounded comrade. Or her. Hadn't the *mec* promised. . . .

Or maybe she didn't want to understand. Didn't want to face the fact that they'd left them to die.

With trembling hands she raised the plastic bottle to Joxi's lips. He gulped, dribbles running down his chin, over the blanket. Again and again, greedy for more.

A small sample-like packet labeled PENICILLIN sat in the stone niche. "How about your medication?"

His dark eyes rolled back in his head. His body arched, then bucked in sharp convulsions. But his grip held like iron. Good god, what could she do?

Was he dying? Having seizures? The fever burned from him like fire.

She lifted his head, opened his mouth, put the antibiotic tablet on his tongue. Closed his mouth. "Chew." Then she emptied the water bottle over his face. Patted his brow, his face, his arms with the now-sopping blanket, trying to cool him down. Phrases in Basque tumbled from his dry lips. Rhythmic, chanting. A Basse Navarre dialect she didn't understand except for occasional Spanish words: tree, boulder, rushing water. What sounded like a child's song.

He lay there, shaking and helpless. White scars ribbed his shoulders, his chest, like welts from an old beating. What kind of life had he lived? she wondered. She'd never nursed her boyfriend like this, or taken care of him. He hated her being nearby if he was sick.

Twenty, thirty minutes passed; she couldn't tell time down here in the dark. She kept on swabbing Joxi down. Finding more bottled water, wetting the blankets until his convulsions subsided into infrequent jerks.

"Hotz . . . no."

Now chills wracked him. His teeth shattered. He grew aware, his eyes darted. For a man of machismo, he acted as helpless as an infant. She didn't know which was worse: his shaking from chills, or convulsing with fever.

How could she find something dry to wrap him in? Why was she doing this when her life depended on getting away?

She found another jacket, a pair of discarded overalls, a stained plastic tarp, and wrapped him as tightly as she could to generate body heat. In the corner she eyed tubes of paper, unrolled them, and covered him like the homeless she'd seen in the doorways covered with newspapers to keep warm. She kept rubbing his arms, his legs, until her shoulders ached. After a while, his shaking subsided; his eyes closed.

She sighed in relief. And realized for the first time that the fear had left her: she'd been too busy. Tired, she leaned down on the earth floor, clasped her arms around her knees to ease her aching back and shoulders.

The kerosene lamp sputtered low on the flickering wick, casting long shadows on the stone. She looked up. Joxi's heavy-lidded, half-open eyes watched her.

"Why?"

She stretched her neck, felt his forehead. "Your fever's down."

"You tied me like a hog for butchering." His one dark eye glittered.

"Against the chills." She tucked the plastic tighter around him. "You were delirious."

His hand shot out, grabbed her hair. Tight. Pulling the roots of her hair. Pain seared her scalp. "Why did you use these?"

"I . . . I took anything to keep you warm." Tears brimmed in her eyes. "You were convulsing with fever, then shaking with cold. That's the thanks I get for. . . ." And then it all hit her: the tiredness, the hunger, being chained up. She burst into sobs.

The look in his eye changed.

"*Miatzte ama,* just like my mother. Shut up." He struggled to sit up. "Roll these up. Put them back as you found them."

She rubbed her head. The chain around her ankle bit and rubbed her skin raw.

"Now," he barked.

She put them together. Diagrams of what looked like train tracks, rail lines. She rolled them back up, slipped them in the tube.

His gaze wavered.

"Why did you help me?"

She blinked. "I don't know. You're a human being?" She shrugged. "Maybe that's stupid. Maybe you're going to kill me."

"That's the plan."

She backed up in fear, shaking her head.

"Will you do two things?" He leaned on his elbow, coughing. "Do them the way I say."

"So I'll die sooner?" She spit on the floor. "Forget it."

He grabbed the lip balm and tweezers from her things. "Slather this in the lock on your ankle chain; twist your tweezers inside until it clicks open."

"Quit playing with me."

"It's gotten me out of jail every time." He looked at his watch on the stone niche. "Now. Do it before they return."

"You don't get it, do you? Your comrades left us to die."

"Comrades? You think a true Basque patriot lines his pockets? Kills an old comrade?" He winced in pain. "I heard the snakes. They thought I'd gone unconscious." He shook his head. "Don't let on. The trick's to act the same. When they load up, make a break."

Surprised, she stared at him.

"How can I get out?"

"You're on your own there." He coughed, a wheezing from deep in his chest. "Now hand me that bag." He pointed to a khaki canvas shoulder bag in the corner.

"Why should I trust you?"

"A life for a life, *compris?*"

"You're making a deal?"

"You're not from the Motherland, eh? Basques always make deals."

Could she trust him? But from the shaking of his hands, the tiny beads of sweat forming again on his brow, she'd gotten the better deal.

WEDNESDAY NIGHT

A lightning chop batted Aimée's arm down. The stinging crosscut to her ribs whipped her against the garage wall. She yelled and toppled into the dustbins. Pain seared her side. Choking for breath, she raised her arm to ward off the next blow.

"Now the other arm. So I can see it."

She heard the flick of a switch, and light flooded the underground stone-walled garage.

René stood, legs spread, arms extended in firing stance with a Beretta aimed at her head.

"Nice, René." She gasped. "Register your arms as lethal weapons. Forget the Beretta."

René's grip wavered. "*Mon Dieu,* with the outfit I thought a man —"

"If you bought it, the EPIGN will. That's what counts."

René pocketed the gun, reached down to help her up. "*Désolé,* Aimée. Are you all right? Does it hurt?"

Only when she breathed. She got to her feet. Staggered.

"Let me wrap your ribs. Come upstairs. . . ."

"No time." She pulled out the video receiver, grabbed the wall as her vision reeled and then righted itself. "I need you to hook this up to your laptop, record and monitor the feed."

René stared at the dim video playing on the palm-sized screen. "But that's the Mercedes. I recognize the roof line."

"That's right, René, parked with stolen plates on rue Copernic." She winced at every breath. "Did you bring me a phone?"

His brow crinkled in worry. He took his cane from the car. "What the hell's going on?"

"I didn't want you involved," she said. "Look, just trust me —"

"Not until you tell me what all this means, why the EPIGN was asking questions."

"There's not much time."

"I'm waiting, Aimée."

So she gave him the short version.

"Kidnapped?" René rocked on his hand-made Lobb shoes. "If Euskadi Action, this ETA group, kidnapped the princess using the Mercedes, are they likely to use it again?"

"The stolen plates." She wished she had one of the painkillers sitting on her bedside table.

"They'll abandon it if they're smart," he said.

"Got any other ideas, René?"

He brushed cobwebs from her coat. "I might. Let's go upstairs."

"What if the EPIGN are watching your place?"

René swallowed. "Good point. But Michou's expecting me next door for a drink."

The blood sample from her Louboutins. She still hadn't heard back from Viard.

"If Viard's there, can you ask him to meet us down here?"

René shook his head but punched in the number and made the call. "What about hooking up the feed? Please, René."

In the back seat of the Citroën, René opened his briefcase, set his laptop on the leather seat, and hooked a cable to the receiver.

Not two minutes later, footsteps sounded on her left.

"Giving Michou a run for her money?" Viard grinned. "I like your androgynous look. Very Helmut Newton. But why the cloak and dagger, Aimée?" Viard dusted his hands in the less-than-clean subterranean garage René rented for half the price of his apartment and felt lucky to have.

"You don't want to know, Viard."

"Again?" He pulled a notebook from the breast pocket of his tweed jacket. "We were swamped. I managed to get to your heels this morning. O-negative blood type. Nothing special. Except for the mucosa traces."

"Mucosa?"

"You know, the lining in the nose. After lunch, we had a lull," Viard said. "Thought I'd put a portion of the sample under the microscope. Interesting."

Anxious and hot in the humid dank garage air, she took off the fedora. Shook her hair. "In what way?"

"The mucosa came from the nose. Along with the blood. I'd say there was a nosebleed."

Surprised, she moved closer. "Not from a gunshot wound?"

"I found no gunpowder residue. Of course, that might not present in such a small sample. But, why someone might have a nosebleed: I looked more closely at the blood — red cells, white cells, platelets. . . ." Viard, enthusiasm creeping into his voice, thumbed to another page in his notebook.

Nodded as he read and rubbed his chin. "Then it got fascinating, or morbid, depending on your point of view."

Why couldn't he just tell her?

"What's your take, Viard?"

"Far too many white blood cells — abnormal ones at that — for a healthy individual. Also not a normal number of platelets."

"Meaning?"

"I'm not a doctor, Aimée," he said.

"Neither am I, remember?" Her ribs ached. She wished he'd get to the point. "I got through a year of premed and never hit the lab. Chemistry and biology did me in."

"Speaking based on the lab smear, with such a high white blood cell count, he's about done in."

She unsnapped the tie. Fanned her neck. "How can you tell?"

"Like I say, I'm not a physician. But symptoms such as nosebleeds, fatigue, weight loss, and high white blood cell count — and abnormal white blood cells — in most cases indicate an advanced stage of disease. Leukemia."

Stunned, she leaned against the wall. Did she need to rethink everything with this revelation?

"A terminal terrorist? Gives him an interesting motive," René said.

"Worse, René," she said, thinking. "Nothing to lose."

She pecked Viard on both cheeks. *"Merci."*

"So when's our dinner?"

"Ask René," she said. "I've got to go."

"But it's safer here," he said. "Stay with Michou."

"My taxi meter's running."

René handed her a red cell phone. "That's your new number. It's programmed in my cell. Keep in touch every twenty minutes."

She paused at the door, a dark unease flooding her. Morbier's weight loss, the hollows under his eyes. "How long does the man have, Viard?"

"I run the lab, but I don't provide diagnoses, Aimée," he said.

"But according to . . . the platelets, your observations. . . ." Her throat caught.

"At this point, I'd suggest he live every day like it's his only one."

Aimée surveilled the winding street, the corners. Deserted except for the taxi. She clutched her side, sinking into the back seat. "Rue Raynouard, *s'il vous plaît.* On the way, stop at the all-night pharmacy on Champs-Elysées."

Ten minutes and three extra-strength Dolipranes — washed down by fizzy Vittel —

later, she crouched in the back seat as the taxi cruised past Xavierre's dark, shuttered town house. She noted the parked cars and the Renault with two heads silhouetted against the darkness. The Renault from the market.

Across the narrow street, she noted a dim glow emanating through Madame de Boucher's second-floor lace curtains. Then a darker curtain blocked the dim light.

A car door slammed, an engine rumbled, and the Renault's headlights flashed on.

"Turn right." Past the steepled church on rue Jean Bologne, paralleling rue Raynouard, she motioned for him to pause. "Wait by the florist's across from the Boulainvilliers Métro." She took his card. "If I don't call you within one hour, erase my record. Put me down as a no-show pickup. You never heard of me."

She passed him two hundred francs.

"Deal?"

He nodded, took the francs, patted a tattered copy of a Simenon novel on his dashboard. "Got an Inspector Maigret investigation to keep me company. Almost as exciting as tonight."

She summoned a smile. "But tonight's far from over, Monsieur."

She knew Madame de Boucher's building

on rue Alphonse XIII overlooked the rear courtyards and gardens of these apartments.

Stepping onto the narrow street, she had a sense of being watched. She heard the crunching of leaves, the heavy tread of measured footsteps.

Her shoulders tightened. She stepped into the building doorway and turned.

Headlights backlit a dark figure: moisture glimmering on close-cropped hair, a martial stride halfway down the street. Hair rose on the back of her neck. No mistaking that cocky assuredness. EPIGN.

They not only were watching Xavierre's house, they were patrolling the *quartier*.

She dug in her purse for the stubby universal mailman's key in the side pocket. The one she'd "borrowed" from Morbier a month ago and "forgotten" to return. The worn key provided *la Poste* universal access to buildings and courtyards. A *passe-partout.* Where was it?

The footsteps crackling over the leaves got closer. She concentrated until her fingers found the key.

Praying that the key still worked, she inserted it and heard the lock tumble. Once inside, she shut the glass door, heading into the marble-tiled foyer toward the rear. She kept going, ignoring the knocking coming from the glass door, almost running into the table with a vase of roses emitting a faint fragrance.

At the door on her right, she slipped off her boots and stuck them in her bag. *Sans* stilettos, she crept across the dark pavered inner courtyard to what had been a carriage entrance. Now a small wooden vaulted door was the only egress.

The door creaked open onto the adjoining courtyard, choked with Land Rovers, a barometer of the *quartier*'s wealth. A high stone wall backed onto Madame's building.

No trees to climb. No outbuilding with a roof. No ladder.

Stuck.

Less than two hours left.

She climbed onto the nearest Land Rover's hood and then to its roof, eyeballed a rough measurement, and wished the Doliprane would dull the ache in her ribs faster. She fashioned a slipknot at one end of her cashmere scarf, knotting the other end to her long, coarser wool scarf. Together they almost reached the top of the wall.

And then she saw the wood wine carton filled with newspapers. Climbing down, she spread old newspapers on the Land Rover's roof, hefted the cartons, and prayed her aim would hit the rusted iron remains of the old gas-lamp fixture topping the wall.

She balanced on the upside-down wine carton and threw the end of her scarf. Missed. Then again. On her third try, the scarf knot caught on the rusted iron and held. She tugged, testing her weight, and climbed, pulling herself up.

Her toes wedged in the stone niches. She tried to ignore the sharp slicing pain as her sore ribs landed on the wall's top ledge. Then she levied herself up. One leg over, and the next. She gasped in pain.

Below her lay a huge drop to Madame's courtyard.

She prayed to god her scarves would hold and rappelled halfway down the wall before the rotted iron in the crumbling stone came loose. She caught the ivy trellis and hung suspended, the pain in her side shooting through her, then eased herself down onto a chipped haloed statue of Mary.

Perspiring, she picked up her knotted scarves, now encrusted with rust. Keep going, she told herself. She had to keep going.

She crept past the concierge's loge and jiggled the inner door lock with the mini-screwdriver on her Swiss Army knife until it clicked open. She slipped on her boots and mounted the staircase to Madame de Boucher's door.

The strains of "Leaves of Autumn" came from the doorway. That damn bird was singing again. She knocked and stuck her fedora over the peephole. Heard footsteps on the other side. She knocked again.

"Madame, please, I must talk with you."

No answer.

"It's vital, Madame. The *quartier*'s thick with police patrols."

"So," came a muffled voice. "You're with the police. I know the law. Go away. You can't barge in here until dawn. Nazis or not, you won't get in here."

Aimée took out her card and slipped it under the door. "I lied. I'm not a *flic*. Look at my card. Irati's in danger. Please, I'm the only one who can help her."

Silence. She removed the fedora and put her eye to the peephole.

"Agustino was murdered not far from here. Tell Irati. But he warned me before her mother's murderer. . . ."

The door opened. Madame de Boucher stood, ice pick raised. "Shhh . . . my neighbors. Quick."

Again in that hallway reeking of old newspapers. But a quivering Irati, her face drained pale, stood by the coatrack.

"But how did you know I'd . . . ?"

"Come here? A good guess. You Socialists

stick together, don't you?" Aimée stepped inside. "Listen, the EPIGN's parked below, watching your house. They're looking for me too." The parrot's singing was louder inside. The shrill notes grated on her taut nerves, and she shut the salon door. "It's dangerous; I know a safe hiding place."

"You're lying." Irati backed up.

"Check for yourself," she said.

Madame de Boucher set down the ice pick and grabbed her walking stick. "I'll see about that."

"This man coerced you, didn't he, Irati?"

Irati backed away. Her eyelids fluttered. "I don't know what you mean."

Of course she did. Just her body movement gave her away.

"Do you want him to get away with your mother's murder? The brutal slaying of Agustino and his nephew . . . ?" She shuddered, remembering the bloodied Adidas. Blood everywhere.

Panic painted Irati's tight features.

"Agustino told me he's called Txili, his ETA *nom de guerre*," Aimée said. "What hold did he have over your mother?"

Irati bit her lip. "*Maman* told me nothing. I saw him, this Txili, yes; but *Maman* told me to get out of the room. I'd never seen him in my life. I didn't know he'd stolen

322

our car or what he wanted until the next morning." A pinprick of blood showed on her chapped lip.

Aimée nodded. "But was he bleeding? Did he look wounded? Could you tell that much?"

She thought, shrugged. "He coughed, I think." Irati's brow wrinkled in worry. "On the phone, he said *Maman* had left the bag for him; I was to do as she'd promised or he couldn't protect us."

"Couldn't protect you from what?"

"The others. The group. That's what he kept saying." Her lip trembled. "They'd place a bomb under Robbé's car, shove me on the Métro tracks, my aunt would return to Bayonne and find my uncle dead. Terrible things. He said he couldn't stop them unless I cooperated."

"And you believed him?"

Irati's eyes batted in fear. "What else could I do?"

"But you're involved with Euskadi Action. This shows all their trademarks."

"Involved?" Irati spread her arms. "I attended one meeting. I wish I never had. Fanatics ranting about reclaiming the Basque homeland, like a religion. They insisted I buy a stupid T-shirt and hound me now with mail."

So that's how they'd gotten her address.

"But what did this Txili hold over your mother?"

"*Zut alors,* we can't get away from them. Anywhere Robbé goes, his car could go up in smoke. If I'm in a crowded station. . . ." She shook her head. "Any time, he said, any place, it could happen."

He'd terrorized her. Irati saw his threats as real. Who was to say they weren't? But how could she break through and convince her?

"I can help you," Aimée said. "Or there's the EPIGN downstairs. The elite assault squad. It's just a matter of time until they find you, like I did. They'll interrogate you, break you down, link you to the princess's kidnapping."

Irati's hand went to her mouth in fear. "The princess . . . what do you mean?"

"I think you know. At least part of it."

She hoped her hunch was right.

Tears brimmed Irati's eyes. "But I never knew. Never. He just told me. . . ." Her shoulders shook. "You think he'll hurt Maria?"

"Not if I can help it," she said, pulling a cane-backed chair toward her. "Sit down. We've got less than two hours left."

"Two hours?"

"His deadline. Have a seat."

Irati collapsed in the chair. "Her father was ambassador here years ago. That's how we knew them. Maria's family comes to Bayonne every summer. We go to my uncle's house in the mountains in Basse Navarre. I've known Maria since we were little. She likes to party, a little rebellious. But still, inside, she's *sympa,* you know; she has a good heart."

"Spoiled brat, I heard."

Irati wiped her eyes. "Her father's so conservative, insists she perform her 'duties' *noblesse oblige.* She hates it. A little wild, yes. But I figured she'd go along with it."

"With a kidnapping by ETA terrorists, a daring escape, followed by a tell-all article and modeling contract?"

"Nothing like that." Irati shook in horror. "He insisted that I ask Maria to meet at this resto and say we'd go clubbing and then . . ." She paused. "It felt wrong. He said *Maman* was a patriot and wasn't I? When I asked him what he meant, he said *Maman* owed the cause from way back. Took an oath. Had vowed support."

"Support that got her killed? How could he explain her murder?"

"At first he blamed Morbier." She rubbed her eyes. "Then he changed his story, said he couldn't control the *ettaras* — the young militants — who took things into their own hands out in the garden."

"A lie," Aimée said. "Like all the lies he's telling you. I only heard one person's footsteps, one car door slam." Aimée took Irati's elbow, stared into her tear-filled eyes. "He's using your fear, I understand. But you can't let Morbier go down for this."

"But he threatened that Robbé would be next if I didn't cooperate, didn't arrange to meet Maria."

"So instead of the Marmottan reception announcing the Basque accord, Maria went to meet you but was kidnapped instead."

"You're sure?" Irati's eyes batted in fear. "I've heard nothing on the radio or *télé*."

"I was there. Before any public announcement was made, her father insisted on a three-hour window, to negotiate in private."

"I don't understand."

"The Basque referendum's dead in the water and Maria's the hostage for release of ETA's political prisoners in France, his goal all along."

Irati blinked. "He's an ETA political militant? You're sure? He seems a business type, conservative. I couldn't believe the way he talked."

Aimée's mind spun into high gear. "As if

his talk doesn't match his appearance?"

"I saw him for only a few minutes before *Maman . . .*" Irati took a breath. ". . . made me leave. At first impression I took him for a banker. Thinking back, yes. Now in his phone calls he uses those old phrases, *passé* ETA slogans, 'militant patriotism' and 'Basque autonomy.' People don't talk like that any more. They're sick of violence."

A front? But for what?

Irati stared at her. "He said he knows you."

The hair stood on the back of her neck. "Me?"

"He must have seen you, I don't know."

Of course: from the window. Or . . . something in the back of her mind niggled, eluding her.

"But at first you didn't recognize me in this outfit, did you, Irati? That's why you're going to get away — you can change clothes like shedding skin, new colors, new hair."

"But for how long?"

Irati had no illusions about the future, but a desperate need to believe. How many more bodies would there be, she wondered, before Irati wised up?

"Long enough for you to —"

The cell phone on the hall radiator trilled. Irati glanced at the number. "It's him." Before she could answer, Aimée grabbed her hand.

"Keep him talking as long as you can," she said. "Agree to anything. Ask to meet him. Just keep him on the line."

Irati nodded and picked up the telephone, her eyes wide with fear.

"Oui?"

Pause. "Look, there's something. . . ."

She pursed her lips.

"What . . . *non!*"

Irati dropped the phone.

Aimée reached down and grabbed it. A buzz. She hit CALLBACK and the number came up blocked. Not even time for Léo to trace it.

Irati looked like she'd been hit by a truck.

"He's got Robbé."

Aimée's heart sank. She was in over her head. All their heads. For a moment she weighed working with Valois and informing the EPIGN, people she didn't trust farther than her little finger.

But doing that would link Irati to ETA, the kidnapping, Agustino's murder, the stolen documents. A barbed-wire tangle of complications. And might get her no further toward finding the murderer or the princess.

"What does he want?"

"He called Robbé 'insurance.' " Irati folded her arms over her chest, rocked. "You see, he told me if talked to anyone, or someone followed me. . . ."

"So you'd get further implicated?" She held the shiny blue virgin passport. "ETA *ettaras* robbed the *Imprimerie Nationale* van, killed a *flic*. They kept their stash at Agustino's. I found this in his atelier."

"I don't know. That's all he said. I heard Robbé shouting. A scream."

She covered her face with shaking hands.

Aimée's new phone trilled. She went into the salon to take the call. The bird, quiet for the moment, pecked at the cuttle bone in the cage.

"See anything, René?"

"I hear something on rue Copernic," he said. "The car door's opening."

Her heart jumped.

"Dim image, distorted pixels," said René. "All sepia, dark. The streetlight's far away. Talking. No response. I think it's a cell phone conversation. But the viewfinder's out of range, just catches dark movement . . . wait, like an arm reaching into the car."

"Can you make out words?"

All of a sudden the bird burst into a shrill "Leaves of Autumn" refrain.

"Wait, I heard the same voice two minutes earlier on the street. I'm recording so I can clean up the audio . . . now a damn truck. . . ."

"But he's in the car? Driving away?"

"*Non.* A head, but I can't make it out. . . . Who's singing in the background?"

"A damn parrot," she said. "Call me back."

Frustrated, she wanted to kick the bird's cage and ruffle more than his feathers. Instead, she covered his cage with the cloth; silence reigned, apart from Irati's muffled sobbing.

"Irati, tell him the truth," she said. "You're being watched, trailed. Would he want you to lead them right to him? What does he want from you?"

Irati averted her eyes. She was keeping something back.

"Do you want Robbé alive?"

She nodded. "I don't have any other choice but to do what he says."

"We all have choices. Just not necessarily the ones we want."

"Easy for you to say."

"The EPIGN want me to work for them. I can easily lean out the window and say, 'Up here.' Should I? They're a trained elite assault unit that tallies the enemy body count as success and victims as collateral damage. Otherwise, by yourself, you're depending on this man who killed your mother and Agustino."

"How do you know he killed *Maman?* Why?"

"I know Morbier didn't. He was meeting an informer on the Paris outskirts." She expelled air from her mouth. "Cooperating with Txili gives neither Robbé nor the princess a shot in hell of living more than an hour and a half."

Aimée took the encryption manual from her bag, thumbed to the blank back page.

"So, three choices: the big boys with big toys, or you on your own playing to Txili's drum, or me," she said. "Me, I guarantee you'll have a shot. Maybe just one, but that's more than zero. So you choose, Irati."

"You think they're dead no matter what, don't you?"

"Going by the statistics so far, a wise assumption."

Irati's face crinkled in pain.

"What's the point now? He'll get to us. I know it. Robbé's diabetic. His insulin —"

"Do you have it?" Aimée interrupted.

Irati's head bobbed. "I always carry extra for him, in case."

Aimée pushed the damp hair from Irati's tear-stained face.

"Then we have to get it to him, *n'est-ce*

pas?" she said. "It's a good bargaining tool. I have an idea. Do you want to hear it?"

Irati wiped her face with her sleeve, nodded.

Aimée took her pencil and started writing.

"First you'll tell him this," she said, "but in your own words."

Irati stared at Aimée's encryption manual. Nodded again.

Now she had her.

"After that, you'll tell me about Robbé."

Madame de Boucher made a tsk-tsk sound. "I saw the scum. Time for you to escape."

Madame stood at the hall armoire, one hand on her ebony walking stick, her other selecting a coat for Irati. She took a seventies belted checked-wool coat — never worn, by the look of it. Sniffed. "A little mothball odor. Not bad." She handed it to Irati with an Hermès scarf.

"This way," Madame de Boucher said. "We used it during the war."

Hadn't been used since, Aimée figured from the rotting timbers, speckled mold, and dirt-filmed broken glass in the back stairs. Madame opened a cobwebbed cupboard, tapped her walking-stick tip inside. Creaking and groaning, the cupboard moved to reveal a blacked-over skylight. "I keep it oiled. *Les Fritz* never found this. Good thing, eh, you never know."

Oiled for more than fifty years. Amazing.

"Too bad it didn't save my brother. Aaah, but that's another story."

Aimée twisted the handle and pushed. The slanted skylight gave a centimeter. "Harder," Madame said.

Using her knee, she wedged it open enough to squeeze through. Cold night air and pigeon feathers met her.

"Follow along the roof line to the last building."

"And then?"

"Find the blacked-out skylight, wedge it open with this." Madame handed Irati a hammer, then tied the Hermès scarf around Irati's head. *"Bon courage."*

Aimée'd need more than that, considering the slick blue roof tiles, a multi-story drop, and a shaking Irati.

She handed Irati the end of her tied scarves. "Hold on. Don't look down. No matter what."

Algae-scented wind from the Seine gusted over her skin, making her lapels fly up. Beyond lay a vista of glittering pinprick lights as she crawled, edging along the narrow rooftop. Caked pigeon droppings, crackling twig birds' nests, and crumbling brick came back on her fingers. She took deep breaths, cold air slicing into her lungs, her gaze focused on the next rooftop. Then the next, inching her way forward along the narrow ridge.

Skittering stucco clumps slid down the roof tiles. She had to keep breathing, keep going, aiming for the dark misted outline of the last roof. Trying to imagine a young Madame de Boucher doing this.

"Almost there, Irati."

No answer. She tugged the scarf and felt the slack.

"Irati?" She turned her head.

A mistake.

Her foot slipped. She scrabbled her fingers over the damp tiles. Her hands and knees were coated with dirt, and she couldn't get a good grip. She felt a sliver of panic, then saw Irati's outstretched hand. But too late. She slid down the slick roof.

Frantic, she reached out for something, anything, and caught a metal bar. Grabbing it with all her might, she held on and dug her pointed toes into a metal rim.

Her slide halted; she took a breath. The distant reverberation in the sky grew louder, turning into the *thupt* of a helicopter. Closer and closer. The sweeping searchlight of the helicopter illuminated the stair-step chimney pots on the roofs of houses on the next street.

Any minute, the search beam would catch them like flies on the roof.

"Hurry, Irati, keep going."

Gritting her teeth, she pulled herself up by the edge of the tiles and metal bar to the other roof. Thank god the Doliprane had kicked in. With each breath, her heart thumped. So did her bag against her hip. An insistent trill was coming from it. Her phone.

She saw a cracked, blackened skylight with its broken wood frame before her. Irati had forced it open. Aimée climbed down, her shoulders heaving, reaching an old iron walkway surrounding a cathedral-ceilinged atelier.

"Let's go, Aimée."

She reached for her phone, finding that René had left a message. That could wait. She punched in a number.

"What are you doing?" Irati's feet clattered down the spiral staircase ahead.

"Calling our taxi."

"Where to now?" said the taxi driver.

"Down avenue Mozart a few blocks," she said. "We'll let my friend off during the red light, then keep going, *compris?*"

"You're not the first passenger to ask that, 'Monsieur,' " he said. "Mind if I smoke a cigar?"

"Go ahead."

He lit up, puffing on a cigar, sending sweet acrid fumes around the car.

Then it hit her. The cigarillo box in the car, the burning cigarillo. "Txili smoked cigarillos, *non?*"

Bars of light and shadow alternated on Irati's tight-lipped face in the speeding taxi.

"Coughing, and he still smoked," said Irati. She patted the insulin kit in Aimée's pocket. "You remember that Robbé needs this shot now."

"Don't worry. And you?"

Irati unfolded the sheet torn from Aimée's encryption manual, her big eyes wide with fear. "What if Txili . . . ?"

"No ifs. At first he'll refuse and give you a hard time. But he'll give in. He has to. Just keep to the plan we discussed."

"The plan, of course." Irati spoke as if convincing herself. "What's Plan B?"

"Plan B?"

"Our backup plan. You said we had a plan B."

She did? At the corner, Aimée saw the light turning yellow. She put Sebastian's key

336

ring in Irati's shaking hands.

"Stay in the apartment, Irati. Wait for my call."

"But what's our Plan B?" Irati insisted.

She had to come up with something.

"Go on the laptop: password GUIMARD. Do a search for Txili, Basque, and ETA sabotage. Get background."

Irati jumped out. Her seventies coat flashed among the parked bicycles on the pavement. The light turned green, and then Irati disappeared through the doorway.

Aimée put in her earbuds and hit CALL-BACK. "Catch his face, René?"

"Why didn't you answer?"

"My hands were full. . . ." Little did he know.

"You missed him."

Merde.

"He spoke with three men," René said. "All of them grunting and hauling bags from the Mercedes trunk."

"To where?"

"Looks like across the street, but on the map I don't see any buildings, any address. Just a dark spot."

"But that's the reservoir." They were hauling the *Imprimerie Nationale* stash beneath the reservoir. Their backup location, after Agustino's atelier. Where they'd keep the princess. And she'd stood right in front of it. Hadn't she seen the workers in the café, the waiter complaining there were more of them?

"René, hack into the Eau de Paris site. Access the Passy reservoir architectural plans," she said. "I need to know the layout in five minutes."

She leaned forward in the taxi. "Place Victor Hugo. Same café and wait, *s'il vous plaît.*"

By the time the taxi let her off, René had informed her he'd entered the Eau de Paris logistics plan.

She ran, her earbud cord bouncing, down rue Copernic, keeping to the wall lining the reservoir. Getting closer, she saw no one at the Mercedes. She crossed the street. Tried the car doors, the trunk. Locked.

What to do but wait? She didn't have long. Voices, footsteps came from behind the green metal door notched in the wall next to the EAU DE PARIS sign. The circular NO PARKING DAY AND NIGHT sign blinked. Scraping noises. She hunched down behind a Fiat not a yard away.

"Talk to me, René," she whispered. "I hear them inside."

"Still searching, Aimée. Stands to reason one of them works there," René said.

"More than one, René. How many levels in the reservoir?"

"Looks like it's several stories high, with a vaulted underground containing the valves and the control station," he said. "Built by Belgrand, the 'father of our sewers,' in 1868. On top are three uncovered pools. There are five in all, fed from the Seine and Montsouris reservoir, *non potable* water used to wash streets and for the parks."

She wished he'd quit the history lesson.

"So how can I get in?"

More scuffling inside the green metal door that must lead to the interior, the underground, the pools.

"Attends un moment," René said, "the plans take time to load."

She heard a man's low voice, accompanied by the scraping of metal on stone. The green door opened. A dim figure in overalls scanned the street and darted past the Fiat in front of her.

Now or never.

She ran and slipped inside before the door closed.

A dark cobbled alley with an old-fashioned gatehouse stood to her right. Potted geraniums on the steps. Voices. The orange glow of a cigarette tip down the alley. The smell of water. She slipped behind a planter trailing ivy on the gatekeeper's wall, crouched under the window shutter, hit MUTE on her phone.

Waiting. They were waiting. The green door scraped open. "*Merde* . . . forgot to lock it," the man in overalls muttered.

His back to her, he inserted a round key, locking the door. She saw a bag under his other arm, the neck of a wine bottle peeking out.

Now inside, how would she get out? Sharp narrow green metal prongs stretched above the door, along the wall. But she'd worry about that later.

Then he disappeared in the dark. She heard a long belch, his footsteps stumbling on the cobbles. *"Zut. . . ."*

The rest she couldn't hear. Drinking. Thank god for small mercies; it would dull his reaction time.

She kept to the shadows, guided by his footsteps. Ahead lay a lighted cobbled space fronted by a second green metal double door, cove-shaped, built into the stone wall. Brown leaves rustled in the overhanging tree. An Eau de Paris van was parked on the side.

She turned off MUTE on her cell. "I'm in. The gatehouse is behind me. There's a door in a wall. Talk to me, René."

340

"Looks like a control center inside, a matrix of water pipes on the second level," said René. "Minimal workforce, according to this. Most of the control's automated, runs itself."

"Where's the storage?" That's where they'd hide the stash, keep the princess.

"I see A1 and A2 maintenance facilities at ground level, tunnel A; that's the first left."

She'd start there. "And a back exit?" He told her before she hung up. But first she had to get in. Now one of the coved doors stood ajar. Light slanted over the cobbles as the three figures René had mentioned pulled something over their heads. One checked his watch, murmured into a cell phone, and clicked it shut.

Work helmets? she wondered, kneeling behind the van. Then she recognized the black ski masks. Her hand shook. She caught her bag just before she dropped it.

She stilled her shaking hand in her pocket. On the bright side, if they were hiding their identities, the princess must still be alive: they hadn't killed her. Yet.

Forty-five minutes to go.

She made out a long row of lights like a seam, punctuating a vaulted stone ceiling trailing down a tunnel.

Two of the men entered it. The other

paced outside under the tree branches, checking his phone. Of course, she realized, there would be no phone reception inside. Bad news; she couldn't keep in contact with René. But neither could Txili call from within. He'd wait nearby, negotiating with the father. He'd use Robbé somehow to offer proof that the princess was alive. That's where Irati came in.

She tried the van door. Locked. She needed a distraction. She felt around. No loose gravel. Just a hose reel mounted on a bracket in the stone. She crawled, inching forward to reach for the nozzle and turn the spigot handle.

The *mec* stood under the branches, drinking from the bottle every so often. She counted on that delaying his reaction time. She turned the spigot handle as hard as she could, heard a slight rumble but saw not a drip. She'd have to let the pressure build up.

She pulled back behind the van, waited until he took another swig, grabbed the hose nozzle, unscrewed it, and aimed. The force of the cold water blast sent him, stumbling, against the wall. "Oie . . . what the?" he shouted. She directed the spray against his arms. Then he slipped and the bottle fell.

If she didn't work fast, the others would

hear — if they hadn't already. With her other hand, she grabbed the bottle and hit him over the head. Then again.

She screwed the nozzle to reduce the water flow to a trickle. Reached for the key ring and cell phone in his pocket. She dried off the phone with her sleeve. Punched in René's number. Busy.

Merde.

She couldn't wait. Inside the tunnel, she veered to the left, passing a series of coved vaulted arches. Moist cool drafts of air hit her face. Then she heard screams.

"My rank carries privileges, eh, Pollard?"

Morbier jerked his thumb at the warden's desk in the dimly lit room, smaller by half than his office in the Commissariat. A subterranean room, dank and pervaded by the wet-wool smell in the adjoining coatroom. Part of *le Dépôt's* underground warren leading to the Tribunal. A place he'd avoided at all costs until now.

"Rank?" Pollard, the police union lawyer, shot him a grim smile and motioned to the wood bench as he took the chair. "Count yourself blessed I noticed my name on your IGS docket hearing tomorrow. No notification came to me, an unusual IGS sabotage tactic." Middle-aged, with thinning blond hair and a suit jacket straining at the middle, Pollard set his briefcase on the stone floor. "My brother-in-law let me 'borrow' his desk. 'Unofficially,' like everything you and I say here."

Tomorrow. He couldn't stand another night, much less another day, down here.

"Rumor's circulating that you're uncooperative, Morbier." Pollard removed his wire-framed glasses, studied them, then wiped the right lens with a tissue. "Quite a handful. And at your age."

"Coming from you, I'm surprised," said Morbier. "You're supposed to be defending me." He leaned against the stone wall; the oval grilled window was above him. "Won't twenty-five years of my union dues cover it?"

"Quit sounding like every corrupt cobble-pounding one-stripe sergeant I've had the unhappy opportunity to represent," Pollard said. "But you're not on the take — or so I hear. What's with you?"

"Besides a big bucket of shit?" Anger flushed his face. He rubbed his chin — two days' worth of stubble. Threw up his arms, the fight gone out of him. "Lucard was talking sentencing terms. What's the use?"

"We'll get nowhere with your attitude." Pollard leaned back in the chair and yawned. "We need a defense. Or had you forgotten this detail in some crusade to topple the Préfecture?"

Morbier snorted. "Not that I envy you, but that's your job, *n'est-ce pas?*"

345

Pollard picked an eyelash from his cheek, flicked it away.

"You're a *flic,* Morbier," he said. "Time you thought like one. Forget the circumstantial evidence, this crime-of-passion charge, for now. Tell me what's twisted. What's wrong here?"

A wave of hopelessness hit Morbier.

"Without the investigation file. . . ." He shrugged, left the rest unsaid.

"We've known each other *alors,* ten, twelve years?" Pollard said, his tone coaxing. "What does your gut say?"

His gut? Jolted to his senses, he stared at his hands, at the cracked concrete floor, the fissures revealing stone. A dawning realization came over him. He'd submerged everything after losing Xavierre. Shocked, he'd wallowed in grief and self-pity, striking out in anger. Hadn't he seen these reactions himself in the families of other victims? But *flics* didn't have that luxury. Not if they were working a case.

For the first time, not sidetracked by emotion, something shifted deep inside him. Like a numbing shot of Novocain at the dentist's, a curious remoteness filled him. He knew the pain would return, but his mind cleared.

It came back to him now.

"Saturday night after dinner, Xavierre received a phone call," Morbier said. He remembered her edginess, the way the muscle in her neck had tightened. The nuance he'd picked up, how she'd brushed it off as "the second crisis with the caterer this week."

Fool.

"On Sunday, she didn't return my calls," Morbier said. "I left her messages. That night, instead of keeping the florists' final appointment she'd insisted we make, she canceled. Just like that."

"Busy with her daughter's wedding plans, from what I understand. Not so unusual, eh?" Pollard pursed his lips. "We married ours off in June. You think they leave, but it's the wedding bills they leave . . . *zut,* they will set me back for years."

"But that's not . . . wasn't like her," Morbier said. "She'd teased me, saying if I didn't approve her mother-of-the-bride gardenia bouquet. . . ." His throat caught.

"Weren't you invited to this wedding rehearsal party?"

"At first, yes. But there were too many deaf old aunts, et cetera. 'Boring,' she said. I wouldn't want to come."

Morbier focused on a large crack, a pattern of smaller branches seaming the floor.

"Think, Morbier."

It played back in his mind like a bad film.

"On Monday afternoon, Xavierre sounded like herself. 'Bring Champagne,' she said. But then the Lyon fiasco kicked in, though I promised to stop by en route. A half hour later, she'd changed her mind: 'Not worth your while, don't come.' But something was terrifying her. I felt the push/pull of her wanting to talk. Almost a warning."

Pollard nodded. "So you went to see for yourself."

"I heard loud voices, shouting, from the back window. An argument in Basque."

"Basque?" Pollard sat up. "But that's not in your statement."

In Morbier's mind, he could see the man now from the back. Tall, dark hair, black coat. Moving around. Restless, he remembered. Coughing.

"Xavierre threw a shopping bag at him. Paper fluttered in the air. But her daughter walked in. She took her by the arm and rushed out. Cars pulled up, the guests . . . that was it."

"What else?"

"I got the call to respond."

"Meaning?"

"High alert, issued in Lyon. I left. Met my driver, then asked Leduc to . . . don't get her more involved." Morbier slammed his fist on the table. "If only I could check. . . ."

"This?" Pollard slid a brown unmarked folder over the desk.

Morbier thumbed open the file. Crisp photocopies of the crime-scene report, *procès verbal* statements, witness accounts, preliminary lab reports.

"How the hell did you get this, Pollard?"

"That's the least of your worries, Morbier." He stood, glancing at his watch. "Time for my hearing upstairs. You've got thirty minutes to read the contents before putting it in here." Pollard indicated the top drawer. "I need to return it today, *compris?*"

"And then?"

"My brother-in-law's shift resumes in thirty minutes. But he leaves *en vacances* as of tonight. You've only got until midnight to pass on a message."

Pollard set down a rectangular gold notebook embossed with the legend *Wedding wishes for your new life together,* a slim gold pen attached. "Take notes, find overlooked details, compare it to what's on the report. Analyze. Do what you always do."

"In this notebook?"

"We've got hundreds left; now my wife uses them for shopping lists."

Never close, often adversarial in cases,

Pollard puzzled him.

"Why do this for me?"

"Let's just say I prefer not to lose cases to the *police des polices.*"

The door shut behind him.

Morbier scanned the file with anxious fingers. Paper-clipped to the last page he found the message. On a torn-out pink WHILE YOU WERE OUT telephone form he saw three handwritten words:

Laguardiere died today.

A man wearing a black ski mask held a gun to the head of the young woman. She lay panting and spread-eagled in the dark coved crevice. Her legs apart, one ankle duct-taped to a door-frame hinge, the other to a wall post. Only a torn chemise-type dress half-covered her thighs.

"Not clever of you to listen to Joxi," he said. "But I'll take care of you like a real man."

Her whimpers echoed off the stone. Her eyes were black points of terror as she writhed back and forth.

Aimée tiptoed closer. Only one more step, and. . . .

Her heel caught on a metal rim protruding from the stone floor.

"Silvio? Took your time. My turn first, then —"

Aimée swung the wine bottle with all her might against his head. The loud crack reverberated as he staggered, wobbling as if dancing. He shook his head, then fell to the ground, his gun clattering by his feet. His body twitched, his fingers scrabbling against the stone.

Aimée pocketed his gun and kicked him in the jaw until his moans ceased. She turned to the shaking young woman whose eyes were wide with fear. "Are you all right?"

A loud scream answered her. Echoing and echoing.

Hair rose on the back of Aimée's neck.

She turned to face a shaking, white-faced Robbé, held by the other ski-masked man. No doubt he had trained a gun on Robbé's back. Had he seen . . . ?

"I don't like you hurting my friend," the man in the ski mask said, his voice deep and gravel-like.

"I don't like rape. . . ." Aimée countered.

A snort. "So you say."

He shoved Robbé to the ground. "Now undo the girl."

"But I've got this boy's insulin. He's diabetic."

"Did you hear me?" The man held his snub-nosed pistol to Robbé's head. "Now!" A beeping came from his wristwatch. *"Merde!"* He checked it, shrugged. "Time flies when you're having fun."

"You call this fun?" She'd edged her hand into her coat pocket. She gripped the pistol that the other man had dropped, angling the barrel nose-up, holding her breath.

He gave a mock sigh. "Seems like he won't need his insulin now."

She edged her forefinger around the trigger. "Why?" She had to keep him talking.

"Plan B."

Plan B again. She perspired under the dress shirt and *le smoking* jacket she was wearing and wished to god *she* had backup.

"So what's this Plan B?"

"Damn hot down here." He pulled off his mask and shook a head of black curly hair, his other hand holding the pistol aimed at Robbé. "That's better." He shot her a grin, revealing a set of silver braces.

A bad sign when a terrorist removed his mask: he didn't care about witnesses.

"I'd like to know Plan B." She caught the girl's eye. Hoped she got her message. "She would, too."

"You'll find out," he said, stepping closer to a shivering Robbé.

Her heart thumped against her chest.

"I'll let him find out first."

She squeezed the trigger, shooting through her coat pocket. There was a deafening crack. He grabbed his chest, his other hand jerking, and fired wildly into the low ceiling. Stone chips and dust rained down. Aimée fired again, hitting his shoulder.

"*Salope,* how did you . . . ?" he asked, a surprised look on his face. Then his legs gave out and he fell backward.

A line of blood trickled over the cracks in the stone.

She tried to ignore the singed odor and the heat in her pocket. She turned to the girl, who'd closed her eyes. "Can you walk?"

A nod. She took the Swiss Army knife from her bag and sawed the duct tape from the girl's wrist. Then she rubbed her ice-cold arms.

Robbé slumped, his eyes flickering in his head.

"Robbé?"

The girl screamed. "He's dead!"

Aimée dropped the knife and felt for Robbé's pulse. Rapid. His hands cold and clammy.

"Please . . . please cut me loose."

No time to finish undoing her. She handed the girl the knife. "Here." Took the insulin kit from her pocket.

"My hand's numb. I can't." The girl broke into tears.

"Try. You have to try."

Robbé mumbled. His legs seized up. He'd

gone into diabetic shock. She pulled out the syringe, flicked the ampoule, and hoped she remembered everything Irati had told her.

She rolled up Robbé's sleeve, stuck the needle into his upper arm muscle, and released the plunger.

The coppery smell of blood mingled with that of the damp in the stone alcove. It made her light-headed.

The girl crawled on the floor, shivering, and tugged her hand. "There's more of them." Her teeth chattered. Her face was smudged with dirt, her hair was matted, and she looked like she hadn't eaten.

"Where?"

"I don't know. One of them's hurt. Joxi. He helped me."

"Then we've got to get out of here. Now."

She rolled down Robbé's sleeve. Why hadn't the color come back to his face?

She took off her coat, draped it around the girl's shoulders. "You can do this. I know you can."

Robbé's eyelids fluttered.

"He's coming around. See?" she said. "Help me get him on his feet."

Somehow, with the girl's help, she got Robbé over her shoulder.

"Which way?"

The girl shook her head.

"Didn't you hear noises?"

"Down there." She pointed to the long tunnel branching into a fork.

Think. She had to think. René had indicated that the way to the reservoir pools was through the outdoor staircase. From the pool level, another way out existed through a now-disused maintenance house exit.

To the right, she saw a sloping cove lined by raised dirt beds. Electrical wires from a switch box in the low ceiling led to a short walkway through thick walls. Beyond was a green door similar to the one at the entrance.

"This way," she said.

At the door, she pulled out the key ring, propping Robbé against the damp wall. She tried each key. The dress shirt plastered wetly to her back; drops of perspiration beaded her brow. The eleventh key clicked and turned. She shoved the door open.

"Someone's coming," the princess said.

She prayed that this led outside and not to a storeroom.

"Let's go."

A dark night and fresh cold air greeted them. A concrete spiral staircase wound upward.

For a thin man, Robbé weighed heavily

on her shoulder. "Can you walk, Robbé?"

He blinked at her, disoriented. "Let go of me." He jabbed her with his elbow and fell back against the railing.

Pounding sounded on the metal door below. She'd locked it. But how long before they located another key?

"You tried to kill me," he said.

"Me?" she asked panting. "If Irati hadn't given me this, you'd still be in diabetic shock." She shoved the kit into his hand and took his arm. "Hurry."

Unsure, he stared.

"Next time you won't be so lucky," she said. "The Basque put a gun to your head, remember?"

"Get going now," the girl yelled. She pushed him up the stairs.

Few stars shone above them in the night sky. A half-moon wisped by clouds hung over the Arc de Triomphe, a postage stamp–sized yellow glow in the distance. Faint lights glimmered on the surface of swimming pool–like reservoirs. She inhaled the algae-scented wind, heard the splash of a fish. To the right, the blue-lit needle of the Eiffel Tower poked behind the building rooftops. From below, one would never know that several stories above the street, a whole other world existed.

"That way. Quick." She pointed toward the far end of the smallest pool, calculating the direction of rue Paul Valéry. They had to escape. A long narrow walkway rimmed the pool at the rear of the dark stone walls of apartment buildings.

Running now, she made out the nineteenth-century two-story mansard-roofed house, quaint and incongruous, at the edge of the water. Unlived-in, dark, with torn shades in the window. It reminded her of a village train station complete with geraniums, similar to the gatehouse at the rue Copernic entrance.

The exit. She had to find the exit to the street. In the crusted brick wall edging the house, she saw another green metal door.

"Hurry. Go to the door."

The girl ran, coat flapping in the wind, Robbé behind, trying to keep up. She took the key ring, tried the larger old-fashioned keys first. None fit.

"I don't like this," the girl said, her voice quavering. "Hear that?"

Shouts carried over the water.

The girl balled her wool sleeve around her fist and punched in the glass panel of the house's door. Glass splintered, caught the light, and sprayed the coat like shiny sequins. She reached in and turned the old-fashioned handle. "Locked," she gasped. "What do we do?"

Aimée's mind raced. Should they try to break down the door, barricade themselves inside, and call for help? Who knew how long she could hold them off?

But she couldn't give up. Finally, the last key clicked and turned. "Let's go."

Running down the narrow, dark stairs between the reservoir foundations and brick walls, she hit the taxi driver's number on her cell phone.

"*Vite!* Rue Paul Valéry, near the corner of rue Lauriston."

If a reception committee was waiting, she hoped the taxi would deter them.

She turned the key in the last door to the street.

"Whatever happens, turn right and get into the G7 taxi."

The girl rubbed her runny nose with her sleeve, nodding.

"Can you do that, Robbé?"

"What about you?" he said sullenly.

She pulled the gun out of the girl's coat pocket. "Just don't look back, okay?"

"Look, I'm sorry I. . . ."

"Forget it. Go."

She stepped out, the gun raised. Four dark figures were in the middle of rue Paul

Valéry, the taxi idling at the corner behind them.

She hit the taxi driver's cell number again. "See those *mecs?* I'm sure you can scare them. There's three of us just beyond them. Whatever you do, don't let them reach us."

A little laugh. *"Pas de problème."*

All of a sudden, the taxi gunned down the street, headlights blinking, horn blaring. The *mecs* jumped and scattered. With a squeal of brakes, the taxi stopped in front of Aimée.

She opened the door and pushed the others into the back seat, then climbed in front beside the driver.

Without a word, he ground into first, tore down rue Paul Valéry and into Avenue Victor Hugo. In a few blocks, he pulled into the roundabout of Place de l'Étoile circling the Arc de Triomphe, a maze of headlights and hundreds of darting cars. He opened his window, stuck his fist out at a driver who slowed, then cut in front of a truck. He grinned at Aimée, his eyes shining. "No one can follow us here. We'll be lucky to get out alive ourselves."

"Great job," she said.

"I haven't had this much fun in years," he said.

"*Bon,* let's keep circling and I'll make

some calls, figure out where we're going next."

She turned to the girl in the back seat. "We haven't been introduced. I'm Aimée, and you are . . . ?"

"Maria."

"I thought so," she said. "Your father's looking for you."

Robbé sat back, rubbing his arm. "That's an understatement."

After circling the Arc de Triomphe for twenty minutes, the taxi turned into Avenue Foch, the wide, tree-lined boulevard radiating from Place de l'Étoile. Town house after fashionable town house and mansion after mansion lined the street. The taxi pulled up to a grilled metal gate. A security guard nodded to the taxi driver. The automatic gates opened to a driveway where there was an ambulance standing. The ambassador paced on the front steps of the town house, which had lights blazing in every window.

Aimée turned to Maria. "Remember what we said? Forget my using the gun. But describe the Basque who helped you, the rail-line diagrams, and everything else you remember."

Maria swallowed. "The ambassador doesn't look too happy. I think I'm in big trouble."

"Wrong. You're giving him a feather in his diplomatic hat. You're safe, Maria. Don't let him forget it."

Maria gave a small smile and struggled out of the coat. "Wouldn't want to forget this." Her torn chemise hung from her thin bruised shoulders.

Aimée pressed a card with Martine's number into her hand. "Call my friend Martine, the journalist, in a little while. You can trust her."

A grim-faced ambassador, in rolled-up shirtsleeves, his tie loosened, opened the taxi door. Without a word, he took Maria's arm, helped her up the steps, and gestured to the waiting paramedics.

He'd left a calling card on the coat. A military-issue satellite cell phone with built in GPS tracking. Courtesy of Colonel Valois.

Just what she'd feared. Sitting in a taxi on the wealthiest street in Paris didn't equate with fighting rebels in the mountains of Afghanistan.

Or did it?

According to Léo, the moment she flicked on the phone it would activate the GPS, alerting the military, who would immediately track her location. Deal with the devil? She needed to think about that. Figure out how to use it to her advantage.

The phone rang.

Of course, the thing was already on.

Robbé handed it to her.

"Mademoiselle Leduc," said Colonel Valois. "Interesting solo operation. Our team would have handled it with more efficiency and a lower body count."

She doubted that. His formerly inviting tone had turned frosty. Maybe he wanted to take back his offer.

"So you say, Colonel," she said. "I guess you had to be there."

Pause. "If my men told me that, I'd remind them of the families left behind."

Sanctimonious bastard.

"Next time a terrorist's ready to rape a young girl and puts a gun to the head of a man in diabetic shock, I'll try to remember that." She bit her tongue. Stupid to provide fodder for an investigation.

"That's besides the point, Mademoiselle Leduc," he said. "Our mission's not accomplished."

"You've got the princess —"

"I'm referring to loose ends," he interrupted. "I think you know what I mean. It's very much in your interest to cooperate."

So now he'd twist shooting a Basque terrorist in self-defense against her? Big boys with big toys, Martine had said, and frustrated at not using them. Her intuition told her to act interested in working for him.

"So, don't I get paid now?"

"Did I imply that?" His tone warmed. "The offer stands. *Bien sûr,* and according to our terms. Our protocol, that's the way we operate."

He sounded like the IT director client at the failing company, whose "protocol" ultimately couldn't pay Leduc's fees.

"I'm listening."

"Keep this phone operational at all times. The moment you're contacted, respond. Oh, and alert me if you get any calls on the phone in your bag." Pause. "No more solo operations. Just keep me informed and we'll take it from there."

In other words, stay glued to them by GPS, every movement tracked.

"You're interested in hearing my terms, Colonel?"

"We've already set up a bank account with —"

"I didn't finish, Colonel," she said. "Commissaire Morbier released and cleared of all charge. *C'est tout.*"

"But that's not my jurisdiction, Mademoiselle."

She stared at the lighted mansions beyond

the trees flashing by.

"I'm sure you can work something out, Colonel."

She flipped the phone closed and hit the OFF button.

She turned to Robbé. "We've got places to go."

Robbé bit his lip. "I want to see Irati."

"Soon," she said. "Let's go, Monsieur. Of course, we never had that passenger, never came here, *compris?*"

The taxi driver put on his driving gloves and shifted into first. "Understood." His eyes glittered. "Any chance of a car chase?"

"I hope not," she said.

He shrugged. As agreed, the grilled metal gate opened and the taxi merged onto Avenue Foch. Ten minutes later, the taxi parked in front of Fondation d'Auteuil, the church-and-orphanage complex off rue de la Fontaine.

She noticed Robbé's whitened knuckles on the insulin kit. "I think you've got things to tell me, *non?*"

"How did you know I live here?"

"Let's talk inside." She nodded to the taxi driver. "Monsieur. . . ."

He took the Maigret novel from the dashboard. "I know. Reading time." He winked. "Wouldn't trade this job for the world. I'm having the night of my life! And call me Théo."

"*Merci,* Théo," she said. "But it's not over yet."

Robbé pressed the numbers on the digi-code pad with shaking fingers. The gate opened to a long park. The secondhand charity shop with donations from the chic parishioners on the left, the faint outlines of *L'église* Sainte Thérèse ahead. The orphanage's workshops, offices, and housing on the right.

"You grew up here, Robbé," she said, pulling the coat back on and buttoning it against the dank chill.

"What's that got to do with anything?" he said.

A sign pointed the way upstairs to the orphanage's housing, indicating a wing of shared rooms for young working apprentices like Robbé. A community setting in which to dwell while mastering a trade and avoid steep Paris rents. Apprenticeships, like those of the traditional guilds. The communal meeting room, with blue and yellow chintz curtains, was dark.

"The Basques sponsored your apprenticeship in the Bayonne printing works," Aimée said. "That's where you met Txili, didn't you? The others?"

"What?"

"Irati told me about you," she said. "Your life." Now she had to press him. Get him to reveal Txili. "That's why you wanted a small wedding. As an orphan, you had no family to invite."

He looked away. "We wanted an intimate ceremony," he said, his lisp more pronounced.

"But Xavierre got involved. Of course she meant well, her only daughter, so excited, but it got out of hand," Aimée said. "Then Txili, your old patron, appeared at the wedding rehearsal party, so happy for you. He wanted to help. He just asked a little favor. After all, you're Basque. Wasn't that what he told you? It was why he'd sponsored you, after all. He knew your ETA patriot parents had been killed in a shootout with the French police."

"*Non . . . non,* I don't know what you're talking about."

"But you do, Robbé. That's why he counted on you with the princess."

"You don't know that. You can't prove that," he said, moving away.

"Not yet," she said. "But what happens when Irati discovers the truth? That you murdered her mother?" she said, trying to provoke him. "Of course, you didn't mean

367

for that to happen, nor for Agustino to die; you didn't know —"

"Stop." He put his hands over his ears.

"But you were worried that Xavierre had told Morbier, a *flic,* the real plan. . . ."

"I didn't kill Xavierre," he yelled. "She helped me, believed in me. Why would I? I give you my word."

She believed him, but his wild eyes and jittery hand movements worried her.

"Then who did, Robbé?" she asked.

His shoulders shook. He opened his mouth to speak. Several short *thupts* sounded, thudding into the arch above them, spitting stone dust over her head. His words froze on his lips.

"Down!" She lunged, pushing him onto the ground.

Another *thupt* and more dust. A high-powered pistol with a suppressor. She crawled under the stone wall. Took a breath and peered over the ledge. A figure flashed under the trees. She heard crunching gravel, the clang of the street gate.

Robbé bolted. She heard his footsteps racing up the stairs.

She took off, skirting the trees, and made it through the gate. Jumped into the taxi. "Which way did he go, Théo?"

She heard the radio tuned low to the talk-radio channel. The open book lay in his lap.

"Théo, wake up." She shook his shoulder. His head tilted, fell onto his chest. The streetlight beam revealed the line of blood running from his ear.

She gasped. Horror-stricken, she put her fingers on his neck. No pulse.

Her fault. She'd caused this poor man's murder. Having the night of his life . . . now she knew what Valois meant. Maybe Théo had grandchildren. She'd been an idiot to think she could do this alone.

Her eye caught on the book. The bright red droplets spattered over the pages. Like the blood pattern on the gravel. As if the killer had leaned in the window to talk to Théo and had a nosebleed when he did the job.

And that's how she could find him.

She jumped out of the taxi and stared at the dim pavement. A faint blood spatter on rue de la Fontaine. Then it stopped at the corner. Which way?

She turned up rue Ribera. A narrow uphill street, cobbled and dark, past the Romanian Maronite church. He'd go slower than her because of his condition, his nosebleed; he'd be trying to stanch the blood. She reached the corner of rue de la Source.

Nothing.

A cough. Faint, as if he was trying to smother it going up the hill. And it hit her.

Of course he knew her. They'd met in the Basque resto.

She ran across the intersection, perspiring now. Up a steeper narrow street, lined by solid nineteenth-century façades with ornate scrolled pilasters, cast-iron balconies, and cherub-adorned portals. Ivy rustled to the right of a boarded-up *hôtel particulier* under reconstruction. Creaking wood, then what sounded like footsteps echoing down a passage between the buildings. She paused, sniffed. A trail of cigar smoke wafted in his wake.

She searched the boarded-up entrance. Fingered the wood and found the handle, sliding open the makeshift entry, and stepped inside. She tiptoed past concrete mixers in the damp narrow walkway to the rear that ended at a crumbling stone wall. On the right, a sagging door in a rotted frame led to what had been a kitchen, the windows broken, now filled with leaves.

She pulled out her penlight, her pulse racing, illuminating a high-ceilinged salon with streaking water stains on the peeling wallpaper. The reek of dampness and rot everywhere was punctuated by the acrid whiff of cigar smoke. Down the creaking hallway, her penlight, a small yellow trail, shone on leaves and more leaves.

A sharp wind sliced from the broken windows with metal bars. Sweat beaded her chin; her body shivered hot and cold. For a moment, she wanted to turn back. Listen to the voice in her head yelling go back. But he'd gotten away from her before. Not this time!

She made her feet move.

She emerged into what had been the ballroom, half roofed, half opened up to the cold sky. Crystals tinkled from the remains of a sagging chandelier hanging perilously from the crossbeams. The dank-walled ballroom's tall doors were boarded up, enclosed on all sides, lit only by the pallor of the moon. Crates and old doors were crammed in the shadows. There were holes in the ripped-up floorboards.

One way in. The same way out. Not good.

Why hadn't she kept that hammer?

The pistol in her pocket contained one more bullet. Where was he? Aiming for a distraction, she shoved the crates aside on her left. Heard the splinter of wood as they crashed onto the floor.

With a quick step she darted in the opposite direction.

"Let's talk, since we're old friends, Beñat,"

she said. "At least that's how you introduced yourself. You were Timo Baptista in your student days, or do you prefer Txili?"

She felt her way along the damp wall. The smell of cigar smoke intensified. He couldn't suppress his coughing. And then she saw his reflection in the cracked, age-spotted, gold-framed mirror propped against the wall.

He shook his head of close-cropped white hair, a sad expression on his face. His expensive coat hung from his shoulders. "I liked you. Chic, edgy, full of *joie de vivre*. What happened?"

As if she'd personally let him down. If she wasn't careful, he'd charm her again, as he had over olives in the Basque bar.

"But you changed," he said, stepping forward. He tossed the burning cigarillo onto the floor. Ground it out with his foot. "You've become a problem."

She leveled the pistol at him, her back pinned against the rotted doors.

The force of his kick knocked the pistol from her hand and spun it to the floor. Before she could reach for it and grab it, he shoved the gun into a hole in the broken floor with his foot. A plunk and splash of water. Now the gun was in the sewers. Stupid. She'd let her guard down. Perspiration dampened her collar; her shirt stuck to her spine.

"But you're full of surprises," Beñat said, his own pistol in his hand now.

"You didn't need to kill Théo."

"The old taxi driver? Not my fault he tried to play the hero." A shrug.

He sickened her.

"Just an obstacle in your way, so you took care of him?"

"These things happen," he said.

She had to think her way out of this. Stop him any way she could. But how?

"You're dying, Beñat," she said, a low throb again in her ribs. "Leukemia. Such a waste. Look at the cost. And for what?"

Shock mingled with irritation on his hollowed-out face. Aimée noticed his thinness. "A cold? You call a chest cold leukemia?"

"It's eating you up," she said. "The coat's hanging off you, with all the weight you've lost."

"So now you're a doctor?" He snorted. "Bunch of quacks. Never listened to one a day in my life."

"But you're tired, *non?* Those nosebleeds, weakness. . . ."

"Weak? I just kicked a gun out of your hands." He gave a short laugh. "I thought

373

you were smarter, Detective. I researched you. I know all about you and the dwarf."

"René?" Her hand went to her mouth.

"He drives a classic Citroën. A collector's item, eh? But for how long?"

René, in danger from the Basque terrorists, a bomb planted in his car? She flicked open the GPS phone in her pocket, hit the ON switch. A beep.

"What's that?"

"Research, you say?" She spoke fast to distract him. "Let's talk about the police lab's research. They've analyzed the blood samples from my shoe. Your blood."

"What the hell are you talking about?" He pointed the pistol at her. Right at her chest.

Her stomach clenched. Talk, she had to talk. Keep his attention.

"Your nosebleed, the night you strangled Xavierre," she said. "I found the telltale little driblets all over the gravel. I stepped on them. There was a sufficient sample to check your blood under the microscope."

"Why would you . . . ? But you want to scare me, I see," he said, not quite hiding the denial and anger in his voice. "A parting shot. Nothing else to fight with, eh, Detective?"

Her turn to shrug. "You want to argue with science?" she said. "Considering your high white blood cell count, the doctor said you didn't have long. Matter of fact, he said, 'I'd live each day like it's his only one if I were him.' "

He shook his head. "Blood's blood."

"That's why you enlisted the terrorists, calling it a patriotic action for the Basque country." She stared at him. "A lie. And their organization, desperate for passports and *cartes d'identités,* agreed."

A fit of coughing overtook him. But he kept a steady bead on her heart. Fear rippled up her arms. She scanned the ground for a pipe, wires, anything.

"Why make Xavierre pay for the *Imprimerie Nationale* heist that went bad? So bad that you killed a *flic.*"

"You talk like she's a saint," Beñat said. "Know anything about her past? She owed me. Owed us all."

"An oath made in her youth?"

He eyed her with a faint smile. "We'll have company soon. Any minute, my backup team will join us."

Bluffing? Her hands shook. She scanned the dark ballroom, the passageway. Doubted she could make a run for it before he got off a shot.

"Let's talk present tense," she said. "The referendum includes the Paris-to-Madrid high-speed rail through the Basque country. And you didn't want that. But why? Bad for your business?"

"You could say that," he said, his tone becoming bored and businesslike. "Revenue losses of seventy-five percent. All that speed, but no local stops for commerce. No access to the region's factories. Makes the Basque countryside a wasteland."

Now she put it together. "So you kidnapped the princess to force a new referendum guaranteeing that the high-speed train would run through your district *with stops.* Millions for you. Hired ETA to sabotage the rail line and make it appear political."

"What do you know of our long struggle, our culture, our heritage?" His eyes glittered as he edged closer.

"And you're preserving Basque culture?"

He caught her wrist in a grip of steel. Shoved her against the dripping corner. "Shut up." His breath reeked of Izarra.

A hypocrite. Greedy, and with his pistol resting cold on her temple.

"Xavierre couldn't see the big picture."

Not his way, she couldn't. And it all made sense.

"She discovered the plan was to line your pocket, not to benefit the Cause. She threatened to expose you."

"She was going to tell the *flic* — her 'man,' she called him. Can you imagine?" he said. "*Et alors,* the richer the woman, the tighter the fist. Me, I only wanted to help Xavierre give Irati this big wedding she was fixated on. I wanted the best for Robbé." He stopped, a genuine look of puzzlement on his face. "That food her sister cooks — awful — you know that. I even offered to pay for catering as a wedding present."

His concerned tone sent shivers up her arms. More than deluded — amoral, a sociopath — he believed what he said. His clawlike hand tightened on her wrist. The other kept the pistol at her temple.

She struggled to breathe. She had to get the gun away from him.

"Xavierre wouldn't listen —"

"But you never planned to kill her, did you?" Her chest heaved. "Or Agustino. After all, the three of you had taken an oath. You thought they'd cooperate. But they saw you for what you are."

The screech of tires carried from the street. Distant dull thuds. Her heart hammered. No way in hell could the EPIGN make it here that quickly.

His men. The Basque terrorists.

"A pity, that," Beñat said. "Agustino, bullheaded as always —" A fit of coughing overtook him. She heard rattling in his chest. For a second, his grip loosened. With all her might, she slammed the gun up into his face. Heard the crack of breaking bones. Her elbow jabbed him in the ribs.

He doubled over, choking, blood streaming from his face.

She grabbed his wrists, tied them behind his back with her scarf, and left him moaning on the floor. Only moments now. Using her coat sleeve, she picked up his bloody pistol, wiped it off, and checked the chamber. Half-full. She tugged the old doors open to use as a shield. Bit her lip, breathing hard.

She heard only the faint rustle of leaves drifting in through the open roof, twisting and spinning in the moonlight. A sixth sense told her the men were there.

She muttered a little prayer, steadied her grip, and took a deep breath. She peered from behind the door. Five black-helmeted men with night-vision goggles in matching assault gear trained Heckler and Koch MP5s at her. She registered the blood-red dot of a laser sight centered on her heart. Her legs wobbled and she grabbed the doorframe.

"You're the good guys, I presume?" she said.

His MP5 still trained on her, one of the men removed his goggles. "Lieutenant Fabard. EPIGN."

She expelled a gust of air. "Took your time, Lieutenant."

"If you'll just lower the barrel and hand me the pistol?" He extended a gloved hand.

"Otherwise you'll need to kill me, right?" Trying to control the shaking of her hand, she complied. "Any trouble on the way in, Lieutenant?"

"Nothing we couldn't handle," he said.

Two of the team had slung Beñat between their shoulders and reached the ballroom door. "Operatives in the van," Fabard spoke into his mouthpiece. "Mission contained." He motioned to the others. "Ready?" Not twenty seconds had passed.

"Beñat needs medical attention before he can furnish a statement," she said. "You did hear his confession to the murders?"

A quizzical look crossed the lieutenant's eyes. "*Désolé,* but with my headgear. . . ."

Panic hit her. Then she smiled. "Trust me, Lieutenant, you heard his confession." She hit the CALL button on the satellite phone. "We'll chat with Colonel Valois and tell him all about it."

THURSDAY MORNING

The iron-studded old jail door clanged shut behind Morbier. He stood, shopping bag in hand, on the quai de l'Horloge, breathing in the mist and damp morning air. Nothing had ever smelled so sweet. A low fog curled under the Pont Neuf, swirling over the khaki-green Seine. A weak November sun struggled above the blue-tiled rooftops.

He was free.

Instead of turning right, to the Préfecture, he had a quick stop to make before reaching his office. He walked over the Pont Neuf among the rush of commuters, across the turmoil of rue de Rivoli clogged with buses, bicycles, and parents taking children to school. The soot-stained façades, the knots of people outside cafés, the shouts of kiosk vendors selling newspapers were pulsing with life. Like every day. But he didn't have Xavierre to share it with, and he felt a pang of sorrow.

He turned onto rue du Louvre, peered under the awning, through the window, into the corner café. He saw her black leather coat, the high-heeled boots, her tousled wispy hair, that shrug of her shoulders. Safe. A little bit of his heart melted.

THURSDAY MORNING

"The bomb squad defused a detonator under René's car?" asked wide-eyed Zazie, the café owners' red-haired daughter, leaning on her mathematics homework.

Aimée snapped her fingers then popped a Doliprane and downed her espresso at the zinc counter. "Just like that. In ten seconds."

Zazie shook her head and looked up. "*Oui, Monsieur?*"

Aimée grew aware of the man standing next to her, setting his bag on the mosaic tiled floor littered with sugar wrappers. That familiar scent.

"*Un double, s'il vous plaît,* Mademoiselle."

Aimée turned and her kohl-rimmed eyes widened.

"*Encore,* Leduc?" Morbier gestured to her empty demitasse.

Her lip trembled. The bags under his eyes were more pronounced, his shirt needed ironing, but Morbier was back.

"I thought you'd never ask." Warmth filled her, and then her arms were around him, hugging him tight, inhaling his Morbier smell. "Why didn't you tell me?"

"Thought you knew, Leduc," he said, pulling out a pack of Gauloises. "Didn't you have something to do with it?"

"A little." She rubbed her rib. Then grinned at Zazie, now open-mouthed, setting down a steaming cup of espresso for Morbier with a small chocolate on the saucer. "As I was telling Zazie, last night when the —"

"Save it, Leduc." Morbier blew a plume of smoke that wavered above the heads of the morning habitués crowded at the counter. "I'm late for the Commissariat." He drained his espresso. Slipped a twenty-franc note under the saucer. "Don't complain I never buy you a coffee."

"You still owe me an *apéritif,* Morbier."

A blast of air from the open door shook the lace curtains. René entered, leaning on his cane, a big smile on his red-cheeked face.

"Good to have you back, Morbier," he said, pumping Morbier's hand. "These three days. . . . Alors, now we'll get some work done." René cleared his throat. "The project report's being printed, Aimée."

"Got to go." She grabbed her bag and

stuck this morning's *Le Parisien* under her arm. "More later, Zazie."

Out on rue du Louvre, passersby scurried, horns blared. René went ahead. Morbier paused in front of Leduc Detective. Fatigue showed in his eyes. His jowls sagged.

"Promise me you'll make an appointment for a checkup, okay?"

He nodded. "I need to talk, tell you some things, Leduc."

"About the letters? My brother?" she asked. A little hope fluttered in her chest.

"As if I knew yet?" He shook his head. Lines creased his mouth. "You see. . . ."

A siren whined and an unmarked Peugeot with a flashing blue light on its roof pulled up at the curb. Morbier turned, cocked his head the way he always did.

She recognized Melac emerging from the car. Felt a lurch in her stomach.

"*Excusez-moi,* Commissaire," Melac said, "but Command thought you'd be here."

She blinked. The leak, the traitor himself. Her mouth went dry and she didn't return Melac's smile.

"Escalating situation in Lyon, Commissaire," Melac said. "It's urgent. They asked me to escort you."

"So you're the branch liaison now, Melac?"

Melac shrugged. "My leave's canceled, so I guess you're stuck with me, Commissaire. A temporary assignment."

Aimée stared at Melac's pale gray eyes, wondering what was going on behind them.

Morbier paused in thought. "Anything to do with Laguardiere's replacement?"

"His replacement, Loisel, sent me, Commissaire."

Morbier nodded. Flicked his cigarette into the gutter. "Good news. Finally. Let's go."

Good news? She pulled Morbier aside. Shot him a look. "But the leak?" she whispered. "Don't you need a plumber?"

"Plumber? But that's *my* job now, Leduc." Morbier gave a little sigh and turned back to Melac. "Life moves on."

Melac was a good guy after all?

"It's an honor to work under you, Commissaire," Melac said.

At that moment, the sun broke over the blue-tiled rooftops. Thin slants of light caught on the wrought-iron balconies above.

"What did you want to tell me, Morbier?" she said, not wanting to let it go.

"Later, Leduc," he said, now in a hurry. "I'm late."

As usual.

Melac shut the passenger door after Morbier. His fingers brushed hers, spreading warmth, and he winked. "How about Fauchon takeout tonight?" he whispered, his breath in her ear.

"I'm on deadline." She paused. "A new client. . . ."

Sunlight dappled the pavers. She inhaled the crisp air that was ruffling the plane-tree branches. Life did move on.

"But I'll keep the Veuve Clicquot chilled."

ABOUT THE AUTHOR

Cara Black is the author of eleven books in the bestselling Aimée Leduc series. She lives in San Francisco with her husband and son and visits Paris frequently.

The employees of Thorndike Press hope you have enjoyed this Large Print book. All our Thorndike, Wheeler, and Kennebec Large Print titles are designed for easy reading, and all our books are made to last. Other Thorndike Press Large Print books are available at your library, through selected bookstores, or directly from us.

For information about titles, please call:
  (800) 223-1244

or visit our Web site at:
  http://gale.cengage.com/thorndike

To share your comments, please write:
  Publisher
  Thorndike Press
  10 Water St., Suite 310
  Waterville, ME 04901